F
ATH

Atherton, Nancy.

Aunt Dimity and the
deep blue sea.

$22.95

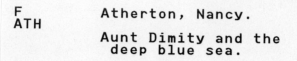

Aunt Dimity and the Deep Blue Sea

Aunt Dimity and the Deep Blue Sea

NANCY ATHERTON

VIKING

VIKING

Published by the Penguin Group

Penguin Group (USA) Inc., 375 Hudson Street,
New York, New York 10014, U.S.A.
Penguin Group (Canada), 90 Eglinton Avenue East, Suite 700,
Toronto, Ontario, Canada M4P 2Y3
(a division of Pearson Penguin Canada Inc.)
Penguin Books Ltd, 80 Strand, London WC2R 0RL, England
Penguin Ireland, 25 St. Stephen's Green, Dublin 2, Ireland
(a division of Penguin Books Ltd)
Penguin Books Australia Ltd, 250 Camberwell Road, Camberwell,
Victoria 3124, Australia
(a division of Pearson Australia Group Pty Ltd)
Penguin Books India Pvt Ltd, 11 Community Centre, Panchsheel Park,
New Delhi – 110 017, India
Penguin Group (NZ), Cnr Airborne and Rosedale Roads, Albany,
Auckland 1310, New Zealand
(a division of Pearson New Zealand Ltd)
Penguin Books (South Africa) (Pty) Ltd, 24 Sturdee Avenue,
Rosebank, Johannesburg 2196, South Africa

Penguin Books Ltd, Registered Offices:
80 Strand, London WC2R 0RL, England

First published in 2006 by Viking Penguin,
a member of Penguin Group (USA) Inc.

10   9   8   7   6   5   4   3   2   1

ISBN 0-670-03476-2

Printed in the United States of America
Set in Perpetua

For
Jim Hudson and Diane Martin,
cherished chums

Aunt Dimity and the Deep Blue Sea

One

$\mathcal{I}$t was far too pretty a day to contemplate violent death. Late April's silken breezes were filled with the scents of spring. Cowslips nodded daintily in the meadow, the oak forest was awash with bluebells, and soft sunlight cast a golden glow over the honey-colored cottage my family and I called home. As I stood calf-deep in the meadow's rippling grasses, playing cricket with my five-year-old sons, the thought of us all being strangled in our beds by a vengeful lunatic was the furthest thing from my mind.

I use the phrase "playing cricket" loosely. Although my husband and I had lived for seven years near the small Cotswolds village of Finch, in England's West Midlands, we were Americans born and bred, and we'd never quite grasped the rules of what was, to us, a peculiar and alien game. Our twin sons, on the other hand, had grown up in England. Cricket was their national pastime. While they took turns bowling and batting, I was good for nothing but fielding balls.

I'd just rescued a particularly soggy specimen from the gurgling stream at the bottom of our meadow when I spotted my husband emerging from the solarium that stretched across the back of the cottage. Will and Rob were the spitting images of their father—dark-haired, brown-eyed, and, to judge by the speed with which they outgrew their clothes, destined to equal if not exceed his lofty height. Whether they would follow Bill into the family business or choose instead to strike it rich on the pro cricket tour remained to be seen.

Bill was a high-priced and highly discreet attorney who spent much of his time drawing up wills for the extremely well-to-do. He ran the European branch of his family's venerable law firm from an office overlooking the village square in Finch, but his work often took him away from home. He'd been in his London office for the past three days, and I hadn't expected to see him for another two. I wondered what had brought him home early.

Stanley, our recently adopted black cat, followed Bill into the back garden, but Bill didn't seem to notice. He didn't bend to stroke Stanley's gleaming coat, or call out to me and the boys, or climb over the garden's low stone wall to join us in the meadow. He simply stood in the shade of the old apple tree, watching us. He stared silently at the boys for a moment before lifting his gaze to scan the tree-covered hills that rose steeply beyond the meadow and the stream. When his eyes finally met mine, I felt a shiver of apprehension so powerful that the rescued ball slipped from my fingers.

My husband looked as though he'd aged ten years since I'd last seen him. His shoulders were hunched, his face was haggard, and his mouth was drawn into a thin, grim line. When our gazes locked, I saw a flame of anger in his eyes, shadowed by bone-deep fear. The sheer intensity of his emotions struck me like a blow.

I must have gasped, because Will and Rob glanced toward the cottage, shouted "Daddy!" and forgot, momentarily, about cricket. They dropped bat and ball, hurtled across the meadow, and bounced over the stone wall into the garden, where they slowed, paused, and finally stood stock-still, peering up at their father. As I hurried over the wall in their wake, they stepped forward and slipped their hands into Bill's.

"What's wrong, Daddy?" asked Rob.

"Is it *very* bad?" asked Will.

Bill dropped to his knees and pulled the boys to him, his head bowed between theirs, his eyes squeezed shut as if he were in pain. When the twins began to squirm, he drew an unsteady breath and loosened his hold. Will and Rob stood back and regarded him anxiously.

"Yes, it's bad," he answered, looking from one solemn face to the other. "But it's nothing for you to worry about. Mummy and Daddy are going to take care of everything."

"We could help," the boys chorused.

"Of course you can." Bill ran his fingers through their dark hair. "You can help me and Mummy by going into the cottage and doing exactly what Annelise tells you to do."

Annelise Sciaparelli was the twins' inestimable nanny. She and I had flipped a coin after lunch to decide who'd pull cricket duty. She'd won.

"There's no need to fetch your toys," Bill said sharply, when the boys turned back toward the meadow. "Just go into the cottage and stay with Annelise. Understand? I want you to stay indoors, with Annelise. You're not to set foot outside of the cottage. Not one foot."

"Not one foot," the boys repeated soberly.

"Mummy and I will be in the study for a while," Bill went on, "and we don't want to be disturbed. I have to speak with Mummy."

Will and Rob exchanged looks that seemed to say, "Something's *always* wrong when Daddy has to speak with Mummy," but they trotted into the cottage without audible comment.

Stanley, who'd been rubbing his head on Bill's hip in a bid for attention, now stood on his hind legs and planted his front paws on Bill's chest. Bill took the hint, picked the cat up, and stood. While Stanley flopped over his shoulder, purring happily, Bill looked down at me. At just over six feet, my husband was nearly a foot taller than I, and he was remarkably fit. His imposing stature usually made me feel secure and protected, but at that moment I felt a strong urge to tuck him into my pocket for safekeeping.

"Bill?" I said.

"Not here." He turned his head to look toward the hills. "Let's go inside."

We passed through the solarium and into the kitchen, where vegetable soup was simmering on the stove and a veal-and-ham pie was baking in the oven. Bill set Stanley down on the floor, near his food dishes, and the cat, satisfied that he'd been given his due, began nibbling. As Bill and I went down the hall to the study, we heard water running in the tub upstairs and Annelise's voice asking the boys if they wanted bubbles in their bath. Everything in the cottage was completely normal, except for my husband.

Wordlessly, Bill closed the study door behind me, turned on the lights over the mantel shelf, motioned for me to take a seat in one of the pair of tall leather armchairs that stood before the hearth, and sat opposite me. His briefcase rested on the small table beside his chair. He gave it a sidelong glance before leaning forward, his elbows on his knees, his hands clasped tightly together.

"Something's come up," he said. "I didn't take it seriously at first, but now I have to, because it involves you and the boys."

"Right," I said. It was all I could manage, because my mouth had gone dry. Bill's fear was contagious.

"Over the past three weeks, I've received a number of"—he hesitated, then plunged on—"a number of threatening messages. They were sent via e-mail, through a complex relay system. We've been unable to trace them back to their source."

"What kind of threatening messages?" I asked.

Bill's gaze drifted back to the briefcase. Then he squared his shoulders, looked me straight in the eye, and said, "Someone wants to kill me."

I blinked. "Death threats? You've been getting *death threats?*" My thoughts spun wildly for a moment before coming to rest on the sheer improbability of what he was saying. "Why? You're not a criminal attorney. You don't deal with violent thugs. You write codicils and clauses and make sure all the wherefores are in place. Why would anyone want to kill you?"

Bill shrugged. "Revenge, apparently. The messages suggest that a former client believes I wronged him in some way. They make it quite clear that he intends to pay me back." He tilted his head to one side and peered at me earnestly. "I would have told you sooner, Lori, but I thought it was a prank. I thought it would blow over. Instead, it's gotten worse. Much worse." He opened the briefcase, removed a sheet of paper, and passed it to me, saying, "This was waiting for me at my London office when I arrived this morning."

I examined the page. It looked like a standard printout of a routine e-mail message, but the words were those of a madman:

> You came like a thief in the night to cast me into the abyss.
> You chained me in darkness, but no earthly chains can hold
> me anymore. I have risen.
> Behold, I am coming soon to repay you for what you have
> done. All that you love will perish. I will strike your children
> dead and give your wife a like measure of torment and
> mourning. I have the keys to Death and Hades, and I will blot
> your name from the book of life forever.
> Your nightmare has begun. There is no waking.
> Abaddon

I looked questioningly at Bill. "Abaddon?"

Bill waved a hand over the note. "It's a mishmash of quotations and misquotations from the Book of Revelations. Abaddon's a pseudonym, of course, but an apt one. In Revelations, Abaddon is the king of the bottomless pit. His minions come to earth to torture sinners."

"It's good to know that our guy reads his Bible," I muttered.

"It's not funny, Lori," Bill snapped.

"I know," I said quickly, "but it's . . . incredible." I reread the unholy epistle before giving it back to Bill, who returned it to the briefcase. " 'All that you love will perish.' I can't believe that any-one would hate us enough to . . . to *kill* us. It's unreal."

"It's real," Bill said heavily. "Which is why you and the twins have to leave the cottage."

"Huh?" I said, taken aback.

"I've spent most of the day with Chief Superintendent Wesley Yarborough at Scotland Yard," Bill explained. "He agrees that we should take the threats seriously. In fact, he was rather annoyed with me for not bringing them to the Yard's attention sooner." Bill sighed. "Yarborough intends to search my work files for clues to Abaddon's identity, and I have to stay in London, to help with the investigation. While I'm there, the chief superintendent and I want you and the boys to be far away from here. You'll leave the cottage tomorrow morning and stay in a safe place until all of this is cleared up."

"We're safe here," I pointed out. "As soon as the villagers find out what's going on, they'll close in around us like a brick wall. If a stranger shows his face in Finch, they'll sound the alarm. All we have to do is put the word out and Abaddon's as good as caught."

"What if Abaddon doesn't come through the village?" Bill countered. "What if he comes over the hills or through the woods?"

"How would he know where to find us?" I asked.

"Lori," Bill said softly, "he's already found us."

Time seemed to stop. My mind went blank. Although Bill had spoken quietly, his words seemed to echo through the room. He reached once more into his briefcase and handed me a sheaf of papers. As I leafed through them, my hands began to tremble.

They were photographs, electronically transmitted digital images of the apple tree in our back garden, the rose trellis framing our front door, the beech hedge flanking our graveled drive. That the pictures had been taken with some sort of telephoto lens afforded me no comfort at all. The images were far too personal. There was one of me, sitting on the bamboo chaise longue beneath the apple tree, and one of Annelise, standing in the doorway of the solarium, but the final image was the most terrifying of all.

"The twins," I whispered. "Will and Rob, on their ponies . . ."

Bill moved from his chair to the ottoman and slid the photographs from my unresisting grasp. He dropped them onto the floor and took my hands in his.

"The photographs came this morning, with the message you've just read," he said. "As soon as they arrived, I sent a security team up from London, to keep an eye on you and the boys while I met with the chief superintendent."

"I haven't seen anyone," I said.

"I told them to keep a low profile," said Bill. "I wanted them to stay in the background until I had a chance to tell you what was happening. They've been patrolling the woods, the hills, the lane. They'll live here, in the cottage, while we're gone, to make sure nothing happens to it."

"'All that you love will perish,'" I repeated numbly. "I suppose that includes the cottage."

"We can't afford to interpret it in any other way," said Bill.

"Where do you want us to go?" I asked.

"Boston," he said promptly. "You can stay with my father."

"*Boston?*" I exclaimed, recoiling. "Are you crazy? You know how much I love your father, Bill, but I am *not* going to Boston. There'd be a whole ocean between us, and the Concorde's not flying anymore. If something happened to you, it'd take me forever to get back."

Bill managed a weary smile. "It was worth a try. But I knew you'd hate the idea of going to Boston, so I've come up with another plan, one that'll keep you on this side of the Atlantic."

"What is it?" I asked.

"I'm not going to tell you," he replied, and when I opened my mouth to protest, he cut me off. "I'm sorry, Lori, but you're a chatterbox. One slip of your tongue and the news would be all over Finch in five minutes. Our neighbors may be well intentioned, but they're addicted to gossip. A casual conversation in the tearoom or the pub would lead Abaddon straight to you. The fewer people who know where you and the boys are, the safer you'll be, so for now I'm keeping your destination to myself. You'll have to trust me on this, love."

Bill gripped my hands more firmly, as if bracing himself for a wave of entirely justified wifely hysterics, but I didn't feel hysterical. I felt cold and still and extremely focused. My husband had shouldered an unimaginably heavy burden. I had no intention of adding to it.

"Right," I said, and got to my feet.

"Where are you going?" Bill asked.

"To pack."

Two

The rest of the afternoon flew by in a flurry of activity. Since it was impossible to select appropriate clothing for an unknown destination, Annelise and I crammed everything from snowsuits to bathing suits into suitcases. And since we didn't know how long we'd be away, there were quite a few suitcases.

The only thing I knew for certain about our secret hideaway was that it was child-friendly, and the only reason I knew that was because Bill assured Will and Rob that there was no need for them to pack every toy they owned, since there would be plenty of things for them to play with where they were going.

At some point Bill called me downstairs to introduce me to Ivan Anton, the head of the security detail from London. The broad-shouldered young man declined my invitation to dinner, telling me that he and his team would be spending the night in the field, as well as on the hillsides and at strategically placed locations along the narrow lane.

"We've set up a secure perimeter around the cottage," Ivan informed me. "No one will get past us, Mrs. Willis."

"Shepherd," I corrected automatically. It was a common mistake. I hadn't changed my last name when I'd married Bill Willis. "I'm Lori Shepherd. But call me Lori. Everyone does."

Ivan nodded. "You can rely on me and my team, Lori. We'll look after your home as if it were our own." He touched his fingers to his brow in a casual salute and went back to patrolling his secure perimeter.

I went back upstairs, to continue packing.

Stanley—wisest of cats—decided to keep clear of our flying feet by curling up in Bill's favorite armchair in the living room. He remained there until dinnertime, when he joined us in the dining room, where he did his utmost to persuade us that the veal-and-ham pie had been baked exclusively for him.

After dinner we gathered around the kitchen table for a spirited game of Go Fish that lasted well past the twins' normal bedtime. When the game ended, Annelise went upstairs to her room to pack her own bags, and Bill went up, too, to put the boys to bed. Stanley went with them—he was, for all intents and purposes, Bill's cat—but I didn't intrude. I knew I'd have the twins with me, wherever we went, but Bill didn't know when he'd see them again. I wanted to give them as much father-and-sons time together as possible.

I put the playing cards away, emptied the dishwasher, and taped notes to the kitchen cabinets, to help Ivan Anton and his team find whatever they might need to make their own meals. It was approaching ten o'clock when I returned to the study.

The lights above the mantel shelf were still lit, but I put a match to the logs in the fireplace anyway. When the flames were leaping, I took from the bookshelves a blue-leather-bound book and settled with it in the armchair I'd occupied earlier, during my disquieting conversation with Bill.

The blue book was a journal of sorts. I'd inherited it from my late mother's closest friend, an Englishwoman named Dimity Westwood. My mother and Dimity had met in London while serving their respective countries during the Second World War. Although they never saw each other again after my mother returned to the States at the conclusion of the war, they maintained their friendship by sending hundreds of letters back and forth across the Atlantic.

My mother treasured her correspondence with Dimity. Her letters were her refuge, her favorite escape from the routines and responsibilities of everyday life, and she kept them a closely guarded secret. I knew nothing about the letters, or her friendship with Dimity, until after both she and Dimity were dead.

Until then I'd known Dimity Westwood only as Aunt Dimity, a fairy-tale figure from my childhood, the main character in a series of bedtime stories invented by my mother. The truth about Aunt Dimity had come as quite a shock, as had the news that my fictional heroine had bequeathed to me a very real fortune along with the honey-colored cottage in which she'd grown up, the precious cache of letters, and a journal bound in blue leather.

It had come as a far greater shock to discover that Dimity, though deceased, had not altogether departed the cottage. Despite having what some might consider a significant handicap, she continued to visit her old home. She was far too civilized to announce her presence by moaning in the chimneys or hovering in a spectral mist at the foot of my bed. Instead, she wrote to me, as she had written to my mother, continuing the correspondence not in letters, but in the blue journal.

Whenever I opened the journal, Dimity's handwriting appeared, an old-fashioned copperplate taught in the village school at a time when indoor plumbing was an uncommon luxury. I had no idea how Dimity managed to bridge the gap between life and afterlife—she wasn't too clear on the mechanics of it either—but the *how* had long since ceased to concern me. My friendship with Aunt Dimity may have been the most surprising of surprise presents, but it was a gift beyond price, and I accepted it gratefully.

The fire crackled and snapped as I curled my legs beneath me in the armchair. I glanced at the diamond-paned window over the old oak desk, half expecting to see the king of the bottomless pit leering at me through the fluttering ivy, and opened the blue journal.

"Dimity?" I said, and felt a knot of tension ease when the familiar lines of royal-blue ink curled and looped reassuringly across the blank page.

Good evening, my dear. How was your day?

"Well . . ." I pursed my lips judiciously. "If you leave out the part where Bill, the boys, and I are being chased from our home by a homicidal maniac who wants to erase our names from the book of life forever"—I took a breath—"it wasn't too bad."

Excuse me?

"It's true, Dimity," I said. "Incredible, but true. Some looney's been e-mailing death threats to Bill for the past few weeks. This morning he expanded the threat to include me and the boys, so Bill's sending us into hiding while he stays in London to work with Chief Superintendent Wesley Yarborough of Scotland Yard."

Good grief. Who on earth would wish to murder Bill?

"A former client, we think," I said. "He calls himself Abaddon."

Ah. The angel of the bottomless pit. The Book of Revelations, alas, provides a wealth of unsavory imagery for the unhinged imagination, and I think we can safely assume that Abaddon is unhinged. Dissatisfied clients don't, as a rule, express their displeasure by threatening to kill one and one's family.

"It's a first for Bill," I acknowledged. "When his clients get mad, they get mad at each other, not at him. They may blame Uncle Hans for leaving ten thousand marks to a shelter for homeless dachshunds, but they don't blame Bill for drawing up Uncle Hans's will."

Abaddon's evidently blaming Bill for something. It may be a case of shooting the messenger, if you'll pardon the unfortunate turn of phrase. What does Bill intend to do in London?

"He's going to help a team of detectives from Scotland Yard," I said. "They plan to go through his work files, to see if they can identify a likely suspect. Bill's not too keen on the idea—the files are highly confidential—but he can't think of a better place to start. He still can't believe that someone he knows—or knew— wants him dead."

Poor man. I do sympathize. When my life was threatened, I found it extremely difficult to—

"When was your life threatened?" I interrupted, startled.

I believe I told you once of a series of poison-pen letters I received when I was working in London?

"Yes," I said. "You told me about them while we were staying at Hailesham House, when Simon Elstyn started getting those creepy anonymous notes. You said that a woman who worked for you, an assistant you trusted, was responsible. But you never mentioned death threats."

I didn't want you to worry retroactively. After all, it happened a very long time ago. Nevertheless, I can remember without effort the overriding sense of disbelief I experienced when I realized that someone, some faceless monster, wished to end my life. Even after the culprit had been appre- hended, the situation continued to seem . . . surreal.

"I know what you mean," I said. "It's the kind of thing that happens to other people. If I didn't have a pile of suitcases in the front hall to anchor me, I'd still doubt that it was happening to us. I'm not used to being hated. Okay," I admitted, after a moment's consideration, "Sally Pyne was annoyed with me when I said that her flower arrangement in the baptismal font at St. George's looked top-heavy, but she didn't *hate* me."

Nor could anyone who knows you. Would it help you to think of Abaddon's hatred as abstract rather than personal?

"Nope," I said. "I feel as if I have a bull's-eye on my forehead, Dimity. It doesn't get much more personal than that."

No, I'm afraid it doesn't. When do you leave?

"Tomorrow morning," I replied.

Will you be safe here tonight?

"Presumably," I said, and told her about Ivan Anton and his crew of security specialists. "And before you ask," I continued, "I don't know where we're going. Bill won't tell me, because he's afraid I'll slip up and tell someone else and then—Finch being the gossip capital of the world—our secret location won't be a secret anymore."

Your openness is one of your most endearing qualities, Lori, but it's a bit of a liability when it comes to the keeping of secrets. I must say that you're responding to the situation with remarkable tranquillity.

"Amazing, isn't it?" I said. "I should be tearing my hair out right about now, but I don't have the energy. There's been too much to do. On top of the packing, I've had to make at least a thousand phone calls to cancel this and reschedule that. I'll tell you, Dimity, you never realize how complicated your life is until you're forced to rearrange it."

Very true.

"I've penciled in a fit of hysteria for tomorrow evening, though," I added. "I think I'll owe it to myself by then, don't you?"

Absolutely. I'm sure it will be most cathartic. Have you told Rob and Will about Abaddon?

"Bill told them that we're going away because a bad man wants to hurt us." I shook my head. "I didn't want to tell them anything, but Bill convinced me that they'd be safer if they were aware of the danger."

How did they react?

"Like five-year-olds," I said with a wry smile. "They went into their twin mind-meld and came out with: 'Don't worry, Daddy, we'll be careful. May we bring our cricket bats?'"

Splendid. They clearly have complete confidence in your ability to protect them, which is as it should be. Will Annelise accompany you?

"No," I replied. "It was a tough decision, and Annelise isn't happy about it—she feels as if she's abandoning us in our hour of need—but it's the right thing to do. We don't want to drag her any deeper into our troubles than she already is. Bill and I decided that her family's farm would be the safest place for her until Abaddon's locked up."

I agree. The Sciaparelli clan knows how to look after its own. At times like this, it's extremely useful for a young woman to have seven muscular and highly protective brothers nearby. What about Stanley? The cats I've known haven't been terribly fond of travel. Are you going to bring him with you? Or will Mr. Anton take care of him?

"Stanley's going into protective custody at Anscombe Manor," I explained. Anscombe Manor was the sprawling home of our closest friends, Emma and Derek Harris, and of their stable master, Kit Smith. "Emma's promised to keep an eye on Stanley, and Kit won't let any harm come to the boys' ponies."

I suspect that Kit will sleep in the stalls, armed with a pitchfork, until the danger passes.

"It wouldn't surprise me one bit," I said. "Kit's a man of peace, except when it comes to people who hurt animals."

Well. You seem to have everything in hand.

"Yep." I nodded.

You've rearranged your affairs with great composure.

"That's right."

The packing is finished, the telephone calls have been made, and every-

thing else has been properly seen to. You've been energetic and sensible and, most important, well organized. I applaud you.

"Thank you," I said, with a little half bow.

Now, my dear child, don't you think it's time for you to tell me what's really going on inside that head of yours?

I studied the question in silence, then lifted my gaze to look slowly around the room. I couldn't count the number of hours I'd spent in the study since the cottage had become my home. I was intimately familiar with each floorboard's creak, each shadowy corner, each whisper of wind in the chimney. As I ran my hand along the armchair's smooth leather, I recalled that I'd been sitting in the same chair the first time I'd opened Aunt Dimity's remarkable journal.

I closed my eyes and let my mind travel through the cottage's other rooms, past the silver-framed family photographs, the piles of stuffed animals, the scrawled notes taped to the living room's mantel shelf—reminders of events and appointments that had seemed important six hours ago but that had since become wholly irrelevant. I saw with my mind's eye the ink-stained cushion on the window seat beneath the living room's bow window, the scratches on the legs of the dining-room table, the overflowing coatrack in the front hall. I saw the twins asleep in their beds, nestled beneath quilts sewn by the village's quilting club, and Bill standing over them, with cold fear in his eyes.

"What's really going on inside my head?" I said softly, and looked into the fire's quivering flames. "I'm being terrorized by someone who wants to kill my husband, my children, and me. I'm being forced to leave the place I love above all others on this earth, and I don't know when I'll be able to come back. I'm keeping calm for Bill's sake and the boys', Dimity, but if you want to know the truth about how I'm feeling, here it is: I want to camouflage my face and go out there in the dark with a machete and a machine gun and a flamethrower. I want to find this evil creep and shoot him and stab him and stomp on him and cut him into little pieces and burn him to ashes and send his ashes into space so they'd never pollute any air I might breathe." I paused to let my thundering heart quieten. "I guess you could say that I'm having a slight problem with anger management."

To the contrary, my dear, I would say that you're managing your anger exceptionally well. You haven't by any chance acquired a flamethrower, have you?

I astonished myself by laughing out loud. "Of course not, Dimity! I haven't had the time. Besides, I wouldn't know what to do with a flamethrower if I had one."

I'm sure they come with instructions. That being said, I believe you'll be better served if you leave all such matters in the capable hands of Ivan Anton and Chief Superintendent Yarborough.

"That's exactly what I intend to do," I said. "I also intend to bring you with me."

I should hope so. You'll need someone to keep you from running amok. And Reginald? You won't leave him behind, will you?

Reginald was a small, pink flannel rabbit with black button eyes, beautifully hand-stitched whiskers, and the ghost of a grape juice stain on his snout. He'd been my constant companion from the earliest days of my childhood, and he remained a cherished chum.

When Dimity mentioned Reginald's name, I looked up at the special niche in the bookshelves where he sat gazing down at me. His black button eyes seemed to dance with impatience in the flickering firelight, as if he were eager to hop into one of the suitcases in the front hall. I hadn't told him yet that he'd be traveling in my carry-on bag, along with the blue journal.

"How could I leave Reginald behind?" I said. "I haven't taken him to bed with me since I was ten years old, but with Bill in London . . . Who knows? I may start sucking my thumb again, too."

I can think of far worse ways to cope with stress.

"Dimity?" I said. "How did you cope?"

I put my trust in the police, consumed vast quantities of chocolate, and tried to get at least eight hours of sleep every night, until the case was solved. I'd advise you to get some rest tonight, if you possibly can. You'll feel much better for it in the morning.

"I'm sure you're right," I said. "Good night, Dimity. I'll fill you in on our whereabouts as soon as we arrive."

Good night, my dear.

I waited until the graceful lines of royal-blue ink had faded from the page, then cast another furtive glance at the ivy-covered window. Dimity had given me sound advice, as always, but I didn't think I could follow it to the letter. Chocolate I could handle—the vaster the quantities, the better—but I doubted that I'd be able to shut my eyes again, much less sleep, until the king of the bottomless pit was behind bars.

Three

An ancient and massive brambly hedge to the south of the cottage separated our property from that of Mr. Malvern, the farmer next door. The hedge was a world unto itself, filled with rabbits, mice, interesting bugs, and a myriad of birds' nests, and riddled with enticing, cavelike hollows that Rob and Will loved to explore on hot summer days.

The hedge was pierced by a sturdy wooden stile that gave us access to Mr. Malvern's north field, a large expanse of tussocky grass usually occupied by his small herd of dairy cows. Daisy, Beulah, and the rest of the herd were grazing elsewhere on the morning of our departure, but the field wasn't empty. Two members of Ivan Anton's security team had, for reasons unknown to me, carried our suitcases over the stile and left them in a neat stack in the damp grass just beyond the hedge. When I asked Bill for an explanation, he said simply that I'd find out soon enough.

Bill and I had spent a restless night bravely reassuring each other that all would be well. We'd checked on Will and Rob at least a dozen times between dozes before rising at dawn to see Annelise off, prepare breakfast, and get the boys up, dressed, and fed.

At seven o'clock Ivan Anton took Stanley, Stanley's bowls, Stanley's toys, and a month's supply of Stanley's favorite gourmet cat food to Anscombe Manor. At a quarter to nine, Ivan's assistants escorted Bill, the twins, and me into the back garden. The two men hopped over the stile, but the rest of us stopped dead in our tracks, transfixed by the astonishing sight of a helicopter landing in Mr. Malvern's north field. When I glanced questioningly at Bill, he swept an arm in the direction of the wind-whipped hedge.

"Your chariot awaits," he said above the noise of the rotors.

As Bill and I guided Will and Rob over the stile, I studied the machine that had come to fly us to safety. To my untrained eye, it looked like the latest model. Big, black, sleek, and shiny, it reminded me more of a cruising shark than a fluttering whirlybird. It seemed to me that only a multimillionaire could afford to own such a fancy plaything, and with that thought comprehension dawned.

"Percy!" I exclaimed, as Bill clambered last over the stile. "You're sending us to stay with Sir Percy Pelham!"

The words had scarcely escaped my lips when Sir Perceval Pelham confirmed my guess by climbing out of the helicopter. Sir Percy and Bill's father were old friends, and Bill had known Sir Percy all his life. He was a huge man, tall and broad-shouldered rather than fat, and although he was in his late fifties, his boundless joie de vivre made him seem years younger. His voice boomed, his step bounced, and his passion for big boys' toys made him extremely popular with the twins. In many ways he was their contemporary.

He was also unspeakably wealthy. Sir Percy had inherited a packet from his father, and he'd multiplied it a hundredfold through clever investments in oil, pharmaceuticals, and various engineering projects all over the world. If anyone could provide my sons and me with first-class protection while Bill was in London, it would be Sir Percy.

The boys let out joyful whoops as the big man approached the stile, pushing his fluffy white hair back from his ruddy forehead and grinning from ear to ear. His copilot, a self-effacing, slender young man named Atkinson, helped Ivan Anton's men load our suitcases into the cargo hold, then came forward to say hello.

"Hullo, Sir Percy! Hullo, Atkinson!" the twins called. "Will you be our pilot, Sir Percy? Can we ride up front with you?"

"You'll ride in the back with me," I stated firmly, and gave Sir Percy a meaningful stare.

"Of course I'll fly the chopper, chaps," he boomed. "Get the best man for the job, I always say. And you'll most certainly ride in the back. Need you to navigate. Vital job, you know. Wouldn't want to come down in the great Namibian Desert by accident, would we?" He squatted and put a hand on each twin's shoulder. "Love to pop in on the ponies and have a tramp round your woods, old things, but time's pressing. Be good fellows, now, and give your papa a proper farewell."

I had to press my hand to my mouth to keep my chin from trembling when Bill knelt to say good-bye to the twins. I could hear the forced cheerfulness in his voice as he told them he'd see them again very soon, and the boys seemed to hear it, too.

"Don't be scared, Daddy," said Rob, patting his father's back consolingly. "Sir Percy will look after us."

Will nodded his agreement. "If the bad man comes near us, Sir Percy will *eat* him."

"With mustard and vinegar," Sir Percy declared. "Run along, now, chaps. Atkinson will get you settled in your seats." He waited until the twins were some distance away, then addressed Bill with unaccustomed sobriety. "Out of the mouths of babes, eh? They're right, you know. You've nothing to worry about. Your family's mine for the duration. Defend 'em with my life, if need be."

"I know you will, Percy." Bill gripped the big man's hand. "Thank you."

"Think nothing of it. I've always wanted to whisk a beautiful woman north of the border. We won't, alas, have time to stop at Gretna Green, which is just as well, since the woman in question is already quite happily married." Sir Percy winked at me, grabbed my carry-on bag, and headed for the helicopter.

"Gretna Green," I said reflectively. "Is Percy taking us to Scotland?"

"My lips are sealed," said Bill.

We turned to face each other. Bill looked suddenly awkward, as if he didn't trust himself to speak.

"Well . . ." he began.

"Look," I broke in hurriedly, "I know what we said last night about not clinging to each other like a pair of needy idiots when it came time to say good-bye, but I don't think it would hurt a thing if we clung like a husband and wife who are fairly fond of each other, do you? Just for a minute?"

"Just for a minute," said Bill, and pulled me into his arms.

The minute lasted a bit longer than the regulation sixty seconds, and I left Bill's shirtfront slightly damper than it had been, but only slightly. After a quick kiss and a wobbly smile, I turned and ran for the helicopter, afraid that if I slowed down, I'd break down.

Sir Percy welcomed me aboard, tucked my jacket into an overhead compartment, and seated me across the aisle from the twins, who were already in shirtsleeves, strapped in their seats, and raring to go. Sir Percy had thoughtfully provided them with child-size headsets so they could communicate with him and Atkinson during the flight. He helped me to don a grown-up set and showed me how to use it, then gave me a double thumbs-up and disappeared into the cockpit.

The entire cabin vibrated when the rotors began to turn, and my stomach plummeted when we shot straight up into the air. I gripped the armrests and took several deliberate breaths, willing my breakfast to stay put, while I glued my nose to the window to watch Bill until we swooped north and he vanished, hidden by the high hedge.

Will and Rob, who'd thoroughly enjoyed our rapid ascent, began calling out familiar sights as we swept over them: Anscombe Manor, the Pym sisters' house, St. George's Church, Hodge Farm. Each place-name brought a neighbor's face to mind, and a host of memories. I thought of how snugly my family fit into the tight-knit tapestry of everyday life in our tiny English village, and my anger at Abaddon surged. With a few malicious keystrokes, he'd robbed us of our home, our village, our place in the world. Using fear as a weapon, he'd torn our family apart and turned us into fleeing refugees. If I ever got my hands on him, I told myself, I wouldn't need a flamethrower. My rage alone would burn him to a crisp.

"Snacks in the overhead for anyone who's peckish!" Sir Percy's voice roared in my headset. "Special treats for junior airmen!"

I'd lost all interest in food, but the boys were perpetually hungry, so I retrieved two bright red plastic boxes from the overhead compartment. I was afraid that the special treats would be sugary concoctions guaranteed to send my overexcited five-year-olds into orbit, so I was pleasantly surprised to find that the boxes contained bananas, nuts, carrot sticks, peanut butter crackers, and small bottles of juice. The special treats turned out to be inedible: two pairs of small but powerful binoculars, two large boxes of crayons, and two sketch pads. The sight of the crayons warmed my heart. Sir Percy might be a busy man, with many irons in many fires, but he'd somehow managed to remember the twins' love of drawing.

I left the boys happily munching, peering, and coloring, and returned to my seat to watch the countryside slide by beneath us.

I knew that Sir Percy owned at least two estates in Scotland and tried for a while to figure out which one he was taking us to, but the helicopter changed directions so often that I soon gave up. It was as if Sir Percy were taking evasive action in order to elude our enemy. I wondered if the maneuvers were necessary—a chilling thought—or if they were just Sir Percy's idea of fun.

"Percy?" I said, pushing a button that I hoped would exclude the twins from our conversation.

"At your service," Sir Percy boomed back.

"Can the boys hear us?" I asked.

"Not if they're wearing their headphones," he replied. "Unless you start shouting, of course, and even then you'd need the lungs of an opera singer to get through to them. The headsets are designed to keep noise to a minimum. What's on your mind, old thing?"

"Are we being followed? By something other than a flock of geese?" I added hastily, to preempt a humorous reply.

"Not as far as I can tell," said Sir Percy, "but one never knows. Better safe than sorry, I always say."

I doubted that he'd ever said such a thing in his life. The Percy Pelham *I* knew drove fast cars, flew jets, scaled mountains, and raced yachts on stormy seas. He'd almost always rather be sorry than safe, but it was possible that he'd curbed his addiction to risk-taking for our sakes.

"How soon will we land?" I asked.

"Impatient, are we?" Sir Percy returned.

"Not impatient," I said, "just curious. Bill wouldn't tell me where we're going because he was afraid I'd tell someone else, but there's no one to tell up here, so I'm sure he wouldn't mind if you told me. Go ahead, Percy, spill the beans."

"Not for a thousand gold sovereigns," he responded stoutly. "It would spoil the surprise. You like surprises, don't you, Lori?"

"Not as much as I used to," I said. "I've had a few too many of them in the past twenty-four hours."

"Courage, my dear," Sir Percy said bracingly. "You've one hundred and twenty channels of music and other entertainment to choose from. Avail yourself of them. It'll do you good to relax."

"If you insist," I said, and after checking in with the boys, who were absorbed in making highly detailed drawings of fantastic helicopters, I followed Sir Percy's advice. Although it felt a bit like fiddling while Rome burned, I pushed buttons on the headset controls until I heard an actor reading *The Wind in the Willows*, settled back in my capacious seat, and confounded my own prediction by falling instantaneously into a deep and mercifully untroubled sleep.

Four

When I awoke, we were flying low over the sea. It had to be the sea, because even the largest lakes in the United Kingdom didn't stretch out to the horizon in endless, rolling swells, but whether it was the North Sea or the Atlantic Ocean, I couldn't tell.

A glance at my wristwatch told me that I'd been asleep for nearly an hour. Will and Rob, who were now engaged in drawing fantastic whales, sharks, and octopi, looked up from their sketch pads and bobbed their heads cheerfully at me. I switched my headset back to intercom mode—cutting off, with some regret, a dramatic recitation of Tennyson's "Charge of the Light Brigade"—and asked them if Sir Percy had said anything about our destination while I slept, but Percy broke in before they could reply.

"Lori, Lori, Lori," he said sorrowfully. "Pumping your sons for information? For shame. For no good purpose, either. I promised your dear husband that I'd keep our destination secret, and secret it shall remain. For a few minutes longer, at any rate."

"A few minutes," I echoed thoughtfully. It was the closest thing to a hint I'd heard since he'd mentioned Gretna Green, though admittedly it wasn't a very helpful one. If we were only a few minutes from our destination, it had to be on a coast, but since Great Britain was an island, there were a lot of coasts to choose from. Sighing, I peered through the window and tried once more to figure out where Sir Percy was taking us.

The sky was a pale, misty blue, but the sea was dazzling, a wrinkled sheet of aquamarine slashed with silver shards of sunlight. I spotted a small fishing boat floating among the glittering waves below us and an enormous oil tanker far out at sea, plowing steadily onward. It wasn't until Will shouted "Land, ho!" that I looked away from the tanker and saw that we were approaching a small island.

"Erinskil," Sir Percy announced through the headphones. "The jewel of the Scottish isles and my little home-away-from-home. Yours, too, until it's time for you to leave."

"The Scottish isles!" I exclaimed. "How wonderful!"

"I'm glad you approve," said Sir Percy.

If I craned my neck to look through the windows on the twins' side of the cabin, I could see a series of larger islands in the distance, but it was difficult to tell how far they were from Erinskil. If I squinted, I could just make out an even larger body of land beyond the islands.

"Is the west coast of Scotland off there to our right?" I asked.

"It is," Sir Percy answered, and continued in the singsong voice of a well-practiced tour guide, "the golden isle of Erinskil lies forty miles west of the Scottish mainland, thirty-two miles from the nearest neighboring island. Fewer than two hundred souls live on Erinskil, spread comfortably over twenty square miles of occasionally arable land. The ferry visits our pleasant shores once a week, but tourists seldom come to call, thanks to our somewhat primitive landing facilities. An ideal retreat for those seeking peace and privacy, wouldn't you say?"

"I would," I agreed wholeheartedly. Sir Percy's solution to our security problem was, to my mind, nothing short of masterful. I'd sleep much better while Abaddon was on the loose, knowing that the twins and I were protected by such a formidable moat.

"Shall I give you an aerial tour?" Sir Percy inquired.

"Yes, please," I said eagerly. I'd been to a good many places in

Great Britain, both before and after I'd chosen to live there. I'd traveled from Lands End to John o' Groats, from Wookey Hole's depths to Mount Snowdon's summit, but I'd never set sail for the fabled Western Isles of Scotland. Although I would have preferred to visit them under less stressful circumstances, I couldn't help feeling a tingle of excitement at the prospect of finally experiencing island life firsthand.

"Look, Mummy!" Rob's voice piped in my headphones. "Windmills!"

Erinskil was longer than it was wide, like an oval platter with a badly chipped rim, pointing north. As we flew over its southwestern tip, I saw a forest of windmills planted on a towering headland. They were modern windmills with long, graceful propellers clearly designed to generate power, but their bases were surprisingly stumpy.

"Why are the windmills so short?" I asked Sir Percy.

"Because they're perched atop three-hundred-foot cliffs," he replied, "in a spot where the wind hasn't stopped blowing since Adam first met Eve. If they were taller, the winter gales would knock 'em over. It'd be dashed inconvenient to be without electricity from September through March, don't you think?"

"Winter lasts from September through March up here?" I said incredulously.

"We're not in the Bahamas, Lori," Sir Percy pointed out. "Even now, in the latter days of April, Erinskil's no place for the fainthearted."

"I guess not," I conceded, and continued to peer downward while Sir Percy flew in a series of S curves that allowed us to view the island from coast to coast.

Erinskil's long central valley was surrounded by a necklace of steep hills. Along the coasts, foaming waves unfurled on white-sand beaches or crashed with a flourish against tall, craggy cliffs. Hundreds of thousands of seabirds rose in swirling clouds from the cliffs as we passed, their beaks open nearly as wide as their wings as they objected raucously to our intrusion.

"Those are the Devil's Teeth," Sir Percy informed me, as we flew over a cluster of stark, jagged stone columns jutting up from the sea, "and that's known as the Sleeping Dragon," he went on, turning to follow the spine of a long, spiky ridge that wound into the island's green interior.

A small, mirror-bright lake lay at the foot of the Sleeping Dragon, and emerald-green fields stretched out beyond it. We flew over pastures hemmed by stone walls and strewn with boulders—though many of the boulders turned out, at second glance, to be sheep. A two-lane paved road ran north to south down the center of the island, with dirt tracks leading off it to what I presumed were farmsteads. We were flying so low that I could plainly see a woman hanging laundry on a line near one whitewashed house. To judge by the way the shirts flapped in the wind, they wouldn't take long to dry.

In the island's northeastern corner, the land dipped down to what appeared to be a natural harbor. At its lowest and most sheltered point, a concrete jetty jutted out from the shoreline and bent at a right angle to form a breakwater. A small construction crane stood at the jetty's elbow, permanently mounted on a concrete base. A few boats lay at anchor inside the breakwater, several more had been drawn up on the slipway, and a collection of whitewashed stone buildings straggled up from the jetty along a cobbled street.

"Stoneywell," said Sir Percy, "Erinskil's harbor and only village. Smaller than Finch it may be, but it possesses all the hallmarks of civilization: church, schoolhouse, post office, pub. My little home-away-from-home stands above the village, in a spot that affords marvelous views of the sea as well as . . ."

The narration continued, but I was no longer listening. I was staring in delighted disbelief at another, much larger building that crowned the grassy headland above the village.

"A *castle!*" I exclaimed. "I didn't know you owned a *castle!*"

It wasn't a fairy-tale castle, with delicate turrets, slender pillars, and pointed arches. The edifice on the headland was a blunt, blocky, businesslike fortification that seemed to grow out of the living rock. An unpaved track wound up from the village to the massive gatehouse in the castle's south wall, and the east wall overlooked the harbor, but its north and west walls had their backs to the sea.

As Sir Percy flew in a wide circle around the headland, I could see that the castle was roughly rectangular in shape, with a squat, round tower at each corner. The gatehouse opened onto a flag-stoned courtyard surrounded on three sides by a U-shaped building, a central block with two wings. The three-story building had evidently been built for durability rather than looks. It sat snugly against the castle's outer walls, as though it had been grafted onto them when the castle had been built.

The outer walls were topped by wide walkways, hung with balconies, and pierced by many windows. I was alarmed to see a half dozen sinister-looking black cannons resting on the lead roof of the northeast tower, their barrels pointing through the crenellations. The bristling weaponry made the castle seem belligerent, as if it were issuing a gruff challenge to would-be pillagers: "Listen up, Viking hordes: No one lands here without *my* permission." From a pole atop the gatehouse, a flag flew, bearing the Pelham family crest.

Sir Percy's voice boomed suddenly in my headphones: *"Surprise!"*

I grinned weakly, glanced at my wide-eyed sons, and began to have second thoughts about the safety of our safe haven. If the boys didn't plunge headlong from the castle walls into the sea, they stood a good chance of blowing themselves to smithereens with Sir Percy's explosive version of patio furniture. I hoped fervently that the big guns were decorative rather than functional, then clutched my armrests as the helicopter stopped in midair, hovered briefly, and began to descend. My heart—and stomach—quaked when I realized that Sir Percy intended to land the helicopter on the edge of a windblown cliff.

I would have shouted "Are you *nuts?*" if I hadn't been terrified of distracting Sir Percy from what I considered to be an unnervingly finicky maneuver. The gusts that drove Erinskil's windmills were sure to flip us over and send us crashing to our doom. I turned to reassure Will and Rob, but their blissful expressions told me that they were in seventh heaven, and I quickly decided to keep my mouth shut. The flight was one big roller-coaster ride to them, and I wasn't about to spoil their fun with boring old intimations of mortality. As the ground rose to meet us, I closed my eyes, gritted my teeth, and hoped for the best.

A gentle bump jarred my seat, but it wasn't until the engines began to wind down that I realized we'd landed. A swift glance through the window told me that my fears had been needless. We were sitting steady as a rock on a helipad of poured concrete surrounded by a smooth, wind-deflecting berm. I smiled sheepishly as Sir Percy emerged from the cockpit, looking buoyant.

"Great landing," I said.

"It *was* rather good, wasn't it?" As he stowed our headsets and helped the boys undo their safety belts, he added over his shoulder, "Glad you're not a nervous Nelly. Some people go all to pieces during the final descent."

"Do they?" I said airily. "I can't imagine why."

Sir Percy dumped the remnants of the twins' snacks into a garbage bag and paused to admire their artwork before putting sketch pads, crayons, and binoculars back into the red plastic boxes, which he presented to them. While he retrieved my carry-on bag from a rear compartment, Atkinson opened the helicopter's exit door, unfolded the steps, and stood by to help the twins and me climb down.

I'd seldom been happier to feel solid concrete beneath my feet, but I didn't have a chance to kiss the helipad. Atkinson unloaded our suitcases at top speed and carried them through a gap in the berm, then climbed back into the helicopter, pulled the steps up, and closed the door behind him. Sir Percy promptly hustled us through the gap, paused, and swung around to salute Atkinson as the helicopter's blades began to turn.

"Where's Atkinson going?" Will asked, as the helicopter soared skyward.

"To the mainland, old son," said Sir Percy. "We can't keep the chopper here for any length of time, unfortunately. The winds can get pretty ferocious. But Atkinson's only a phone call away, weather permitting. Come along, now. . . ."

Sir Percy ushered us out of the landing area and into a strange little vehicle into which Atkinson had already loaded our luggage. The vehicle looked like a cross between a golf cart, a Jeep, and a grape. Its roof and chassis were painted a bright, metallic purple, and its windows were slightly convex, like bugs' eyes. Sir Percy pushed a button on the dashboard to start it, and when he put his foot on the accelerator, the engine produced only a faint hum.

"Electric," he said proudly. "Designed it myself. Too flimsy for the Peking-to-Paris race, but just the ticket for short hops on the island. On we go!"

We bumped along the unpaved track from the landing pad to the castle, and as we approached the gatehouse, Sir Percy pushed another button on the dashboard and the iron-banded wooden gate blocking the entrance slid up and out of our way as easily as if it had been an automatic garage door.

"Good, eh? Designed it myself," said Sir Percy, pointing to the gate as we passed beneath it. "It's a type of plastic—stronger, lighter, more fireproof, and less prone to rot than wood. But it looks the part, doesn't it?"

Sir Percy parked the purple car in the courtyard and told me not to bother with the luggage.

"My housekeeper will see to it," he said, and turned to the boys. "Sorry, chaps, but I have no ponies to offer you. There haven't been horses on Erinskil since before the war. You'll have to use your feet while you're on the island."

Will and Rob favored the grape car with speculative glances, and I made a mental note to ask Sir Percy to lock it up. It was too easy to imagine the thrilling adventures my sons would have, joyriding in a push-button car.

The courtyard was paved in gray flagstone and decorated with a menagerie of gargoyles that won the twins' devoted admiration. Will and Rob spun in circles, trying to decide which grotesque beast they liked best as Sir Percy led us to the staircase of the U-shaped building's central block. He sprinted ahead of us up the broad stone stairs, pushed open the pair of studded wooden doors, and stood aside while we filed past him into an entrance hall that looked as though it hadn't changed much since the Dark Ages.

Everything seemed to be made out of dull gray stone—the floor, the walls, the staircase that rose from the center of the hall to the upper stories. Sunlight filtered dimly through a stained-glass window at the staircase's first landing, illuminating the few things that weren't made from stone: two tarnished suits of armor, a few pieces of ponderous wooden furniture, and tapestry drapes behind which, I imagined, there would be dim passages leading to other parts of the castle. The overall effect was gray, grim, and distinctly chilly. When Sir Percy closed the studded doors behind us, I had the queer feeling that he was sealing us into a tomb.

Sir Percy seemed undaunted by the entrance hall's funereal ambience. He dashed past me, leapt onto the staircase's bottom step, and flung his arms wide. With his twinkling blue eyes and fluffy, windblown hair, he looked like a slightly mad Santa as he proclaimed, "Welcome to Dundrillin Castle!"

His words were still echoing from the walls when a tapestry drape was pushed aside and a gray-haired, angular woman strode across the entrance hall to join us at the bottom of the stairs. She wore a pale gray twinset, a tweed skirt, and sensible shoes, and her long, pointed face was dominated by a long, pointed nose. She was as thin as a rail and almost as tall as Sir Percy, and she wore her iron-gray hair in a neat, chin-length bob that only served to emphasize her bony jawline.

"Ah, Mrs. Gammidge," said Sir Percy. "Lori, Will, Rob—this is Mrs. Gammidge, my housekeeper."

"How do you do, Ms. Shepherd, Master Will, Master Rob?" she said, nodding to each of us in turn.

"Mrs. Gammidge manages all of my estates," Sir Percy explained. "We don't usually come north until late May, but she and a few of the staff traveled up from Kent early, to make the castle ready for you."

An unexpected lump rose in my throat. Kent was in the south of England, hundreds of miles from Scotland's Western Isles.

"That's a long way to go at a moment's notice," I said, much moved.

"We had nearly a week's notice, Ms. Shepherd," Mrs. Gammidge put in. She had a clipped, no-nonsense manner of speaking and the faint trace of a Scottish accent. "We could have made the journey and prepared for your arrival in far less time, had the need presented itself. We are a well-organized household."

"Bill rang me ten days ago and asked me to be on standby, just in case," Sir Percy informed me. "We would have made the move next month at any rate, and what's a few weeks between friends? Mrs. Gammidge has been apprised of the situation, of course, and has taken appropriate action."

"What appropriate action?" I said, puzzled.

"It's not uncommon for a man in Sir Percy's position to become a target for all manner of unpleasantness," said the housekeeper. "Corporate espionage, blackmail, and kidnappings as well as the occasional death threat are not unknown to us. Security, therefore, is our watchword. I've swept your room for bugs—"

"Bugs?" I interrupted, more puzzled still.

"Listening devices," she explained. "I've swept your sons' rooms, too, and I'm pleased to report that I've found nothing suspicious. Cook, of course, has been with us for nearly forty years, so there's no need to worry about the food. Won't you come this way?"

As she led our little group up the staircase, I stared at the back of her head in dismay. I hadn't been worried about food until she'd mentioned it. It had never occurred to me that Abaddon might try to *poison* us, and the thought of him spying on us electronically hadn't crossed my mind. As the boys and I raced to keep up with Mrs. Gammidge, it struck me that Sir Percy Pelham inhabited a world quite different from my own. In mine, housekeepers checked under the beds for dust bunnies. In his, they looked for concealed microphones.

Mrs. Gammidge turned right at the second-story landing, strode down a red-carpeted corridor, and came to a halt before a pair of rough-hewn oak doors with elaborate black iron handles.

"I'm sure your guests will wish to see their rooms and freshen up after their journey," she said, addressing her remarks to Sir Percy, "but I thought it advisable for them to meet Mr. Hunter and Mr. Ross straightaway."

"Hunter and Ross here already?" said Sir Percy. "Good. We're on schedule."

"We are *ahead* of schedule, sir," said Mrs. Gammidge. "Mr. Hunter and Mr. Ross arrived last night. I've set out a little light refreshment in the parlor, and lunch will be served in the dining room at one o'clock. Would you care to advise Cook on dinner, or shall we leave it to her to decide the menu?"

"Best leave it to Cook," said Sir Percy. "She'll know what we have on hand."

While they discussed household affairs, the boys and I surveyed the corridor. Although carpeted, it had a stark, slightly spooky feel to it. The ceiling was arched in a barrel-shaped curve, and the stone walls were rough and unfinished, like those in the entrance hall. Wrought-iron torch brackets fitted with electric bulbs had been mounted on the walls at regular intervals, but the bulbs flickered so erratically that they seemed to shed more shadow than light—they made Mrs. Gammidge's angular face look positively skeletal. The eeriness did not go unnoticed by Will or Rob. Although they didn't breathe a word, they edged so close to me that they were nearly standing on my feet.

"Shall I send Mr. Hunter and Mr. Ross down now, sir?" Mrs. Gammidge inquired.

"The sooner the better," said Sir Percy. "Thank you, Mrs. Gammidge, I'll take it from here."

The housekeeper nodded and sped off down the corridor. Sir Percy took hold of the black iron handles and pushed the oak doors inward.

I winced, and the boys cried out in pain.

Five

The light was so bright it hurt.

"Jeez, Percy," I complained as the twins pressed their faces to my sides. "You could have warned us."

"Awfully sorry," he said contritely. "I'm accustomed to the parlor, but of course you've never been here before. Bit of a shock to the system, eh?"

"A bit," I granted, blinking.

We'd stepped directly from the murky corridor into a room flooded with sunlight. The oak doors faced an uncurtained wall of mullioned windows. The leaded panes of wavy antique glass that would normally fill the Gothic frames had been replaced by single sheets of clear, modern glass that overlooked a vast expanse of blue sky and sparkling sea. The results were blinding.

When my eyes had adjusted to the glare, I realized that Sir Percy's idea of a parlor, like his notion of a housekeeper, was very different from mine. The room was at least fifty feet long and thirty wide.

"It used to be twice as large," said Sir Percy, following my astonished gaze. "Looked like an airplane hangar and cost a fortune to heat, so I lowered the ceiling and added a couple of walls to break up the space." He pointed to a door on his left. "New dining room's through there."

The parlor no longer looked like an airplane hangar but like a homely, if grandly proportioned, living room. The walls had been smoothly plastered, painted a warm, buttery yellow, and hung with gilt-framed seascapes. Flower-filled vases set here and there filled the air with fragrance, and a dozen well-worn Turkish carpets covered the planked floor, overlapping each other in a muted riot of color.

None of the furniture matched, and all of it was slightly shabby. Assorted tables, sofas, and overstuffed armchairs were clustered around the stone hearth at the east end of the room or placed in half circles before the windows, as if Sir Percy could think of no finer entertainment than to spend a quiet evening watching the waves.

A refectory table sat opposite the oak doors, covered with a white linen cloth and set with Mrs. Gammidge's light refreshment. Once the boys' vision had returned to normal, I had to physically restrain them from launching themselves onto the piles of crustless sandwiches and mounds of fruit that had been arranged on china plates.

"You'll spoil your lunch," I said repressively, and limited them to one sandwich and one piece of fruit apiece. They took their booty with them to the deep window ledge behind the refectory table, removed their binoculars from the red plastic boxes, and curled up on the ledge to keep a lookout for pirates while they ate.

I dropped my carry-on bag on a nearby chair and asked if it was safe for Rob and Will to sit so near the massive pane of glass.

"Perfectly," Sir Percy replied. "We've used tempered glass throughout the castle. An absolute necessity. Seagulls turn into cannonballs during a gale."

"Speaking of cannonballs . . ." I began, recalling the weaponry on the northeast tower.

Sir Percy seemed to read my mind. "The cannons are purely ornamental," he assured me. "I've sealed the barrels."

"Good." I looked around the room and shook my head. "You certainly know how to take a girl's breath away, Percy. I'm flabbergasted."

"Dundrillin's a useful retreat," he acknowledged, helping himself to a cucumber sandwich. "My sons and I use it during the summer months for business conferences, corporate powwows, and the like. Well-behaved clients are rewarded with holidays here. Everyone likes to say they've slept in a castle, Americans especially. We've made a number of quite lucrative deals while my guests have been under Dundrillin's spell."

I nodded. Sir Percy was a widower with four grown sons, all of whom held key positions in the flourishing Pelham business empire.

"How long has Dundrillin been in the family?" I asked.

"Hmmm, let me see. . . . " He rubbed his chin thoughtfully, as though casting his mind back over the centuries. "Dundrillin's been in my family for at least . . . three years." He laughed at my confusion. "Bought it when I got out of the oil business, dear girl. That's where the name comes from, you see. Dundrillin Castle. Get it? Dundrillin? *Done drilling?*"

"I get it," I said, with an obliging chuckle. "Why did you get out of oil?"

He shrugged. "It wasn't fun anymore. "Too many cutthroats with too little finesse—just bullyboy tactics and greed. I'm as game as the next man, but I don't relish gunplay during business hours. That's how I met Hunter and Ross, in fact. Ah, speak of the devils. . . ."

Before I could sputter *"Gunplay?"* the oak doors swung inward and two men entered the room. The first was tall and beefy, with short red hair and a freckled face. His eyes were pale blue, and he was dressed casually, in khaki trousers, a striped rugby shirt, and track shoes. He looked as though he might be a few years younger than me, in his late twenties or early thirties.

The second man was more interesting to me, in part because of his bearing, but mostly because of the jagged scar that ran along his left temple and back into his hairline. He was older than the red-haired man—in his mid-forties, at a guess—not quite as tall, and trim rather than beefy, but he radiated an air of command.

He was dressed in dark blue blazer, brown twill trousers, polished brown leather shoes, and a light blue button-down shirt that fit his tapering torso like a glove. His dark hair was clipped short and flecked with gray, and his face was as lean and weathered as a mountaineer's. He had a straight nose, a strong jaw, and a pair of piercing blue-gray eyes that shone almost silver in the sunlight. He seemed to have no trouble making the transition from darkness to light. His intense gaze moved from one end of the parlor to the other before coming to rest on me.

"Ms. Shepherd?" he said. He had a lovely, deep voice, and his accent was that of an educated, middle-class Englishman. "I'm Damian Hunter, and this is my colleague, Andrew Ross."

"Hullo, Ms. Shepherd," said the red-haired young man. He spoke with an unmistakable Scottish lilt. "I'll be looking after your sons during your stay on Erinskil."

The twins swiveled around on the window ledge to peer at Andrew Ross. He smiled and gave them a friendly wave, but they didn't return it. They stared at him appraisingly, as though they were reserving judgment until further evidence of his good intentions surfaced.

"Hullo, lads," Andrew said. "You look just like your snaps."

"Who showed you our snaps?" Rob demanded.

"Sir Percy," Andrew replied. "He's keen on photographs."

"We're keen on drawing," Will informed him loftily.

"So I've heard," said Andrew. "Sir Percy's stocked the nursery with paints and colored pencils and stacks of paper. I could take you up there now, if you like."

Will pointed at Andrew. "Is he going to be our nanny, Mummy?"

"Is he a man-nanny?" Rob added doubtfully.

"My name's Andrew," Andrew growled, glowering, "and that's what you're to call me. If either of you mentions the horrible word 'man-nanny' again, I'll dangle you by your heels from the castle walls!"

Andrew Ross couldn't have thought of a better way to win the twins over. Nothing tickled them more than outrageous threats. They stared at him wide-eyed until he grinned again, then chortled with glee, scrambled down from the window seat, and ran to him, giggling wickedly. I think they were half hoping he'd follow through on his threat.

When Andrew went on to inform the boys that Sir Percy had packed the nursery with surprises, they couldn't wait to leave. I, on the other hand, wasn't about to entrust my babies to anyone without asking a few questions first.

"Have you worked with children before?" I inquired.

"I've had a fair amount of practical experience with the male sort," Andrew replied cheerfully. "I'm the oldest of nine boys."

"Good heavens," I said faintly.

Sir Percy stepped forward. "Andrew's also had specialized training that fits him for the job. Damian and I will tell you all about it *after Rob and Will leave.*"

"Okay," I said, getting the message. I gave the boys a hug and a kiss apiece, reminded them to be on their best behavior, and promised to inspect their rooms as soon as I'd finished speaking with Sir Percy.

They each took hold of one of Andrew's large, freckled hands and marched off with him into the dark corridor, bombarding him with questions about the surprises that lay in store for them in the nursery.

When they'd gone, Sir Percy led Damian Hunter and me to the nearest cluster of armchairs. Sir Percy and I sank comfortably into ours, but Damian sat rigidly on the edge of his. He was also careful, I noticed, to select the chair that gave him the broadest view of the room.

"Right," said Sir Percy, after we'd taken our seats. "Time to get down to brass tacks. I've hired Hunter and Ross to act as your bodyguards while you're at Dundrillin, Lori. Andrew has been assigned to guard the twins, and Damian will keep an eye on you."

"Bodyguards?" I said doubtfully. "Percy, we're in a castle on an island forty miles from the Scottish mainland. Why do we need bodyguards?"

"You may not need them," Sir Percy said, "but as a wise man once said, it's better to have and not need than to need and not have."

"Seems like overkill to me," I muttered.

"Ms. Shepherd," Damian said quietly, "has your life ever been threatened before?"

"No," I said, "but—"

"Have you ever come face-to-face with a madman intent on murdering you?" he broke in.

I eyed him uncertainly. "Well . . . no, but—"

"I have," he said simply.

My eyes flickered to the scar on his temple, but I was nettled by his interruptions and retorted irritably, "Be that as it may, I still think it's a bit much. I mean, how's our madman going to find us?

My husband isn't going to tell him, and I doubt that Percy advertised our flight plan."

"You must not underestimate your adversary." Damian's blue-gray eyes never wavered from my face as he continued. "You've seen only one of the e-mail messages sent to your husband. I've seen them all, and I've seen how well Abaddon covers his tracks. Abaddon may be insane, but he's intelligent and he's in no hurry. He'll bide his time, make his plans. If he gets the chance, he'll come at you when you least expect it—in the night, perhaps, or while you're strolling on the beach. He may torture you first, or he may simply cut your throat. It's impossible to predict, because I suspect he's obeying voices no one else can hear. If I'm frightening you, I'm glad. I want you to be frightened enough to realize that you need my protection. You must be willing to do exactly as I say, when I say it, without hesitation. I can do my job only if I have your full cooperation. Do I have it?"

For a moment I could do nothing but stare at the man in stunned silence. He'd spoken calmly, without raising his voice, but his words conjured nightmarish images that paralyzed me. The hairs on the back of my neck rose, and I had to search to find my voice.

"I . . . I won't let you scare my sons," I stammered. "If Andrew's up there telling them horror stories—"

"He's not," said Damian. "We do know what we're doing, Ms. Shepherd. Andrew's job is to bind Will and Rob to him with affection rather than fear. He's doing his utmost at the moment to become their favorite uncle." He leaned forward, his elbows on his knees. "What about you? Will you let me do my job?"

"Yes." I took a shaky breath. "Yes, of course I will. I'm sorry if I sounded skeptical. It's just . . ." I fumbled for the right words and finished lamely, "It's all new to me."

"That's all right." His mouth turned up briefly in a humorless smile. "It's old to me."

"A few ground rules, I think," Sir Percy suggested, crossing his legs.

Damian sat back in his chair. "Andrew and I will accompany you and the twins at all times. I'll explain the sleeping arrangements when we get to your suite. You may go where you wish on the island, as long as I'm with you. You are, of course, to send no mail, and you are to make no outgoing calls. I assume you've brought a mobile telephone with you."

I nodded.

"Turn it off. Put it away. If you think you might be tempted to use it, give it to me. Satellite signals can be traced. When necessary, your husband will ring you on my mobile. I've already contacted him, by the way, to let him know of your safe arrival."

"Thanks," I said, but I didn't mean it. I'd wanted to speak to Bill myself.

"Any questions?" Damian asked.

"Are you . . . armed?" I sat up as an even more alarming thought presented itself to me. "Is *Andrew?*"

"No," said Damian.

"It's the twins," I said, with a weak smile. "They get into everything. If the cannons worked, I'd advise the village to build bomb shelters. While we're on the subject," I added, turning to Sir Percy, "I'd appreciate it if you'd lock up your electric car. If the twins get behind the wheel—"

"They'll have a jolly good time," Sir Percy declared, thumping the arm of his chair.

"You needn't worry about the car," Damian said. "Andrew won't allow the twins to drive it, Ms. Shepherd."

"Lori," I said automatically. "Call me Lori. Everyone does. Except Mrs. Gammidge."

"Mrs. Gammidge is a stickler for formalities," Sir Percy observed. "I believe she addressed her husband as Mr. Gammidge until the day he died. And they were married for thirty-four years!"

I chuckled raggedly.

"That's more like it." Sir Percy patted my knee. "Damian's paid to be solemn, but I can't have you looking like grim death the whole time you're here, Lori. It's a serious business, no doubt, but you're in good hands. Hunter and Ross are the best in the business. I should know. They've saved my bacon more times than I care to recall."

I twitched as a knock sounded on the parlor's double doors, and two people came into the room, a bespectacled young man and a young blond woman. Both were dressed in business attire and carrying PDAs.

"Sorry to disturb you, Sir Percy," said the woman, "but the call's come in from Beijing, and we've had another offer on the Sydney property."

"And Stockholm's waiting for a reply," added the man.

"Lori," said Sir Percy, bounding to his feet, "let me introduce you to my personal assistants: Kate Halston and Elliot Southmore. Flew in yesterday to set up my office. You won't see much of them, I'm afraid. Their boss is a tyrant." He clapped Damian on the shoulder. "Must dash, old bean. Profit waits for no man."

"I'll show Lori to her suite," said Damian.

"Excellent," said Sir Percy. "We'll take the grand tour of Dundrillin after lunch. And now, if you'll excuse me . . ." My host swept his young assistants through the double doors and out of sight.

I got to my feet, grabbed my carry-on bag, and followed

Damian into the murky corridor. We walked in silence until we reached the curved wall at the end of the passage, where a battered wooden door concealed, of all things unexpected, a modern elevator. I laughed out loud when I saw it.

Damian looked at me inquiringly.

"Whoever heard of a castle with an elevator?" I said as we stepped aboard.

"Sir Percy altered the castle a great deal after he purchased it." Damian pushed the third button in a row of five, and the elevator began its smooth ascent. "It's difficult to find employees who are qualified to provide the kind of maid service his guests require. It's impossible to find maids willing to climb hundreds of stairs several times a day." The elevator stopped, and his tone became instructive. "There are five levels in the northwest tower. Your suite is on the third. It's known as the Cornflower Suite. The nursery is one floor up, on the fourth level."

The metal doors slid apart to reveal a white-painted foyer with a terra-cotta-tiled floor and a frosted light fixture in the ceiling. The foyer had no windows, but it did have some unusual furnishings.

A pole lamp and a leather armchair sat to the right of the elevator, and a folding cot had been erected against the wall on my left, beside a small table equipped with a reading lamp and a battery-powered alarm clock. The cot was furnished with blankets and a pillow, and a well-worn canvas duffel bag had been stowed beneath it.

I turned to Damian. "Your bedroom?"

He nodded. "When you're in your suite, I'll be here."

I formulated my next question carefully before asking, "What about . . . um, bathroom facilities?"

"A powder room is connected to the foyer," he replied, gesturing to a door in the right-hand wall.

I eyed the door doubtfully. "Does it have a shower or a bath?"

"It's sufficient for my needs," Damian said shortly. "Shall we move on?"

He opened a door opposite the elevator and ushered me into one of the most extraordinary rooms I'd ever seen.

The Cornflower Suite was, essentially, one large round chamber. A massive fireplace built of smooth river stones stood in the center of the room, rising from the floor to the plastered ceiling. The ceiling's exposed beams radiated from the chimney to the tower's exterior walls like spokes in a wheel.

The huge fireplace divided the room into two distinct spaces: a sitting room and a bedroom. We'd entered the sitting room, which was as light and airy as the entrance hall had been oppressive. The floor was covered with a thick, cornflower-blue carpet, the walls were papered with a pretty blue-on-white floral print, and the furniture was white French Provincial. A writing table sat beneath a pair of narrow windows set deep in the tower's external wall, and a heavy-duty glass door opened onto a half-moon balcony. The glass door and the decor's pale shades gave brightness to a room that would otherwise have been as dark as a dungeon.

The blue carpet and flowery wallpaper continued in the bedroom, which was furnished in the same style as the sitting room. A drift of muslin hung in a half canopy over a king-size bed dressed with blue-and-white sprigged bedclothes and banked with lacy pillows, and a comfy armchair with a cushioned hassock sat before the fire. A full-length, gilt-framed mirror hung on the wall near the entrance to the bathroom, reflecting the light from windows that overlooked the sea.

My clothes had been put away in the bedroom's wardrobe and chests of drawers, and my suitcases had been stashed on top of the wardrobe, presumably by Mrs. Gammidge's minions. I hung my jacket in the wardrobe and placed my carry-on bag on the bed before I continued exploring.

The curved wall that would have stood at the bed's head had been squared off to form a compact but well-equipped modern bathroom with a deep tub and a separate, glass-walled shower stall. A small mahogany bureau had been retrofitted with a basin and taps to serve as the sink, and the toilet was in its own half-walled space beside it. My toiletries had been stowed in the bureau.

I emerged from the bathroom to find my bodyguard waiting for me in the bedroom.

"It's lovely . . ." I began, but my maternal autopilot had clicked into gear. "But what if there's a fire? We won't be able to use the elevator, will we?"

"Sir Percy left the tower's original staircase in place." Damian laid his hand on the ornate gold frame of the full-length mirror. "The mirror's hinged, like a door. Pull it away from the wall and you'll see the staircase. You'll find the same arrangement in the nursery. The staircase leads to a ground-floor exit. If you open the door, you'll set off alarms throughout the castle, so please use it only when necessary."

I ran a hand along the mirror's frame. "Does the alarm go off if someone tries to open the door from the staircase?"

"Of course," said Damian. "The entire castle's wired."

"Why?" I said, taken aback. "Doesn't Percy trust the islanders?"

"He trusts them as much as he trusts anyone," said Damian. "Sir Percy believes, as I do, that human nature is frail and that it's far easier to prevent a crime than to solve one."

I surveyed the bedroom, then looked back at Damian, smiling sheepishly. "I feel kind of guilty, enjoying so much comfort while you're camped out on a cot."

"You needn't," he said. "I've had to make do with far less. I'll leave you to freshen up, shall I?" He nodded briefly and retreated to the sitting room.

When he was out of sight, I took Aunt Dimity's journal from my carry-on bag, went into the bathroom, and closed the door.

"Dimity?" I said in an undertone. "You're not going to *believe* where we are."

The Tower of London? The fine, old-fashioned copperplate looped and curled sedately across the journal's blank page. *I've heard that it has a fairly competent security system.*

"Close but no cigar," I said. "Sir Percy Pelham's flown us to a castle on an island forty miles off the west coast of Scotland. Pretty cool, huh?"

Bone-chilling, when the north wind blows. Still, Sir Percy has out-done himself. It's helpful to have friends with handy hideaways. Are you whispering because there's a chance you might be overheard?

"My bodyguard's in the next room," I whispered.

Bodyguard? Another of Sir Percy's clever ideas, I presume. He really is a most useful man.

"Security is our watchword," I said, echoing Mrs. Gammidge. "I can't talk now, because I have to see the nursery, go down to lunch, and tour the castle, but I'll bring you up to date this evening."

A castle tour? What fun! I look forward to hearing every detail.

I closed the journal and, after some deliberation, deposited it in the drawer in my bedside table. Then I pulled Reginald from the carry-on bag, smoothed his somewhat rumpled pink flannel ears, and placed him atop the lacy pillows.

"Nice digs, huh, Reg?" I murmured, and his black button eyes seemed to twinkle with approval. After a quick wash and brush-up, I hastened into the sitting room, but Damian had elected to wait for me on the balcony. I pulled open the heavy glass door and raised my voice, to be heard over the rush of the wind.

"I'm shocked, Damian," I said. "I thought the balcony door would be welded shut."

"There's no need," he said. "Come and see."

Six

*D*amian beckoned to me to join him. I crossed to the waist-high stone parapet that served as a balustrade, peered downward, and felt my legs turn to jelly.

There was nothing between me and a sandy beach riddled with vicious rocks but a few hundred feet of thin air and six inches of balcony floor. My head swam, my vision blurred, and my knees wobbled, but I gripped the parapet firmly and eventually got a grip on myself as well.

I refused to swoon. If Damian Hunter was testing my mettle, I intended to pass with flying colors. Instead of drawing back, I leaned farther out over the parapet to examine the tower's smooth stonework.

"Abaddon would have to be a fly to scale the wall," I observed, with a nod of approval. "And I'm in no position to play Rapunzel." I ran a hand through my short crop of dark curls and gave Damian a playful, sidelong smile. "Even if my hair were blond, there wouldn't be enough to make a golden stair."

He glanced briefly at my hair, then looked back out to sea. "I'd like to think that you wouldn't help Abaddon climb the wall, no matter what the circumstances."

"Right," I said, and lapsed into silence. If Sir Percy was paying Damian to be solemn, he was getting his money's worth. The man seemed incapable of banter. I gave a tiny, exasperated sigh, lifted my gaze, and caught sight of a small islet protruding from the waves a half mile beyond the sandy shore. "What's that little island out there? Does it have a name?"

"It's known as Cieran's Chapel," Damian told me. "It's a well-known landmark in these parts. According to local legend, an eighth-century monk named Brother Cieran used to row out there from Erinskil's monastery in order to meditate in solitude."

I cocked my head to one side. "Yes, I can see how the hurly-burly of eighth-century monastic life could get a man down. All those loudmouthed monks rattling their rosaries and chanting at all hours . . ."

"I imagine it could be very distracting." Damian looked at his watch. "We should be going, Lori. Lunch will be served soon, and we still have to visit the nursery."

"Lead on," I said, and as I followed Damian into the sitting room, I wondered if reclusive Brother Cieran had been as impervious to humor as my bodyguard seemed to be.

By the time Will and Rob finished showing me the nursery, I was convinced that they'd never want to leave Dundrillin Castle. The fourth-floor suite was, under normal circumstances, known as the Rose Suite, and pale rose-petal pink was the dominating color. Its floor plan was exactly the same as the Cornflower Suite's, but safety bars had been affixed to the windows, the balcony door had been bolted shut, and a fender had been placed around the huge fireplace. The sleeping area held twin beds as well as Andrew's folding cot, and the sitting room had been transformed into a child's wonderland.

Brightly painted cupboards spilled over with games, puzzles, building blocks, sticks of modeling clay, stuffed animals, and a mad assortment of toys. Bookcases groaned under the weight of story-books, easels held sketch pads of varying sizes, and an entire table was devoted to watercolor paints, finger paints, colored pencils, and crayons. My favorite feature in the room was a pair of rocking horses that bore a striking resemblance to the boys' gray ponies, Thunder and Storm. I had no idea how Sir Percy had produced such plenty on such short notice, but my gratitude to him rose to new heights.

While Will and Rob introduced Damian to a collection of small knights in armor, Andrew Ross pulled me to one side.

"Your sons have offered to read bedtime stories to me," he said. "Are they having me on?"

"No," I said. "They can read. We're not sure when they learned, but we first noticed it last June." I lowered my voice. "There was an embarrassing incident at the general store in our village, involving the twins, a tabloid headline, and a visiting bishop. They're keeping the newspapers under the counter now."

Andrew roared with laughter. He was a much easier audience than Damian.

"I see you're bunking in together," I said, nodding toward the sleeping area.

"We'll take most of our meals up here, too," he said, "with your permission, of course."

"I don't mind if the boys don't," I said, and turned to the twins. "Rob? Will? Do you want to come downstairs with me?"

"Do we *have* to?" the twins chorused. "We're having fish fingers for lunch!"

It was transparently obvious that a lifetime of maternal love was as nothing when compared to the joys of fish fingers for lunch. I left the twins in the nursery without the slightest twinge of conscience.

Sir Percy had hung a Waterford crystal chandelier from the dining room's ceiling and covered the walls in crimson silk. The hearth had been walled off, he explained, when he'd moved the kitchens from their traditional location belowstairs to rooms adjacent to the dining room.

"Ridiculous to transport meals down miles of drafty corridors," he opined, with impeccable logic, "unless you have a taste for tepid soup and congealed gravy."

The polished mahogany table was large enough to seat twenty, but Sir Percy, Damian, and I clustered at one end of it, in the shadow of a silver candelabra, to eat a lunch fit for a highly successful business mogul: pea soup with truffle oil; seared salmon with grilled eggplant and hollandaise sauce; and sticky lemon cake drizzled with heavy cream. The meal was served by Mrs. Gammidge.

Sir Percy had changed for lunch. He looked every bit the country squire in a tweed blazer, a yellow waistcoat, a pair of tweed plus fours, and argyle knee socks. I'd done nothing more than replace my jacket with a cable-knit cardigan before leaving the suite. Although the rooms were warm enough, Sir Percy had been correct in describing Dundrillin's corridors as drafty.

As Mrs. Gammidge made the rounds with the soup tureen, I couldn't help wondering why a housekeeper taxed with the enormous job of running a castle would add waitressing to her list of responsibilities. My puzzlement must have shown on my face, because when Mrs. Gammidge returned the tureen to the kitchen, Sir Percy answered my unspoken question.

"I have a staff of twelve in residence at the moment," he explained, "but Mrs. Gammidge *insists* on serving meals. She's a perfectionist, of course—wants to see the job done right—but she's also an unrepentant nosey parker." He leaned toward me and added in a stage whisper, "She likes to listen in on conversations."

I laughed and spread my napkin on my lap. "Will Kate and Elliot be joining us?" I asked, although the answer was self-evident: Only three places had been set.

"Good heavens, no," said Sir Percy. "Time is money, my dear girl. They'll eat at their desks and like it." He noted the flicker of disapproval in my eyes and laughed heartily. "I jest, Lori, I jest. I have tried many times to pry my young assistants away from their desks but have yet to succeed. Cook sends bounteous feasts to them in the office, I promise you."

I smiled ruefully. I should have known that he'd been joking. Sir Percy Pelham was many things, but a tyrant he was not.

"Sir Percy," said Damian, "might I add a few comments about security?"

"Fire away," said Sir Percy, and turned his attention to the pea soup.

Damian turned to me. "You and your sons are Sir Percy's only guests at the moment. There's no need for you to memorize the staff's names and faces. Andrew and I know who belongs here."

I hadn't planned to memorize any names or faces, but I nodded wisely.

"Andrew and I have familiarized ourselves with Erinskil's residents as well," Damian went on. "You needn't worry about them."

"There are bound to be travelers visiting the island," I pointed out. "Maybe I shouldn't leave the castle. Abaddon might come to Erinskil disguised as a tourist."

"He might," Sir Percy acknowledged, looking up from his soup, "but we don't get many tourists. Just the odd bird-watcher and a handful of island-baggers."

"Island-baggers?" I said.

"Tourists who collect islands," Sir Percy translated. "They have to be jolly intrepid to collect Erinskil. The interisland ferry can't land here, you see. Visitors have to take a launch from the ferry to the concrete jetty—a bit of a challenge in rough seas. Apart from that, there aren't many places for them to stay. They can either pitch a tent—an unpleasantly damp choice—or use one of the two guest rooms at the pub. No, Erinskil will never play host to a horde of tourists, and we can easily keep watch over the few that do come."

"No tourists?" I said, surprised. "I would have expected the place to be crawling with them. The island looked amazing from the air. Don't people come here just for the scenery?"

"Other islands have dramatic scenery and more besides," said Sir Percy. "Stately homes, gardens, distilleries, stone circles . . ." He shrugged. "We have a ruined monastery, of course, but otherwise it's just birds, sheep, and rocks."

"If there's no tourism," I said, "how do the islanders make a living?"

"Now, that's a *most* interesting subject." Sir Percy the businessman waxed enthusiastic. "Feel the sleeve of this jacket," he said, holding his arm out to me. "The fabric was woven right here on Erinskil. Supple as cashmere and tough as nails."

"It's beautiful as well," I said, admiring the tweed's heathery shades.

Sir Percy planted his elbows on the table and tented his fingers. "The islanders formed a cooperative some sixty years ago, to make tweed. They raise the sheep, process the wool, and weave it in Stoneywell, using traditional tools and techniques. It's terribly exclusive and therefore frightfully expensive. They sell it via the

Internet these days. As Erinskil's laird, I'm pleased to say that it all seems to tick along quite happily."

I looked up from my salmon. "Did I hear you right, Percy? Did you call yourself the laird of Erinskil?"

"Indeed I did," said Sir Percy proudly. "Bought the title off the Earl of Strathcairn when I bought the island from him. Dundrillin was originally known as Strathcairn Castle. It was built by the ninth earl, a chap who took the role of laird to heart. He was a bit of a loon, if truth be told. He constructed the castle and armed it with cannons to protect his people from marauding Norsemen, blithely disregarding the fact that he was some eleven hundred years too late."

I smiled inwardly. My first impression of the castle had been more accurate than I'd realized. "Why did the Earl of Strathcairn decide to sell the island?"

"He was strapped for cash," Sir Percy replied. "Couldn't maintain his ancestral seat, let alone a castle that had seen better days. Dundrillin took a bit of a battering during the Second World War, you see, when the island was evacuated and used by the Royal Navy for target practice. A bomb-disposal unit was stationed here for several years after the war, to rid Erinskil of the unexploded ordnance that kept popping up in odd places."

I glanced at the crimson-clad walls and the deep embrasures surrounding the windows. Everything seemed to be intact. "Why wasn't the castle pulverized?"

"The navy was ordered to avoid direct hits on Dundrillin," Sir Percy explained. "There were a few unfortunate mistakes, naturally, but Dundrillin was made to last. It rests on solid bedrock, and the walls are twelve feet thick at their base. The ninth earl may have been daft as a badger, but he knew how to build a castle."

"I feel sorry for the people who were forced to leave the island," I said, with sincere fellow feeling. "The evacuation must have been wrenching for them."

"Needs must in times of war," Sir Percy said breezily. "Erinskil's families returned to rebuild their homes shortly after the war, but the castle was left to rot. The Strathcairns couldn't afford to repair it, but I could." He winked. "The oil business was very kind to me."

"It must have been," I said, bemused. "What's it like, being a laird?"

"The islanders gave me a chilly reception at first," Sir Percy admitted. "They'd put in an offer of their own for the castle, you see, and I'd outbid them. But they warmed to me as soon as they understood that I wanted nothing from them and had no intention of changing their way of life, except for the better. I modernized the windmill farm, for example, made it ten times more efficient than it used to be."

"I assumed the windmills were your idea," I commented.

"The islanders installed the original system twenty years ago," said Sir Percy. "They're quite keen on self-sufficiency. They're keen on hard cash, too, and I employed quite a few of them to work on the castle's renovation. Cal Maconinch and his good wife act as caretakers when the castle's vacant. Cal's the local harbormaster, and he appreciates the extra income."

"Don't certain responsibilities go along with being a laird?" I asked.

Sir Percy nodded. "It's like being a rather grand landlord, but my tenants have been gratifyingly undemanding so far. Haven't had to repair so much as a dripping tap in the past three years, except for the ones in Dundrillin."

"One more question," I promised, "and then I'll let you eat in peace."

"I'm yours to command," said Sir Percy, with a gentlemanly bow.

"The parlor and the dining room are charming," I said. "And the tower suites are lovely." I rested my chin on my hand. "So why is the entrance hall so . . . dreary?"

Sir Percy's amiable smile became a sly grin. "I take a certain perverse pleasure in seeing the looks of dread on my guests' faces when they first arrive. *You,* for example, looked like a condemned prisoner on her way to the gallows. I think you'll agree that the entrance hall makes the rest of Dundrillin come as a delightfully cozy surprise."

"You're a bad man, Percy." I clucked my tongue, then settled down to enjoy the rest of the marvelous lunch. When I asked Mrs. Gammidge if I could have the recipe for the sticky lemon cake, she obligingly retrieved it from the kitchen.

"It's been Sir Percy's favorite pudding ever since he was a boy," she told me, gazing indulgently at her boss.

"It's wonderful," I said. "I'm going to make it for my husband as soon as I . . ." My voice faded and my spirits faltered. Sir Percy's lively account of the island's history had helped me briefly to forget the true and terrible reason for my visit to Dundrillin, but thoughts of home brought it rushing back.

"As soon as you get home," Sir Percy finished firmly, "which will happen before you know it." He wiped his mouth with a linen napkin and pushed his chair back. "Please thank Cook for an excellent meal, Mrs. Gammidge. My guests are going to help me walk it off. Come along, you two. Come and see my castle!"

Sir Percy had poured his heart and soul—not to mention quite a big chunk of change—into Dundrillin. What had once been a virtual ruin was now a leisure palace so complete that only die-hard nature lovers would ever feel the need to leave it.

His guests could view movies in the forty-seat screening room or swim in the heated pool. If they preferred a good read, they could lose themselves in the library. There was a computer room for those who wished to keep in touch with the outside world, and an observatory at the top of the southwest tower for those who wished to keep in touch with worlds beyond their own.

The workout room would satisfy all but the most demanding fitness freaks, and the sunroom would provide a happy retreat for those who liked to loll. The wine cellar seemed to go on forever, and if guests needed to clear their heads after an evening spent imbibing, they had only to stroll out onto the battlements and breathe in the crisp, clean air.

We bypassed the business offices and the family's private apartments but walked along the battlements to look in on the rest of the guest suites, which were located in the other towers. As we moved from room to room Sir Percy kept up a running commentary on the improvements he'd made in the castle, and the engineering feats that had made the improvements possible.

Although the tour was fascinating, it left me feeling unsettled. Rooms not needed for our immediate use had been left under dust sheets, and the hearths had been cold and bare. The corridors seemed to go on forever, and the thick stone walls deadened even Sir Percy's oversized voice. A scant handful of guests wasn't enough to fill a place designed to entertain dozens, and a staff of twelve was hardly adequate to guard it. As our footsteps echoed hollowly in the stairwells, I began to wonder if the castle was as secure a refuge as it had at first seemed. Abaddon might have trouble getting through the gate, I thought, but once inside, he'd find no end of hiding places.

I glanced at Damian and felt a little better. He was, without doubt, the most humorless, paranoid, cold fish of a man I'd ever met, but even so, it was comforting to know that he was watching my back.

Seven

The castle tour lasted long enough for me to be glad that I'd worn comfortable shoes. We met up with Andrew, Will, and Rob in the parlor for tea, and after surveying the substantial repast Cook had provided, I decided that it would also serve as the twins' dinner. They'd been far too enthralled by their new surroundings to settle down for naps, so an early night was in order.

After they'd eaten their fill and told me every detail of their fabulous afternoon, I returned with them to the nursery, stopping on the way to show them the Cornflower Suite. I wanted them to know where to find me in case homesickness struck before morning.

Damian remained in the sitting room while Andrew helped me to get the boys bathed, in their jammies, and in bed. I answered their questions about Daddy, Annelise, Stanley, Thunder, and Storm as best I could, listened while they took turns reading a chapter of *The Black Stallion* to me, and stayed by their sides until they fell asleep.

When I thanked Andrew for taking such good care of the twins, he thanked me in return for raising them properly.

"They're fine lads," he told me. "Bright as buttons and good as gold."

Andrew Ross, I decided, was a young man of great discernment.

It was half past six when Damian and I returned to the Cornflower Suite. As I crossed the foyer to enter the sitting room,

Damian's cell phone rang. He answered it, murmured a few terse words, then held it out to me.

"It's your husband," he said.

I snatched the phone from his hand, ran with it into the sitting room, and closed the door.

"Oh, Bill," I exclaimed, flopping onto a soft armchair, "if I'd known you were going to call, I would have let the twins stay up. They fell asleep five minutes ago."

"Don't wake them," he said. "I'm sure they're tuckered out."

"Where are you calling from?" I asked.

"Chief Superintendent Yarborough would rather I didn't tell you," he replied, "but it's quite comfortable."

"Good," I said. "Any progress on the . . . case?"

"Not yet," he replied. "Yarborough and I have examined about twenty client files today, but no outstandingly suspicious characters have revealed themselves so far. Please tell me that you and the boys are having a good time. I need to know that at least one part of my plan is working."

I spent the next half hour telling him about the helicopter ride, the nursery, the excellent food, and the grand tour. I also told him about Damian and Andrew, but they weren't news to Bill.

"I asked Percy to hire bodyguards for you," he informed me. "We've worked out a system of daily passwords. Your man won't put me through unless I give him the right one. Now," he continued, "on the home front: Annelise is fine if still a bit irritated with us for leaving her behind, Ivan Anton reports that all is well at the cottage, and Emma Harris says that our menagerie is thriving, so you can tell the boys not to worry about Stanley, Thunder, or Storm."

"I will," I said. "We miss you a whole bunch, by the way."

"I miss you even more." Bill sighed dejectedly. "I just want this to be over."

"It will be," I soothed. "One day we'll look back on this and . . . Okay, we'll probably shudder and shriek, but at least it'll be over."

Bill's chuckle brought a smile to my face. After we'd said our good-nights, I sat for a moment, curled around the phone, replaying in my mind the sound of his laughter. We'd been apart for less than twelve hours, but it seemed much longer. It wasn't fair, I told myself. Bill and I were good people, or at least we tried to be good. We'd done nothing to deserve Abaddon.

The puddle of self-pity was ankle-deep and rising by the time I pushed myself out of the chair and knocked on the foyer door. Damian called for me to come in, and I found him sitting in the leather armchair next to the elevator, a laptop computer open on his lap.

"Answering e-mail?" I asked.

He turned the laptop so that I could see the monitor. The screen was divided into four sections. Each showed a different black-and-white image of a specific place in the castle—a door, a corridor, a staircase, the courtyard. As I watched, the images flickered and changed to show other corridors, doors, and staircases.

"There's a man in the main control room monitoring activity in and around Dundrillin," he explained, "but I like to keep my hand in."

I made a mental note to be on my best behavior when wandering the corridors, then leaned against the doorjamb and said gloomily, "Abaddon's still at large."

"It's early days yet." Damian looked up from the computer

screen and regarded me intently. "And if Scotland Yard doesn't stop him, I will."

The steely glint in his eyes frightened me a little. I couldn't keep myself from glancing at his scar. I wanted to ask him if he'd ever killed anyone, but I held back. I wasn't sure I wanted to know the answer.

I had just enough time left after Bill's phone call to take a hot shower and change into a fine woolen dress before going down for dinner. Damian didn't change. I doubted that there was enough room in his duffel bag for evening dress, but it didn't matter. Sir Percy, unlike Mrs. Gammidge, wasn't a stickler for formalities. He showed up for dinner wearing a bulky black turtleneck and dark tweed trousers, both of which, he informed us, had been made on Erinskil.

We were deep into our leek-and-potato soup when Sir Percy asked about our plans for the following day. My mouth was too full for polite speech, but Damian answered readily.

"If the weather holds, I thought we might go down to your cove in the morning, sir." He turned to me. "The water's too cold for swimming, but I imagine your sons will be able to find other ways to amuse themselves."

"It's a great idea," I said. "Will and Rob love beach-combing."

"You must take them to the observatory one night while you're here," Sir Percy advised as Mrs. Gammidge cleared away the soup bowls. "The sky is as clear as a newborn's conscience. I've seen comets, meteor showers—if you're lucky, the aurora borealis will show herself." He heaved a dramatic sigh as Mrs. Gammidge began serving the rack of lamb. "If I needed one reason to return to Erinskil, it would be the night sky. Or the ghost," he added, after a reflective pause. "I'm rather fond of our ghost."

I was glad that I'd finished my soup. If I hadn't, I would have sprayed it across the linen tablecloth. As it was, my voice rose a few octaves as I squeaked, "Is Dundrillin *haunted?*"

"Not as such," Sir Percy said. "But we're not far from a place that is." He swallowed a forkful of sautéed spinach and jutted his chin toward the windows. "There once was a chap, you see, named Brother Cieran——"

"The meditating monk," I broke in, nodding. "Damian told me about him. He used to row out to the islet I can see from my balcony. It's called Cieran's Chapel, isn't it?"

"It is," said Sir Percy. "Local legend has it that he was out there praying when Vikings came ashore at the harbor. They pillaged the village and killed everyone, then moved inland to attack the monastery. The marauders were gone by the time Brother Cieran returned, but the monastery had been looted and the monks had been slain. After giving his brethren and his flock a decent burial, Brother Cieran rowed back to the little island. Once there, he released his boat—to punish himself, some say, for not perishing with the others. It's said that his tormented spirit lingers there still, praying through all eternity for the souls of the dead."

I suppressed a shudder and asked, "Have you seen the ghost?"

"Alas, no," said Sir Percy. "But a few of my guests have. The apparition either frightened or thrilled them, but I'd like to think it would inspire pity in me. The Earl of Strathcairn's grandfather—the tenth earl——was so moved by the tale that he elected to have himself buried on Cieran's Chapel. He told his grandson that he wanted to keep poor Brother Cieran company."

"How splendid," I murmured.

Sir Percy waved his knife in a vaguely southerly direction. "The ruined monastery is just over a mile from here, above the overlook on the coastal path. Legend has it that if you stand inside the ruins on certain nights, when the moon and stars are just so, you can hear the screams of the dying monks."

His macabre words were still echoing in my mind when the chandelier flickered and went out, plunging the room into darkness. I gasped, nearly stabbed myself in the face with a forkful of lamb, and knocked over my water glass.

"Calm yourself, Lori."

A match flared, and the sight of Sir Percy's face, lit eerily from below, made it absolutely impossible for me to follow his advice. I quivered like a cornered rabbit while he leaned forward to light the candles in the silver candelabra.

"Happens all the time." He puffed on the match to extinguish it. "Why do you think we have so many candles about the place? Had to rewire the whole castle, you know. Things are bound to go pop now and then. The lights should come on again shortly. Mrs. Gammidge knows the fuse box like the back of her hand."

My own hands shook as I picked up my water glass, which had, fortunately, been empty. When I'd stopped quaking, I eyed Sir Percy suspiciously.

"Are you sure you didn't have Mrs. Gammidge pull the plug on purpose?" I asked. "You *were* telling a spooky story, after all."

"Wouldn't dream of it, my dear," said Sir Percy. "The legend's quite ghoulish enough without adding special effects."

"I agree," Damian said severely. "And if you want Lori to get any sleep at all tonight, sir, I'd suggest that you change the subject to something *less* ghoulish."

"Quite right," said Sir Percy, chastened. He thought for a moment, then began, "Did I ever tell you about the tone-deaf goatherd I came across in China? Well, this fellow *loved* to sing . . . ."

By the time the lights came back on, I was wiping tears of laughter from my cheeks.

Sir Percy invited me to view a film after dinner—"A light comedy, I promise!"—but I gave him a rain check and returned with Damian to the Cornflower Suite. I left him at his post in the foyer and went alone into the suite, where the bed had been turned down, lamps had been lit, and a turf fire had been laid, ready to light. A porcelain box on the mantel shelf held wooden matches.

I touched a match to the tinder, watched the flames rise, and decided to step out onto the balcony. Although midnight was approaching, I needed to collect my thoughts before sharing them with Aunt Dimity. Apart from that, Sir Percy had piqued my curiosity. I wanted to see if the night sky was all it was cracked up to be.

It was everything he'd promised and more. I'd thought the sky above the cottage was crystalline, but it was murky compared to the sky above Erinskil. I'd never seen so many stars. The heavens were strewn with a million pinpoints of light, and each pinpoint was reflected in the restless waves. The waxing moon could do nothing to diminish their brilliance. I stared openmouthed, unaware of the chill night air, lost in awe and delight. It was like being inside a glitter-filled snow globe. Could there be a more perfect spot, I wondered, to teach Rob and Will about the constellations?

The thought gave me pause. I hesitated, then went to knock on the foyer door.

"Come in," Damian called.

He was still fully dressed and awake, watching the flickering images of Dundrillin's entrances and passageways on his laptop.

"I'm sorry to bother you," I said, "but do you know how to find constellations?"

A moment later we were both on the balcony and Damian was pointing out shapes in the star-crowded sky: Cassiopeia, Orion, Taurus, Gemini—he would have gone on much longer if I hadn't stopped him.

"Whoa," I said, laughing. "I think that'll do for now." I leaned on the stone parapet and lowered my gaze until it came to rest on the dark contours of Cieran's Chapel. "I can usually find my way around the night sky, but I can't do it here."

"Too many stars," he said, still peering upward. "The constellations are hidden in plain sight."

He seemed in no hurry to leave, and I couldn't blame him. Who'd sit in a windowless room when there were such riches to behold?

"How long have you been a bodyguard?" I asked.

"Twenty years." He rested his hands on the parapet and scanned the sea. "I'm an old man compared to many of my colleagues."

"I'd say that getting older is a definite plus in your line of work," I said. "It proves that you're good at your job."

"No." He shook his head decisively. "If my *clients* get older, it proves that I'm good at my job."

I smiled wryly. "How did you meet Percy?"

"He hired me." Damian shrugged. "The oil business took him to some dodgy parts of the world. I helped him out of a few tight corners."

"Sounds very cloak-and-dagger," I said. "Would I be right in describing you as a real-life action hero?"

Damian's silvery eyes flashed dangerously as he turned to face me. "The last thing on earth I want to be is a hero. I do not want to be forced to do what I do best. I do everything in my power to make sure I'm not."

"That's . . . er, good," I stammered, cowed by his intensity. "I'm fond of dullness myself. If you ask me, excitement is highly overrated."

"Highly," said Damian, and turned to go. "Good night, Lori."

I shook my head, wondering if he'd ever lighten up, took one last look at the moonlit sea, and saw a dim golden glow illuminate the jet-black silhouette of Cieran's Chapel. I blinked, and it was gone.

"Damian!" I cried.

He spun around in the doorway. "What is it?"

"I thought I saw . . ." I stared hard, but the light had vanished. "A meteor. I thought I saw a meteor. I wanted you to see it, but it's gone." I could sense the tension draining from his body.

"It was a kind thought," he said, "but——"

"I know," I interrupted. "I shouldn't have shouted. I'm sorry. Go to bed."

"You should do the same," he advised, and left the balcony.

I remained at the parapet, staring at Cieran's Chapel.

Had I seen what I thought I'd seen? Perhaps a rogue wave had tossed a sliver of moonlight into the air, or perhaps—and the thought never would have occurred to me if not for Dimity—perhaps I'd joined the ranks of the privileged few who'd witnessed Brother Cieran praying through all eternity for the souls of the dead. I couldn't be sure, and until I was, I wasn't going to say anything to Damian. I didn't want him to think that I'd been unduly influenced by Sir Percy's story.

I retreated from the balcony to the bedroom, took Aunt Dimity's journal from the bedside drawer, and sank onto the edge of the bed.

"Dimity," I said, opening the journal, "would you do me a favor?"
To my relief, Dimity replied promptly.

Certainly, if it's within my power.

"I'm pretty sure it is." I thought for a moment, then repeated everything Sir Percy and Damian had told me about Brother Cieran. It wasn't until I finished telling Dimity about the tenth earl's final resting place that I hesitated.

Two words appeared on the page: *Go on.*

"When I got back to my room after dinner," I said slowly, "I went out onto the balcony. I was about to come back in when I saw a light on Cieran's Chapel. It was there only for a moment, but it was definitely there."

Have you told your bodyguard about the light?

"Sort of." I frowned worriedly down at the journal. "I said I'd seen a meteor because . . . because I don't want Damian to think . . ."

You don't want Damian to think that you believe in ghosts. Should I be insulted?

"Damian hardly knows me," I said hastily. "I don't want him to think I'm . . . impressionable."

His opinion of you is unimportant at the moment, Lori. Damian Hunter is responsible for your safety. I'm sure he'd want to know about any unusual events you might witness, and since the islet is uninhabited, the light surely counts as an unusual event. You should tell him about it.

"I will," I said, "as soon as I've eliminated Brother Cieran from my list of suspects."

Ah. I see. I believe I can guess what favor you wish to ask of me.

"Could you check it out for me, Dimity?" I asked. "Would you . . . er, ask around and find out if Brother Cieran's still . . . um, in residence?"

It might not be Brother Cieran, you know. Perhaps you saw the tenth earl taking the night air. But rest assured, I will make inquiries.

"Thanks, Dimity." The weight of the day descended on me suddenly, and I gave a tremendous yawn.

It's time you were in bed, my dear. We'll speak again tomorrow.

"Good night, Dimity." I watched the lines of royal-blue ink fade from the page, then returned the journal to the drawer and got ready for bed.

It wasn't until I was lying beneath the blankets, gazing into the moon-washed darkness, that I became aware of a sound I hadn't fully noticed before. The regular thud and boom of the surf came to me, as if from a great distance, like the pounding of a gigantic fist on solid rock.

It should have been a soothing sound, but it wasn't. A wave of loneliness began to close over me, and I reached for Reginald. My pink bunny wasn't a perfect substitute for Bill, but he'd serve until the real thing came back again.

Even with Reginald cradled in my arms, I should by rights have lain awake late into the night, haunted by visions of Abaddon climbing through my window with a knife clenched between his teeth. I should have tossed and turned, tormented by the muted screams of massacred monks. Instead, I drifted into sleep thinking only of Brother Cieran. Was he still chained by guilt to his lonely sanctuary? What, I wondered, would release him from his vigil?

Eight

When I awoke, bars of sunlight were falling across my bed. I squinted at the mullioned windows, peered muzzily at the massive fireplace, and gradually remembered where I was and how I'd come to be there.

A glance at the clock on the bedside table told me that it was seven o'clock. I stared drowsily at the raftered ceiling for a while, wondering what my neighbors in Finch were saying about the strangers who'd moved into my cottage. Devoted gossips one and all, the villagers were no doubt having a field day inventing stories to explain our departure. I took some pride in knowing that we'd provided them with such a rich, ongoing source of entertainment. Compared to their inventions, the true story would probably fall flat.

Chuckling quietly, I placed Reginald on the bedside table and reached for Aunt Dimity's journal, curious to find out what, if anything, she'd learned about Brother Cieran while I slept. I leaned back against a heap of pillows and opened the blue journal on my lap, but before I'd opened my mouth, Aunt Dimity's fine, old-fashioned copperplate flew across the page.

You must tell Damian about the light.

I sat up a bit straighter. "It wasn't Brother Cieran?"

Definitely not. Much of what Sir Percy told you about Brother Cieran is true, but the poor soul left the islet some centuries ago. He is no longer "in residence," as you so tactfully put it, nor is the old earl. I don't know what created the light you saw, and I don't like not knowing. If Abaddon is hiding out on Cieran's Chapel,

"How could he be?" I cut in. "How could he know where we are? Even if he did find out, how could he follow us so quickly? We've been here for less than twenty-four hours, Dimity. And how on earth could he get out to that forsaken chunk of rock?"

Anyone can hire a boat, Lori, and e-mail can be sent from anywhere. Abaddon may have already been in Scotland when he started sending his vile messages to Bill. I don't know how he could have discovered your present location, but you mustn't assume he hasn't. You must tell Damian about the light. Let him investigate it. It may have nothing to do with Abaddon, but surely it's better to know one way or the other.

I leaned my chin on my hand, grimacing. "Damian's going to be incredibly unhappy with me for not telling him the truth right away."

Are you a timid mouse quaking in the corner or a bold lioness defending her cubs? Put some starch in your backbone, Lori, and tell Damian.

I cocked an ear toward the foyer and heard the familiar thunder of little feet. "I'll tell him, Dimity, but I have to go now. My cubs are on the prowl."

I managed to stash the journal in the bedside drawer mere moments before Will and Rob came scampering into the bedroom. Clad in sweatshirts, jeans, and sneakers, they bounced onto the bed, demanding that I get dressed.

Rob sprawled across the duvet and kicked his heels in the air. "We've been awake for *ages,* Mummy."

"Andrew wouldn't let us come down until a decent hour," Will informed me.

"It's a decent hour now," Rob pointed out.

"Time to rise and shine," Will declared. "Andrew's taking us to the *beach* after breakfast."

"And the sun doesn't last all day," Rob concluded sagely.

"Andrew?" I called. "May I speak with you?"

The young man came into the bedroom. He was wearing another colorful rugby shirt, jeans, and sneakers, and looking rather anxious, as though he expected me to scold him for setting the boys loose on me.

"Thanks for keeping Rob and Will occupied for so long," I said. "I haven't slept past six since they were born. When's breakfast?"

A relieved smile swept across Andrew's freckled face. "It'll be here in ten minutes. Rob and Will thought it would be a nice surprise."

"Ten minutes is all I need." While Andrew retreated to the sitting room, I shooed the boys off the bed and got ready to face the morning.

Damian joined us for breakfast in my sitting room, and although he wasn't the life of the party, he'd at least dressed down for the day, in a blue crewneck sweater, khakis, sneakers, and a loose-fitting rain jacket. I'd followed my sons' example and donned sweatshirt, jeans, and sneakers. After we'd eaten, I followed Damian's example and added a rain jacket.

Andrew hoisted a large day pack to his back. He'd filled it with plastic buckets and spades, the twins' cricket bats, and their rain jackets. When I asked if he'd included a bottle of sunblock, he nodded.

"Rain gear and sunblock," he said, chuckling. "Tells you all you need to know about April in Scotland."

"Which is why we should be going," said Damian, getting to his feet. "The weather could turn ugly in an instant."

On that optimistic note, we boarded the elevator, descended to the tower's ground level, and entered a circular chamber that had been converted into a changing room for beachgoers. It held a shower stall, curtained cubicles, marble benches, and open shelves filled with fluffy towels. There were no windows, but the plastered walls had been decorated with trompe l'oeil paintings depicting seaside scenes.

Damian led the way to a side door and nodded casually at another door half hidden in shadows on our left.

"The emergency stairs," he explained. "They lead here, and from here you can get outside." He tapped a sequence of buttons on a wall-mounted keypad, presumably to disarm the alarm system, and pushed the side door open.

We stepped out into the cool, sunlit morning. When I glanced upward, I realized that we were standing on the strip of headland directly below my balcony. I was surprised to see how low the cliffs were—they'd looked much higher from above. The strip of headland looked different, too, now that I was standing on it. It was wider, and slashed by a sunken path that ran in both directions along the cliffs.

"The coastal path," Damian explained, following my gaze. "It goes all the way around the island."

"Sounds scenic," I said as the brine-scented breeze tossed my curls. "Could we walk it tomorrow? If we're still here, that is."

Damian tilted his head back to look at the sky. "I don't see why not, if the fine weather holds."

"We want to go to the beach," Will reminded us determinedly.

"So you shall," said Andrew, and he crossed the sunken path to a pair of stone pillars that stood at the grassy strip's outer edge.

The pillars marked the top of a set of stairs that had been cut into the cliff. Although the staircase was equipped with a rope railing threaded through a series of iron posts, I took hold of Rob's hand and Andrew grabbed Will's before we started down. Damian took up the rear.

Andrew used the time we spent on the stairs to lecture Will and Rob about the dangers of rip currents and the way high tides could creep up and swallow unsuspecting little boys. Before our sneakers touched the sand, he made them vow solemnly that they would never go to the beach on their own. I could have kissed him.

I was even more grateful to him once we'd reached the beach. Although the tide was on its way out, the belt of broken shells and drying seaweed left behind by the high tide was well up on the sand. Anyone caught in the cove when the tide was in would have to scramble to reach the safety of the stairs or risk being drowned, swept out to sea, or battered to death on the jagged rocks I'd seen from my balcony.

The sun had not yet climbed over the cliffs, so the cove was still in shadow, but the sea glittered and the white sand glowed invitingly. Will and Rob swiftly divested themselves of shoes and socks and engaged their grown-up companions in a fast-paced game of tag that somehow turned into a cricket match with driftwood wickets and Mummy fielding balls. Once the twins had burned off their excess energy—and batted three balls into the surf—they settled down with the buckets and spades and began to construct a miniature version of Dundrillin Castle. Andrew and I acted as architectural consultants, but Damian strolled away on his own, to stand at the edge of the sea.

When we finished the sand castle, Andrew headed off with the boys to search for seashells and tide pools. I waited until they'd disappeared behind a cluster of barnacle-encrusted rocks, then took a deep breath and walked over to stand beside Damian.

I had a strong suspicion that my bodyguard was about to lose his temper, and I didn't want him to lose it in front of my sons.

Damian acknowledged my arrival by pointing to a flock of small birds skimming the waves between the beach and Cieran's Chapel.

"Puffins," he said.

"Oh, how splendid!" I watched in delight as the flock flew in tight formation mere inches above the foaming crests. "I wish I'd brought my camera."

"You can bring it when we walk the coastal path," he suggested. "I'm sure we'll see them again. They nest in the western cliffs."

"You know a lot about Erinskil," I observed. "Have you been here often?"

"I've never been here before," he replied, "but I can read and I know how to listen. Sir Percy provided Andrew and me with detailed dossiers on Erinskil. We supplemented the dossiers by spending a few hours in the pub on the night we arrived."

"Good thinking," I said. "If you want to know what's going on in a place, spend time in the local pub. Church bulletin boards are helpful, too, and a post office can be almost as helpful as the pub, especially if the postmistress is as nosey as the one in my village. She's better than a local newspaper for—"

"Lori." Damian interrupted the flow of nervous babble before it could become a torrent. "Is something bothering you?"

"Well . . . yes." The moment of truth had come. "Remember last night, when I told you I'd seen a meteor? It wasn't a meteor."

"What was it?" Damian asked, frowning slightly.

"A light. I saw a light on Cieran's Chapel. It came and went so quickly that I wasn't sure I'd seen it, but I am now." I hunched my shoulders and braced myself for a tongue-lashing. When nothing happened, I added, in a small voice, "I'm sorry, Damian. I shouldn't have lied to you. Feel free to yell at me."

To my utter amazement, Damian simply rocked back on his heels, shook his head, and smiled.

"I'm not going to yell at you, Lori," he said. "I'm not surprised that you thought you saw something on Cieran's Chapel last night. I wouldn't be surprised if you'd seen a chorus line of chanting monks. You're under a great deal of mental stress at the moment. Sir Percy's story was bound to affect you. I thought it ill-advised of him to share it with you, and you've proven me right."

"But . . . but I *did* see a light," I protested, but I got no further, because the twins chose that exact moment to shout *"Mummy!"* at the tops of their lungs.

Damian and I took off at a run, spraying sand in our wake as we rounded a massive outcropping of rock. Andrew, Will, and Rob were standing together at its base, staring upward. I looked up, too, and felt a sliver of ice slide down my spine.

A human skull sat wedged in a crevice near the top of the rock, well above the high-water line. It stared down at us, grinning its timeless, maniacal grin, and for a shattering moment I thought that its fleshless maw had emitted a cackle of laughter, but it was only the shriek of a passing gull.

I drew a quick, shallow breath and forced a smile.

"My goodness," I said shakily. "That certainly beats the lobster pot Daddy found in Skegness."

If I was worried about my sons' being traumatized for life, I was overestimating their sensitivity. As it turned out, the little ghouls were thrilled by their find.

"Andrew won't let us fetch it down," Will complained.

"He says it's dirty," said Rob, "but we can wash it in the ocean, can't we?"

"When it's clean, we can take it home," said Will.

"No, we most certainly cannot," I stated firmly, and quickly improvised a reason for the ban. "It's . . . not ours. It belongs to Sir Percy."

"Sir Percy will let us keep it," Rob said confidently, and he was probably right.

"I'm sorry, boys," Damian interjected, "but I can't allow you to take the skull home with you. Andrew, would you please get it down?"

Andrew tipped seashells from the plastic bucket he was carrying and hooked the handle over his wrist. While he climbed up to the skull, I scanned the looming cliff tops, then backed slowly away, pulling Damian with me.

"It's *him*," I whispered urgently when the twins were safely out of earshot.

"Whom?" he asked.

"*Abaddon.*" Dimity's words came flooding back to me in a panicky torrent. "He followed us to Erinskil yesterday, camped out on Cieran's Chapel last night, and left the skull here this morning as a . . . a sick, demented calling card."

Damian glanced toward Rob and Will, then pulled me even farther away from them.

"Lori," he said, with the patient air of one pacifying a frantic toddler, "I want you to calm down."

"*Calm down?*" I snapped. "*You're* the one who said he might cut my throat on the beach!"

"But he couldn't have known you'd be on the beach this morning," Damian pointed out. "He couldn't have known it would be such a fine day."

"Look," I began testily, but Damian cut me off.

"Hold on, Lori," he said. "Let's ask ourselves a few questions, shall we? How did Abaddon follow you to Erinskil? He didn't come on the ferry—it's not due for another four days. If he acquired a boat privately and dropped anchor in the harbor, I'd have heard about it—the harbormaster reports to me. Sir Percy's private cove is the only other reasonable landing place on the island, and it's been under electronic surveillance since Mrs. Gammidge arrived. No boat has come ashore, and no one's been seen decorating the beach with skulls."

"There are other beaches," I said. "I saw them from the air."

"Beaches, yes. Landing sites, no." Damian shook his head. "It's not easy to land a boat in Sir Percy's cove, Lori. It's ten times worse at the other beaches. They're fenced in by all sorts of underwater obstacles—rocks, reefs, snags. I wish Abaddon *would* try to land at one of them. He'd drown before he ever stepped ashore, and we'd be finished with him."

I folded my arms and eyed him skeptically. "I suppose the skull sprouted wings and flew up there?"

"The tide washes up all sorts of strange objects," said Damian in an infuriatingly reasonable tone of voice. "Storms deposit them in unexpected places."

I recoiled, aghast. "Are my sons likely to find *more* body parts?"

"It's not as uncommon an occurrence as you might think," Damian explained. "There's a small section in the Stoneywell churchyard reserved for the burial of bones returned by the sea."

"Oh," I said, momentarily taken aback. "Is that why you asked Andrew to get the skull? Are you planning to bury it?"

"I'll send it to the forensics lab in Glasgow first," said Damian. "If they can't connect it with a crime or an accident, it'll probably end up in the churchyard." He put a hand on my shoulder. "Are you okay now?"

"No, I'm not," I said crossly, and shrugged off his hand. "What about my light? Someone should investigate it. Abaddon could be out there, spying on us!"

"I doubt that Abaddon would choose such a prominent landmark as a hiding place," said Damian. He peered at me closely, then seemed to reach a decision. "But of course we'll look into it. If it will put your mind at ease, we can go out to Cieran's Chapel right now."

"How?" I asked.

He pulled out his cell phone. "Say the word and I'll have a boat pick us up in thirty minutes."

I looked over my shoulder at the expanse of choppy water stretching between me and the wave-lashed islet, then looked back at my precious babes, who were bent low over Andrew's bucket, holding a cheerfully bloodthirsty discussion about the skull's possible origins. Was I a timid mouse or a bold lioness?

"Make the call," I said.

Nine

Favoided mentioning the upcoming boat ride to Will and Rob. They were so eager to show the skull to Sir Percy that they didn't object to being sent back to the castle, but if they'd known what they were about to miss, they wouldn't have gone quietly.

I was raring to get out to the islet. I didn't particularly want to discover Abaddon's campsite—I wanted my insane stalker to stay far away from Erinskil—but I hoped we would find *something*. If Damian went on treating me as if I were an excitable schoolgirl, I wouldn't be responsible for my actions. I had to prove to him that the dim golden glow hadn't been a figment of my overstressed imagination.

My determination was shaken slightly when the boat Damian had ordered came into view, bouncing from wave to wave as it rounded the headland. I'd expected some sort of fishing vessel, not an inflatable rubber dinghy with an outboard motor. I zipped up my rain jacket and glanced nervously at the whitecaps blooming between the cove and the islet. The wind was picking up.

Damian seemed to sense my misgivings. He pointed to a line of swirls and eddies about twenty yards offshore.

"You see those little ripples out there?" he asked. "The snags beneath them will tear the keel out of a boat faster than you can say snap. Luckily, we're nearing low tide, when they're easier to avoid, but finding the right channel still requires local knowledge, a high level of seamanship, and a boat with an extremely shallow draft. Sir Percy's yacht wouldn't be any good to us at all."

"Who's our . . . er, driver?" I asked.

"Mick Ferguson will be our pilot," Damian informed me. "Mick was born and raised on Erinskil. He knows what he's doing."

I watched in consternation as Mick Ferguson threaded the dinghy through the swirls and eddies, then drove it at full speed straight at the beach. At the last minute, he cut the power, tilted the motor up out of the water, and allowed momentum to carry the dinghy onto the sand. It was a virtuoso performance and did much to restore my confidence.

Mick Ferguson was a short, burly man with curly salt-and-pepper hair, a grizzled beard, and bright blue eyes set deeply in a face pleated with wrinkles. He was wearing a fluorescent orange rain jacket with matching rain pants and a pair of black rubber boots that reached nearly to his knees.

"Mick, this is Lori," said Damian, when we reached the dinghy. "Lori's a guest of Sir Percy's."

"You'll be the one who came yesterday, in the helicopter." Mick's blue eyes narrowed shrewdly. "With the two wee lads."

"That's me," I acknowledged. I wouldn't have been shocked to discover that Mick already knew what I'd had for breakfast and possibly my shoe size. I'd lived in Finch long enough to know how quickly news spread in a small community.

After Damian and I had zipped and snapped our rain jackets, Mick put out a hand to help me aboard, directed me to sit on the wooden bench that straddled the dinghy's midsection, and passed me a life vest. He checked to make sure I'd fastened the straps correctly, then hopped out of the boat to help Damian push it back into the water. Damian's khakis were wet to the knees by the time the two men climbed aboard, but I felt no guilt. The dinghy rode so low in the water that my jeans wouldn't stay dry for long.

Damian sat beside me and suggested that I take hold of one of the nylon loops dangling from the boat's sides. Mick started the outboard motor and backed away from the shore before turning the dinghy toward Cieran's Chapel.

"Thanks for coming to get us, Mr. Ferguson!" I bellowed, half turning to face the pilot. I had to shout to be heard above the motor's roar.

"We won't be able to stay long!" Mick shouted back. "Weather's moving in."

I didn't see a cloud in the sky, but I wasn't about to question Mick's expertise, and the information didn't seem to bother Damian one bit.

"We won't need much time," he said complacently.

Once we left the shelter of the cove and entered open water, conversation became impossible. Mick seemed determined to get us out to the islet as fast as he could, so the boat leapt through the choppy water, hitting wave crests with bone-jarring smacks that sent streams of salt water splashing over us. It was like riding a bucking bronco through a car wash, and although a certain fun-loving portion of my brain was squealing "Whee!" the rest of it was entertaining profoundly covetous thoughts about Mick's rain pants.

We slowed to a crawl as we approached the Chapel, and I wondered how on earth we would get ashore. The islet rose some forty feet straight up from the sea, a sheer-sided monolith festooned with bird droppings and slimy seaweed. But Mick was on home surf, and he knew his way around. He steered the boat to the islet's north side, where a cleft in the rock held a series of broad shelves that stepped down to the water's edge.

Mick guided the boat onto the lowest shelf and made a line fast to an iron ring that hung from a bolt driven into the solid rock. Damian paused to give the ring a tug before turning to supervise my death-defying hop from the boat onto the next shelf up. As I scrambled to the top of the cleft, using my hands and knees as well as my feet, I decided that if Abaddon had chosen Cieran's Chapel as a campground, he was an even bigger nutcase than I'd supposed.

When I emerged from the cleft onto more or less level ground, I saw that the Chapel was neither as exposed nor as barren as I'd expected it to be. The sheer stone walls formed a notched and irregular windbreak around the edge of the islet, and the uneven ground was covered with a tough, springy mat of low-growing plants that were spangled here and there with minute blossoms.

Mick waited in an elbow of rock, hunched against the freshening breeze, but Damian walked with me while I slowly crisscrossed the islet, scanning the ground for traces of a campsite. I saw none— no scorch marks, no ashes, no footprints, and no sign of crushed foliage where a tent might have been pitched. Damian squatted down now and then to study the local flora, but he didn't say a word. He didn't have to. I could hear him *thinking,* "I told you so."

I finished my search at the edge of a bowl-shaped depression on the east side of the islet. There, at the bottom of the bowl, lay a stone slab the size of a large door. An inscription had been carved into the slab, in Celtic lettering:

> James Robert, tenth Earl of Strathcairn
> 1854–1937
> The heart benevolent and kind
> The most resembles God

"It's from Burns," I said to Damian. "The quotation, I mean. It's from a poem by Robert Burns."

"It describes the old laird well," Mick said, coming up behind me. "James Robert was a good man."

I remembered why the tenth earl had asked to be buried on Cieran's Chapel and smiled sadly. "I'm sure he was."

"Is that why you came out here?" Mick asked, watching me carefully. "Did you want to pay your respects to the old laird?"

"Lori's interested in folklore," Damian answered smoothly. "After Sir Percy told her the legend of Brother Cieran, she couldn't wait to visit the Chapel."

"You should have known better," Mick muttered.

"I beg your pardon?" I said.

"You're a mother," he said forcefully, and shot a reproachful glance at me from beneath his bushy brows. "You're responsible for two young lives. You shouldn't be taking such risks."

I didn't know what had angered the old man, but I tried to mollify him.

"Damian wouldn't have called you if he didn't think you could get us out here safely," I said. "And I don't mind getting wet."

"I'm not talking about getting wet," Mick growled. "Brother Cieran went mad, you know. He marooned himself and lost his mind. Did Sir Percy mention that?" He thrust a calloused finger toward the stone tablet. "It's said he died right there, driven mad by grief and thirst and loneliness. That's why the old laird chose the spot for his tomb."

I looked down at the stony ground surrounding the old laird's grave and felt pity well up in me. Of course Brother Cieran had gone mad, I thought. He'd glanced up from his prayers one sunny day to see black smoke billowing from the island. He must have known what it meant, yet he'd scrambled into his small boat, rowed hard to shore, and climbed the steep path to the monastery, where he'd found a smoldering ruin and, one by one, the bodies of his friends. How long had it taken him to dig their graves? How long had he stood staring out to sea before making the decision to return to the islet, release the boat, and condemn himself to death? Of course it had driven him mad.

Mick's voice broke into my reveries.

"It's said that Brother Cieran never left the Chapel," he murmured hoarsely. "It's said that his ghost wanders here still, suffering the torments of the damned. There're those who wouldn't come out here for love or money."

Mick spoke with such conviction that I wondered if Aunt Dimity had been mistaken when she'd told me that Brother Cieran had left the islet long ago.

"Have you seen his ghost?" I asked.

"That's none of your business," Mick said gruffly, leaving me with the clear impression that he had and that it hadn't been an experience he cherished. He cast a glance skyward, then stumped off toward the cleft, saying, "It's time we were going. I'll have to take you to the harbor, Mr. Hunter. Sea's too rough to drop you at the cove."

"That'll be fine, Mick," said Damian. "We can walk up to the castle from the village."

While the two men were talking, I noticed a band of high, white clouds sailing across the blue sky. When I looked toward the northern horizon, I saw a line of much darker clouds that seemed to be moving rapidly in our direction. Damian, too, took note of the oncoming storm. Alarmed, we hastened back to the dinghy, with Mick urging us on, and braced ourselves as he gunned the motor and went full bore around the headland to Stoneywell's tiny harbor.

We almost made it. We were thirty yards from the L-shaped jetty when the heavens opened. Mick steered the boat through curtains of driving rain onto the slipway, and Damian and I helped him pull it clear of the high-water mark.

"Can I buy you a drink, Mick?" Damian offered, shouting this time to be heard above the pounding rain.

"Thanks, no," said Mick. "I'd best be off home. Wife'll be worried about me. She doesn't like me going out to the Chapel." He gave me a surly glance, turned on his heel, and strode up the cobbled street.

"Thanks again, Mr. Ferguson," I called to his retreating back, but he didn't respond.

I pushed my sodden curls back from my forehead and sighed. The only good thing about the rain was that it was washing some of the salt out of my jeans. The thought of slogging up the long, muddy track to the castle did not fill me with glee.

Damian had no trouble interpreting my mood.

"I'll ring for a car," he said. "We can wait for it in the pub."

He took me by the elbow and steered me over the slick cobbles past several rain-blurred buildings and into the dimly lit and wonderfully warm pub. It was a fairly spacious one-room establishment, with a low ceiling, whitewashed walls, and a floor of wide planks. The bar was to our left, the open hearth to our right, and assorted tables and chairs had been placed between them. We hung our streaming jackets on hooks just inside the door and claimed the table closest to the fire.

Two men sat at the bar, nursing whiskeys, and two others shared a table near the back wall. They all stopped talking and turned to stare at us as we took our seats, then turned back to their drinks and their low-voiced conversations. A moment later a motherly, middle-aged barmaid came bustling up to us, wiping her plump hands on a white apron.

"Mrs. Muggoch," said Damian, "may I introduce Ms. Lori Shepherd?"

"Call me Lori," I said, smiling up at the barmaid.

She smiled back. "You'll be staying with Sir Percy, you and those adorable wee lads of yours. Will and Rob they're called, is that right?"

"That's right," I said. I doubted that there was a soul on Erinskil who didn't know my sons' names, heights, weights, and date of birth.

"Ach, Sir Percy's wonderful with children," said Mrs. Muggoch. "Well, he's never really grown up himself, has he? I don't mean to criticize," she added hastily. "You'd be hard-pressed to find anyone on the island who'd criticize Sir Percy. He's a good man. We all think so."

"I think so, too," I said. "And I couldn't agree with you more. Sir Percy will never grow old—or up. I wouldn't change him for the world."

"Nor would we," said Mrs. Muggoch.

"Are your guests keeping you busy, Mrs. Muggoch?" Damian turned to me and explained, "A young couple—a pair of birdwatchers—arrived on the last ferry. They're staying here at the pub."

"Ach, they're nice kids, and considerate, too." She bent low and murmured mischievously, "Took the room with separate beds. Who's to know if they stay in them all night long, but it's thoughtful of them to spare my tender feelings, don't you think?" She straightened and looked us over from head to toe. "How on earth did you get so wet?"

"Mick Ferguson took us out to Cieran's Chapel," said Damian.

Mrs. Muggoch gave a startled gasp. "Did he? You wouldn't catch me out there. It's terrible bad luck to set foot on the Chapel."

"Why?" I asked.

"Brother Cieran killed himself," said Mrs. Muggoch. "It may have happened a long time ago, but suicide's a mortal sin, and

Brother Cieran left the stain of it on those rocks. Ask anyone on Erinskil. They'll tell you that bad things happen to people who go out there. I could tell you tales that would keep you awake nights, and they're all of them true. If I were you, I'd be careful for the next little while." She shook her head. "It's cursed, that place."

Mick Ferguson's strange outburst suddenly made sense to me. He'd considered my trip to Cieran's Chapel risky, not because of the wind and waves but because of the curse that hung over the islet.

"The tenth earl didn't think Cieran's Chapel was cursed," I pointed out to Mrs. Muggoch.

"Ach, no, but James Robert was a saint, and there're special rules for saints," she said. Her smile returned. "Now, what can I get for you?"

Damian ordered a large pot of tea and a plate of Mrs. Muggoch's homemade shortbread. She bustled off to the kitchen, and he pulled out his cell phone.

"Wait," I said, and nodded toward the rain-dashed windows. "I'd like to warm up a bit before we step outside again."

"Mrs. Gammidge will expect us in the dining room at one o'clock," he said. "I'll ask her to send a car in"—he consulted his watch—"half an hour. We'll be back in time to shower and change before lunch."

I nodded happily, and Damian made the call.

When the tea and the shortbread arrived, we sipped and nibbled in silence, staring fixedly into the fire. I didn't know what was on Damian's mind, but I knew what was on mine: Our trip to Cieran's Chapel had been a colossal waste of time. I'd searched the stupid rock from end to end, but I still couldn't explain the mysterious golden glow. To make matters worse, Damian had been wonderful from start to finish. He'd organized the pointless expedition at the drop of a hat, even though he hadn't believed a word I'd said about the light. He'd allowed himself to be drenched, chilled, and buffeted without complaint, and when my search had proven fruitless, he'd gallantly refrained from crowing. I had to give credit where credit was due.

"Damian," I said, leaning forward, "you were right. About the light, I mean. I must have imagined it."

"Do you think so?" Damian raised an eyebrow enigmatically but said nothing more.

The fire guttered as the front door opened, admitting a gust of wind and a bedraggled young couple dressed in the traditional garb of bird-watchers: well-worn day packs, bobble caps, bulky anoraks, sturdy walking shoes, and wool trousers tucked into woolly knee socks.

The young woman had cameras and binoculars slung on straps around her neck, and the young man held in one hand a clear plastic bag filled with field guides, notebooks, and maps. Both were tall, slender, dark-haired, and good-looking, though the young man's good looks were diminished slightly by a pair of severe-looking black-rimmed glasses that were far too large for his fine-featured face.

They called hello to Mrs. Muggoch, left their packs, caps, and anoraks at the door, and made a beeline for the fire. The young man was two steps away from me when I blinked in amazement. I saw a flicker of recognition in his eyes and felt my own widen, but before I could speak, he stumbled, lost his grip on the clear plastic bag, and sent an avalanche of field guides tumbling onto our table. My teacup toppled into my lap and the saucer went skittering off into space, but before it hit the hearthstone there was a blur of movement and Damian was standing in front of me, his arm outstretched, his palm planted firmly on the young man's chest.

"Back off," he said quietly.

"Gosh, yes, of course," the young man said, backpedaling a step or two. "I'm so sorry. It's these frightful boots. They're splendid in the wild, but they trip me up the moment I return to civilization." He peered through his rain-blurred lenses at me. "I really am most awfully sorry."

"You might try cleaning your specs, Harry," muttered the young woman, who was clearly mortified.

Mrs. Muggoch hurried over with a towel, and while I blotted the spilled tea from my jeans, the embarrassed young woman asked Damian if she might retrieve the items Harry had dumped on the table. Damian studied her briefly, then stepped aside and allowed her to gather up the notebooks.

Harry, in the meantime, had dried his glasses and put them on again. He peered at me anxiously.

"I haven't scalded you, have I?" he asked. "I really am the most *appalling* klutz. Shall I fetch the doctor?"

"No, don't," I told him. "The tea wasn't hot. I'm fine."

"I'll pay for the saucer, of course," he said, turning to Mrs. Muggoch.

"There's no need for that, Harry," she said, patting his shoulder. "Accidents will happen." She picked up the bits of broken china and returned with them to the bar.

"You're all being far too kind." Harry glowered at his treacherous boots, then looked at me, his face brightening. "You're not interested in birds by any chance, are you? If you are, Cassie and I could show you some really smashing nesting sites. Please say you'll come. It's the only way I can think to make things up to you. Oh, excuse me. . . ." He thrust a hand toward me. "Harry Peters—that's me, the clumsy oaf—and this is my friend, Cassie Lynton."

"Lori Shepherd," I said. Damian was scowling mightily at me, but I ignored him, shook Harry's hand, and gave Cassie a friendly nod. "I've just arrived on Erinskil, and I'd love to see the nesting sites. Where and when shall we meet?"

Young Harry looked as though I'd given him absolution. "On the coastal path, below the old monastery? Cassie and I will be there at seven tomorrow morning. It's best to get out early, you know."

I winced inwardly at the thought of rising with the dawn but promised Harry that Damian and I would be there at the appointed hour.

"Grand," said Harry, beaming.

Damian intervened. "If you'll excuse us, we really should be going."

"What about our ride?" I asked.

"The rain's let up," he said. "We can walk back to the castle."

"Gosh," said Harry, his eyes widening. "Are you staying at the castle? How *marvelous*."

"If we don't leave now, Lori, we'll be late for lunch," said Damian, tapping his watch.

I said good-bye to Harry and Cassie, donned my rain jacket, and stepped out into the drizzle, with Damian breathing fire down my neck. He was radiating displeasure, but he waited until we'd reached the muddy track above the village to vent his spleen.

"For God's sake, Lori," he expostulated, "I expect you felt sorry for the young idiot, but it was irresponsible of you to accept his invitation. I don't know anything about him."

"That's okay," I said. "I do."

Damian stopped short. "I beg your pardon?"

I swung around to face him. "I know for a fact that Harry Peters doesn't wear glasses, he's not a bird-watcher, and he's never made a clumsy move in his life. Harry Peters's real name is Peter Harris. And he grew up next door to me."

Ten

*D*amian's brow creased angrily.

"Calm down, Damian," I said, imitating the soothing croon he'd used on me.

"I'll calm down," he snapped, "when you've told me exactly what the boy next door is doing on Erinskil."

"I don't have a clue," I admitted. "I've never been more surprised to see anyone in my life. I honestly don't know why Peter's here, and I have absolutely no idea why he's using an assumed name, but I *think* he dumped the tea in my lap to keep me from blowing his cover."

"*Why* is he traveling under cover?" Damian asked, his voice creaking with exasperation.

"Not a clue," I said serenely, "but I'm sure he'll tell me all about it tomorrow. That's why he offered to meet me. The nesting sites were his idea, remember, and they're not near the village. Peter wants to tell me, in private, why he's here."

I began slogging uphill again. My sneakers, I decided, would be unwearable by the time I got back to Dundrillin. They were good shoes, but they hadn't been built to withstand the triple threat of sand, salt water, and mud. Damian trudged beside me, scanning the scrubby shrubs and tumbled rocks that littered the hillside. It was a pity no passing assassin appeared. My bodyguard looked as though he needed to hit something.

"Chance meetings make me nervous," he grumbled. "I don't believe in coincidence."

"It's not as coincidental as it seems," I assured him. "Peter's spent the past year in the Western Isles, studying seals. Maybe he had a few days off and decided to explore Erinskil."

Damian gave a snort of incredulity. "Ah, yes, the top-secret, hush-hush seal study—*that* must be why he's traveling incognito. Do you know anything about the girl?"

"Any friend of Peter's is a friend of mine," I said staunchly. "Stop fussing, Damian. If Peter Harris were American, he'd be the ideal Eagle Scout. I'd trust him with my life."

"I hope you don't have to," Damian said grimly, and walked on in silence.

Sir Percy's seldom-seen assistant, Elliot Southmore, met us halfway up the hill in the purple car. I took the front seat, and Damian rode in the back. The track was so narrow and the verges so slick that Elliot had to drive all the way back to the village in order to turn the car around.

"Am I late?" he asked as we bumped downhill. "I understood that I was to pick you up at the pub."

"We decided to leave early," said Damian.

"Tidy little place," Elliot commented when we reached the top of Stoneywell's main street. "The natives are none too friendly, though."

"Really?" I said. "The barmaid at the pub seemed nice enough."

"Oh, she's all right," said Elliot, "but the rest of them gave Kate and me the cold shoulder when we stopped in there last night. Clammed up the minute we walked in and stared at us until we left. We felt like exotic specimens in a zoo."

"You probably did seem exotic," I said. "Percy told us that they don't get many visitors here."

"Well, they won't see Kate and me again," said Elliot. "We'll have our evening drinks in front of the fire in the library from now on. We don't mind being stared at by Sir Percy's portrait collection."

He dropped us off at the castle's main entrance, and we hurried up to the suite to shower and change. I showered, at any rate. Damian must have worked contortionist miracles in his powder room, because he was clean as a whistle and neatly dressed when we went down to join Sir Percy in the dining room.

We took our places at the table, and Mrs. Gammidge entered, carrying a tureen. As she removed the lid, the tantalizing aroma of crab bisque wafted through the air. My stomach growled its approval—our seafaring adventure had sharpened my appetite to a fine point.

Sir Percy opened the mealtime conversation in his own unique way by offering to replace the skull from the cove with one he'd received as a gift while visiting Borneo—"I don't want Will and Rob to go home empty-handed!"—but I politely refused.

"The Borneo skull was a gift, Percy," I said. "You're not supposed to give away gifts."

"True enough," he agreed philosophically. "It's the skull of an old chieftain, you see. Loaded with magic. I'd probably bring a curse down on my head if I gave it away. Still, it's a pity the twins can't keep the one they found. Boys like that sort of thing." He turned to Damian. "Must you send it off to Glasgow?"

"It may aid the police in solving a crime," Damian reminded him.

"Not likely," said Sir Percy. "Not unless they're still working on a case that's several hundred years old."

"What are you talking about, Percy?" I asked.

"The skull's ancient," he informed us. "You can tell by its color. I'm surprised you didn't spot it, Damian."

"I haven't had a chance to examine the skull closely," Damian pointed out.

"We have," said Sir Percy. "God alone knows where it came from, but the poor blighter whose brains it once protected suffered a rather nasty end. Cranium cracked like a soft-boiled egg. It's a wonder it held together all this time."

"Sir Percy." Mrs. Gammidge eyed her employer reprovingly. "There are more suitable subjects for discussion at table. I'm certain you can find one."

"What? Oh, yes, sorry. Forgot myself." Sir Percy supped his soup in silence for a moment before beginning again. "Andrew told me of your impromptu visit to Cieran's Chapel. Did you enjoy the trip, Lori?"

"It was too wet to be enjoyable," I replied. "But it was interesting. The barmaid at the pub thinks I've brought a curse down on *my* head by going out there."

"The islanders are a superstitious lot," Sir Percy acknowledged. "Erinskil's not so different from Borneo when you get right down to it."

"Did you know that a curse was associated with the Chapel, sir?" asked Damian. "It wasn't mentioned in the dossier."

"If I'd included every queer story I've heard about Cieran's Chapel since I arrived on Erinskil, the dossier would have weighed more than I do," said Sir Percy. "But now that you mention it, I'll tell you a curious thing. A guest of mine—a chap who runs a major corporation—went out there once. Broke his leg two days later." He shrugged. "Make of it what you will."

"I'll watch my step," I promised.

"A bit too late for that." Sir Percy waggled his soup spoon at me. "I heard about your run-in with the young oaf at the pub. Spilled tea all over you, didn't he?"

"I'll take spilled tea over a broken leg any old day," I said, laughing. "And he's not an oaf—he's my next-door neighbor."

"He's . . . what?" asked Sir Percy, nonplussed.

"My neighbor," I replied. "His name is Peter Harris, and he grew up next door to me. His parents are my closest friends in England."

"Did they send him to keep an eye on you?" asked Sir Percy.

"How could they?" I said. "They don't know where I am. Peter's been away from home for the past year, studying seals on an island not too far from here. I don't know what brought him to Erinskil, but I plan to find out. Damian and I are going to join him for a spot of bird-watching tomorrow morning." I looked up at Mrs. Gammidge as she removed my empty soup bowl. "Would it be possible to have an early supper on a tray in my room tonight, Mrs. Gammidge? Damian and I are meeting Peter at seven, so I'd like to get to bed at a reasonable hour."

"Nothing could be simpler, dear girl," Sir Percy boomed. "Make a note of it, Mrs. Gammidge. An early supper on a tray for our esteemed guest."

"If I might make a suggestion, sir," said the housekeeper. "Ms. Shepherd could dine with her sons this evening. Dinner is served at six o'clock in the nursery."

"A perfect solution," I said.

"I'll ask Cook to send breakfast up to you and Mr. Hunter at half past five tomorrow morning," Mrs. Gammidge continued. "I'll also ask her to pack a hamper for you, so you won't have to hurry back to the castle for lunch."

"Would you ask Cook to pack something for our friends as well?" I asked. "They're young, so they're bound to be hungry."

"Of course," she replied, and served the fillet of sole.

Damian withdrew from the conversation halfway through the main course and scarcely spoke a word as we rode the elevator up to the nursery to check in with the twins. He was clearly preoccupied, but when I asked if he was worried about anything in particular, he shook his head.

"Nothing in particular," he answered distantly. "Something's not right, but I can't quite put my finger on it."

"At the risk of sounding self-centered," I said, "may I ask if this something has to do with me and the boys?"

"I don't think so." His eyes focused sharply on my face. "But I would appreciate it if you'd remain in your suite or in the nursery for the rest of the day. I'll arrange for tea to be served in the nursery."

"No problem," I said, and refrained from quizzing him. I didn't know what was bothering him, but I was confident that our early-morning rendezvous would allay any misgivings he might have about Peter Harris.

I spent the rest of the afternoon playing with Rob and Will in the nursery. Sir Percy had provided them with so many different games and toys, and Andrew was such a clever ringmaster, that they didn't mind being cooped up. When I explained to them that Damian and I would be going out the next morning, they informed me that they'd be busy, too, playing knights-in-armor on the battlements with Andrew. As I watched them race their rocking horses, I became more convinced than ever that they'd beg Sir

Percy to adopt them when it came time for them to return to their humdrum home.

After tea, dinner, baths, and bedtime stories, I returned to my suite and a phone call from my discouraged husband. Bill had spent another long day going through client files with Chief Superintendent Yarborough and would spend much of the night doing the same thing. Not a single lead had raised its ugly head.

"I feel so stupid, Lori," he said. "I *know* my clients. I should know who Abaddon is by now, but I can't for the life of me point to a likely suspect."

"Don't beat yourself up," I told him. "If one of your clients has gone bonkers, then you don't really know him anymore."

"True, I suppose," he said glumly.

"Has Abaddon sent any more e-mail?" I asked.

"Not a single line," said Bill. "Yarborough's concerned. He thinks it means that Abaddon's moved from one phase to the next—from *sending* threats to *acting* upon them."

I clutched the phone more tightly. "Is everything okay at home?"

"Yes," Bill assured me. "I've touched base with Ivan Anton, Emma Harris, and Annelise. They're fine, the animals are fine, and the cottage is still standing."

"Let's count our blessings, then," I said, "and keep working to nail this creep. I know you'll figure it out, Bill."

"Time isn't on our side, Lori. If Yarborough's right about the e-mail, I have to find Abaddon quickly or—" He caught himself, took a steadying breath, and asked, "How was your day?"

He sounded so low that I didn't have the heart to tell him about the skull, the ghost, the grave, the curse, or the unnamed "something" that was troubling my bodyguard. Instead, I gave him a jolly version of the day's activities, beginning with the cricket match in the cove and ending with Peter Harris's surprise appearance at the pub.

"Peter!" Bill exclaimed. "Are you kidding? Why in the world—"

"I don't know," I said for what seemed like the hundredth time that day. "He's traveling incognito, so I didn't get the chance to ask him why he's on Erinskil."

"*Peter Harris* is traveling incognito?" Bill said wonderingly. "*Our* Peter Harris? The dutiful, hardworking young man we know and love?"

"Yep," I said. "That's the one. Pretty incredible, huh?"

"Utterly incredible," said Bill.

"We've arranged a clandestine rendezvous for tomorrow," I said, "and I promise you, I'll get the whole story out of him."

"I'm sure it will be very interesting," Bill understated. "Give him my best."

After a fond good-night, I returned the phone to Damian, who was sitting in his armchair watching the flickering images of Dundrillin on his laptop.

"Have you put your finger on what's wrong?" I asked.

"Not yet," he replied. "But I will."

"If you need a sounding board," I told him, "I'm available."

Damian looked up from the computer screen, and a faint but genuine smile touched his lips. "Thank you," he said. "I'll bear that in mind."

I left him in the foyer with his laptop, crossed the sitting room, and stepped onto the balcony. The afternoon's storm had blown itself out, the moon was rising, and stars were brightening in the twilit sky, but I had eyes only for the saw-toothed silhouette of Cieran's Chapel. I stared at it until my eyes watered, but no light appeared. Finally I gave up, went back inside, and got ready for bed. Then I reached for the blue journal. It was time to bring Aunt Dimity up to date.

I curled myself into an armchair in the bedroom, with Reginald nestled in the crook of my arm, opened the journal, and said, "Dimity? Are you sure Brother Cieran has left the Chapel?"

Her reply came swiftly, curling across the page without hesitation.

Quite sure. Why do you ask?

I began at the beginning and went on describing the day's events until I reached my conversation with the barmaid at the pub.

"Mrs. Muggoch agrees with Mick Ferguson," I said. "They're both convinced that Brother Cieran's still haunting the Chapel. Mrs. Muggoch told me outright that the islet is cursed, tainted by the mortal sin of Brother Cieran's suicide."

How intriguing. Do Mick Ferguson and Mrs. Muggoch speak for the rest of the islanders? Do they all believe that Cieran's Chapel is cursed?

"Mrs. Muggoch thinks they do," I said. "According to her, everyone believes that bad things happen to people who go there. Mick Ferguson said his wife didn't like him going out there, and Percy told us that one of his guests broke a leg two days after visiting the Chapel."

Sir Percy added to the legend, did he?

I gazed down at Aunt Dimity's words in puzzlement. "Do you think an evil spirit has taken over the Chapel, Dimity?"

I do not. There are no spirits, evil or otherwise, inhabiting the Chapel. If there were, I'd know it. The islanders and Sir Percy are either suffering from a mass hallucination or they're telling fibs.

"Why would they lie to me?" I asked.

I have little doubt that our dear Sir Percy is exercising his well-known sense of humor. As for the others, it may be that they're trying to frighten you.

"Frighten me?" I said. "Why?"

It's a common ploy, one that's been used throughout history. If you want to keep people from visiting a place, you scare them off. You tell them the place is haunted or cursed or unlucky. If you wish to take the scheme a step further, you use visual or auditory tricks to authenticate your claim. It's been done more times than I care to count.

"The light I saw," I said slowly. "Do you think an islander was out there waving a lantern just to spook me?"

It's possible. If everyone on the island knew of your arrival, you can be sure that some, at least, know that your balcony overlooks the Chapel.

"But I didn't find any footprints on the Chapel," I protested.

Footprints wouldn't be easy to find in the springy vegetation you described.

I shook my head. "I don't know, Dimity. It sounds far-fetched to me. Why would the islanders want to scare people away from the Chapel? There's nothing out there except the old laird's grave. Unless . . ." I paused as a new line of reasoning began to take shape in my mind.

Unless? Dimity prompted.

"The island's not set up for tourists," I said, thinking aloud. "There's no proper landing facility for the interisland ferry, and there's no hotel, just Mrs. Muggoch's two guest rooms." I sat forward as my thoughts crystallized. "Maybe the islanders *don't like tourists*. Sir Percy said that they were keen on self-sufficiency. Maybe they don't want day-trippers littering their fields or hogging their favorite tables at the pub."

The so-called curse could be part of a general antitourism campaign. Is that what you're suggesting?

"Sure," I said. "Why not? I've seen what the summer crowds leave behind in Finch. The twins and I spend weeks picking trash out of the hedgerows. I think the people of Erinskil have come up with an extremely clever way to protect their island from the ravages of tourism. I only wish someone in Finch had thought of it a long time ago. I suppose it's too late to put a curse on Sally Pyne's tearoom."

I doubt that Sally Pyne would thank you for it.

"No, probably not," I conceded. "But it makes sense, doesn't it, Dimity? As you said, if you want to keep people from visiting a place, you scare them off."

It does make sense. I'm sure you're right. My goodness, it has been an eventful day.

I grinned. "I haven't even told you the best bit yet. You'll never guess who I ran into in the pub. . . ."

After she recovered from her initial shock, Dimity was enchanted to hear of my encounter with Peter Harris.

Peter Harris, incognito and in disguise, for I think we may consider the glasses a disguise—how perfectly glorious! He was such a solemn, conscientious little boy. I'm utterly delighted to hear that he's being so very devious. And it's simply delicious to think of him traveling incognito with a girl.

"A very pretty girl," I said. "Hardy, too, if she was tramping around the island in that storm. Her name may or may not be Cassie Lynton. We'll find out tomorrow." I leaned back in the chair and looked at the bedside clock. "I'm sorry, Dimity, but if I don't hit the sack soon, I'll be too tired to walk the coastal path tomorrow."

Good night, my dear. Do try to remember everything the young rascal tells you. I want to hear every word of it.

When the lines of royal-blue ink had faded from the page, I climbed into bed, turned out the light, and smiled sleepily at my pink rabbit.

"Reginald," I said softly, "I'm really looking forward to my date with Harry Peters."

Eleven

*F*pried myself out of bed at five o'clock the following morning, showered, and dressed with an eye toward the changeable weather. I layered a fleece pullover on top of a T-shirt and pulled on a pair of trousers I could convert into shorts if by some lucky chance the day became uncomfortably warm. Although a genius in the laundry room had restored my abused sneakers to good health, I elected to wear hiking boots. Damian, too, dressed in sensible outdoor clothes: a tightly woven black wool crewneck sweater, freshly laundered khakis, and hiking boots.

A sturdy, red-haired maid named Pamela arrived in my sitting room on the dot of five-thirty with breakfast for two as well as a pair of oversized day packs so stuffed with picnic provisions that Damian and I had to remove some of them in order to make room for our rain jackets. I could live quite happily without an extra jar of caviar, but my trip to Cieran's Chapel had taught me never to step outside Dundrillin Castle without rain gear.

We didn't talk much during breakfast. I was still groggy—I was not a naturally chirpy morning person—and Damian was still absorbed in his private reflections, so our discourse consisted mostly of "More tea?" and "Pass the marmalade."

We left the castle by the side door we'd used the day before, headed south along the coastal path, and stopped almost immediately to put on our jackets. The pellucid sky held no hint of rain, but the morning air was crisp and the breezes swirling up the cliffs went right through my fleece top.

The fresh air cleared the drowsy cobwebs from my brain, and

I began to take note of the landscape. The view from the headland was so stupendous that it would have been nerve-racking if the sunken path hadn't been so deeply sunken. Centuries of passing feet had worn a wide groove in the rocky soil, with curving, grass-clad banks that were nearly waist-high. It would require a conscious effort to stray beyond the path, and it drifted so close to the cliffs in some places that only the suicidal would make the effort.

From Sir Percy's headland, all of Erinskil lay before us, glimmering emerald-green in the early-morning sun, but as the path descended, our spectacular view of the island was cut off. To our left, the land rose steeply to form a low range of boulder-strewn hills. To our right, the ruffled ocean stretched out to the horizon. Dundrillin loomed behind us, adding a dash of drama to the headland, and the path meandered ahead of us like a verdant, roofless tunnel suspended between land and sea.

It was just as well that the sunken path kept me from straying, because I could scarcely take my eyes off the birds. There were thousands of them, perched on tiny ledges, taking off or landing, swooping, wheeling, and soaring in crazed, kaleidoscopic patterns that would have made an air-traffic controller throw his hands up in despair. I realized too late that I'd forgotten to bring my camera—again—but consoled myself with the thought that it would have delayed our meeting with Peter. I would have spent far too much time trying to capture still images of the birds' fantastic flights.

Thirty minutes of brisk walking brought us to a place where the coastal path opened out onto a broad, flat shelf overlooking the sea. A prodigious heap of boulders straggled along the back of the shelf, and there, sitting atop a large, flat-topped boulder at the base of the rockfall, were Peter Harris and his pretty, dark-haired companion.

"Lori!" cried Peter. He hopped down from his perch and enveloped me, oversized day pack and all, in a hug. "I'm so glad to see you! I can't believe you're here. It's magic, isn't it? I'm sorry I knocked the tea into your lap, but I had to do something. I saw that you'd recognized me, and I was terrified that you'd call out my name."

"It's great to see you, too, Peter." I stepped back to take a good look at him, for his parents' sake. He was a handsome young devil, even taller than Bill, trim, fit, and glowing with vibrant good health. Although he was still dressed in the guise of a bird-watcher, he'd removed his black-framed glasses, so it was easier to see the strikingly beautiful cobalt-blue eyes he'd inherited from his father. "Is it my imagination, or have you grown since I last saw you?"

"Two inches," he acknowledged. "But I think I'm finished now."

"Good," I said. "Any more would just be showing off."

"But what are you doing here, Lori?" Peter exclaimed. "Are you on holiday? Is Bill here? Are the twins?"

"Forget it," I said, wagging a finger at him. "You don't get to ask any questions until you've answered mine . . . *Harry*." I looked past him at the young woman, who'd climbed down from the flat-topped boulder and walked over to stand behind him. "Is your name Cassie, or do we need to be reintroduced?"

"Yes to both questions, I'm afraid," she replied with a wry smile. "It's a rather complicated story."

"Damian and I have all day." I reached back to pat my day pack. "And we've brought enough food for lunch, tea, *and* dinner. The cook at the castle doesn't know the meaning of the word 'moderation.'"

After a brief exchange of greetings, Damian stood back to study his new subjects and, as always, to keep an eye on our surroundings.

"You've chosen a good spot for our rendezvous, Peter," I said. "Lots of birds for us to watch and no people around to watch us."

"It's historical as well." Peter strolled over to lay a hand on the flat-topped boulder he and Cassie had just vacated. "This, my friends, is known as the Slaughter Stone."

"Charming," I said, eyeing the boulder doubtfully.

"Historically significant," Peter corrected. "The pre-Christian residents of Erinskil used to come up here and sacrifice . . . well, one hopes they sacrificed animals as opposed to fellow pre-Christians, but no one knows for certain. At any rate, they made their sacrifices on the stone and chucked the carcasses into the sea."

"How efficient," I said, retreating a step.

"Who told you about the Slaughter Stone?" Damian asked.

"Our landlady," Peter replied. "Mrs. Muggoch heard me telling you where to meet us and volunteered the gory story. You see the gutters?" He ran his fingers along four faint grooves at the front edge of the boulder. "Designed for the convenient drainage of sacrificial blood."

"Good grief, Peter," I said, grimacing. "You were *sitting* there."

"I don't think it's been used recently." Peter drew a fingertip along one of the gutters, then raised it for me to examine. "You see? Spotless. But don't worry, Lori, I won't make you sit there. The overlook is a bit too exposed for comfortable conversation. Cassie and I have found a better spot, a pleasant little nook the wind can't reach."

"Before we go, however . . ." Cassie pulled two pairs of binoculars from her anorak's cargo pockets. She hung one pair around Damian's neck and the other around mine, as if she were presenting us with leis. "For verisimilitude," she explained, "on the off chance that an islander happens by. We're supposed to be bird-watching, after all, and we'd rather not give the game away until we have to."

"Now we're all in disguise," I said, fingering the binoculars. "Wish I'd brought my false mustache."

"It wouldn't suit you," said Peter, laughing.

Damian and I followed the young pair as they scrambled over the Slaughter Stone, climbed halfway up the rockfall, and dropped down onto a circular swath of turf enclosed by boulders. Peter spread a waterproof groundsheet on the damp turf, and we sat facing each other, with our backs to the boulders and our day packs resting by our sides. Apart from the odd gull passing overhead, we were alone.

"Before you get started," I said, "I should tell you that my friend Damian has serious doubts about you. He's convinced that you're a pair of master criminals hiding out from the law."

"Are you really?" said Peter, beaming delightedly at Damian.

"Lori exaggerates," Damian said repressively. "But I am curious to know the reason for your charade. And I'd be grateful to you if you'd explain what you're doing on Erinskil."

"We *are* hiding out," Cassie admitted, "but not from the law."

"Hold on, Cassie," said Peter. "If we start the story in the middle, it'll become irretrievably tangled. Let's start from the beginning and go on from there." He pulled his knees to his chest and wrapped his arms around them. "Cassie and I have been working for the Seal Conservation Trust for the past year. We've been conducting population and migration studies with a team of students and scientists at an observatory in the Outer Hebrides. Everything was going along splendidly until nine days ago, when Grandfather decided to trumpet my accomplishments to the press."

I leaned toward Damian. "Peter's grandfather is Edwin El-styn, the seventh Earl Hailesham."

"Ah." Damian nodded knowingly, as though a piece of the puzzle had fallen into place. He looked at Peter and said, "You're *that* Peter Harris. The one mentioned in the letter."

"You saw the letter?" said Peter.

"I did," Damian acknowledged.

"Letter?" I said, looking confusedly from him to Peter. "What letter?"

"Don't you read the *Times?*" asked Damian.

"Lori avoids newspapers whenever possible," Peter explained. "She finds them depressing."

"They *are* depressing," I muttered.

"They're also filled with useful information," said Damian. He turned to Peter. "Your grandfather must be very proud of you."

"He is, bless him." Peter heaved a forlorn sigh and spoke to me. "Grandfather's so proud of me that he wrote a letter to the *Times*. He wanted the world to know that not *all* children of priv-ilege are brainless wastrels whose pointless lives revolve around cocaine, clubs, and haute couture. He held me up as a shining ex-ample of how *some* of us are doing useful work, far from the lime-light. He thought more attention should be paid to those of us who are involved, hands-on, in worthy projects, and concluded by saying that praise should be given in public to those who've earned it." Peter sighed again. "Grandfather meant well, but I've never been so embarrassed in my life."

"My dad chimed in the next day," said Cassie, rolling her eyes.

"Who is your dad?" I inquired.

"Festhubert Thorpe-Lynton," she answered. "I'm Cassandra Thorpe-Lynton. Dad's in the House of Lords. He read Lord Elstyn's letter aloud in Parliament and followed it with a long-winded speech extolling the unsung virtues of privileged youth."

"In which Cassie featured prominently," Peter added.

"And from there things simply spiraled out of control," Cassie went on. "No one wanted to be shown up. Every peer with a hard-working son or daughter came out of the woodwork to make a statement for the public record. Those without could do nothing but sit and steam."

"Cassie and I were suddenly at the center of yet another debate about the role of the nobility in the modern world," said Peter, cringing.

"We don't get newspapers at our observatory," Cassie went on, "so we had no idea of the whirlwind that was beginning to swirl around Lord Elstyn's letter and my father's speech."

Peter nodded. "It came to our attention a week ago, when boatloads of reporters—"

"And photographers," Cassie inserted.

"—came flocking to our research station to grab a story," Peter finished.

Cassie pressed a hand to her breast. "I'm the peer's do-good daughter."

"I'm the hope for Britain's future," said Peter, laughing.

"And, naturally, we're hopelessly in love." Cassie buried her face in her hands, though she, too, was laughing. "It's been simply too ghastly for words."

"The story must be all over Finch by now," I commented.

"It is," said Peter, and his laughter died. "I rang Mum and Dad on my mobile as soon as I realized what was happening, but they knew about it already. They've had a knot of paparazzi lurking at the end of their drive for nearly a week."

"I wouldn't worry about it," I said. "If the paparazzi sneak up the drive, Bill will be happy to help Emma and Derek sue them for trespassing. In fact, he'll be ecstatic. He's always wanted to take a tabloid twit to court."

Damian regarded the two young people somberly. "I imagine the media invasion made it difficult for you to work."

"It was impossible!" Peter burst out. "The idiots zoomed around the observatory in their rented boats, frightening the wildlife and our colleagues. We prayed that a storm would drown them or at least drive them back to the mainland, but our prayers went unanswered."

"We didn't know what to do," said Cassie. "We considered giving an interview, but we knew that whatever we said would be twisted beyond recognition, so we decided instead to run for it. Jocelyn Withers, our boss, was incredibly understanding. He smuggled us to the mainland on a supply boat, and we spent a day there, kitting ourselves out as bird-watchers."

"Cassie dyed her lovely blond hair brown," said Peter, casting a fond look in Cassie's direction, "and I purchased my horrible specs. Cassandra Thorpe-Lynton became Cassie Lynton, Peter Harris became Harry Peters, and we boarded the ferry for Erinskil."

"Why Erinskil?" Damian inquired.

"We'd heard that it was friendly to bird-watchers," Cassie replied, "but that it didn't attract many casual tourists. We hoped we could hide out here for a week or two without being recognized."

"Once the paparazzi give up on us—or a gale sinks their blasted boats—we'll return to the observatory and continue our work unmolested." Peter straightened his legs and leaned back against his boulder. "There you have it, the whole absurd story. I don't mind telling you, Lori, that it gave me a very nasty turn to see you in the pub."

"I didn't recognize you at first," I admitted, "and when I *did*, you managed to shut me up pretty effectively."

"Sorry about that," said Peter, "but I couldn't let you call out my real name. We've been lucky so far. No one on Erinskil has connected us to the tabloid stories, and no reporters have come hunting for us."

"I won't give you away," I assured him.

"Nor shall I," said Damian.

"Never crossed my mind that you would," said Peter.

"Do Emma and Derek know you're here?" I asked.

Peter nodded. "I rang Mum and Dad as soon as we boarded the ferry. Cassie rang her parents, too. We've sworn them to secrecy, of course, but we didn't want them to worry."

I reached over to pat Peter's boot. "I hope my sons grow up to be just like you, Peter—thoughtful, considerate, kind to their parents. You really are the hope for Britain's future."

"Don't *you* start," Peter pleaded, wincing. "I don't want to be anyone's poster child. The hours are terrible and the rewards, nonexistent." He eyed our day packs with sudden interest. "I know it's a bit early for lunch, but I could do with a midmorning snack. It's hungry work, recounting our misadventures."

I opened my pack and handed out sandwiches while Damian pulled the large thermos from his and poured hot tea for four. Cook had outdone herself. The sandwiches weren't the dainty wafers she produced for tea but thick, hearty slabs of fresh-baked bread filled with smoked ham, nutty cheese, and cold chicken. No one wanted caviar, but the homemade pickles and chutney were a welcome addition to the meal.

I split a giant sandwich with Damian while Peter and Cassie consumed one apiece, made a serious dent in the chutney, and emptied the pickle jar.

"Isn't Mrs. Muggoch feeding you?" I asked.

"Not enough," said Peter, swallowing manfully. "Cassie and I have been hiking all over the island since we arrived. Our appetites have exploded."

I kept the tea flowing while they demolished their midmorning snack, but Damian left the sheltered circle of turf to survey the sunken path and the overlook. He returned shortly thereafter to report, quite literally, that the coast was clear.

After forty minutes' steady gorging, Peter and Cassie were replete. They helped me gather the sandwich wrappings and tuck them into my day pack, then leaned back against their boulders with contented sighs.

"Now that we've satisfied your curiosity," said Peter, "it's your turn to satisfy ours. What brings you to Erinskil, Lori?"

The sunny day seemed to darken. The cool air seemed to grow cold. The sound of the crashing surf was suddenly loud in my ears, and the screams of the hovering gulls became harsh and eerie. I'd enjoyed a brief respite from fear, but it was back again, closing its clammy hand around my heart.

"Lori?" Peter said encouragingly. "Are you on holiday?"

"Not even remotely," I said, and told him everything. If Damian had voiced an objection, I would have talked over him. I had no choice but to tell Peter the truth. He knew me so well that he would have spotted a lie the moment it passed my lips.

"Oh, Lori . . ." Peter said in a hushed voice when I'd finished. He'd drawn his knees to his chest again and leaned over them, taut with concern. "I'm so sorry. You must be going through hell."

"Only when I let myself think about it," I said with a weak smile.

"Is there anything we can do?" Cassie asked.

"Yes," Damian cut in. "You can keep your eyes open and your mouths shut."

"Don't be stupid," Peter snapped. His grandfather's fiery temper blazed suddenly in his blue eyes. "Lives are at stake. Do you think we'd take something like that *lightly?*"

"No," said Damian, chastened. "Of course you wouldn't. I apologize."

"It's all right," said Peter, his fury fading as quickly as it had flared. "You're here to protect Lori and the boys. I do understand."

Damian took a pen and a small pad of paper from his breast pocket, jotted a note, and passed it to Peter. "Here's the number for my mobile. Please ring me if you notice anything out of the ordinary."

"Here's mine," said Peter, tearing the paper in half and scribbling his number on the slip. "In case you need an extra hand. I'd do anything for Lori."

"We already have, by the way," Cassie said casually. "Noticed something out of the ordinary, I mean."

Damian's eyes narrowed. "What have you noticed?"

"There's a little island off to the west of Erinskil," said Cassie. "It's called Cieran's Chapel."

"We know it," I said, nodding.

Cassie leaned forward. "We were up on the coastal path the night before last, looking at the stars, when we saw a light out there—several lights, in fact. They were no more than faint flickers, but we thought it odd."

I shot a triumphant glance at Damian. "I *told* you there was a light."

"You saw one, too?" said Cassie.

"Yes," I said, "but I only saw one brief flash."

"What time did you see your lights, Cassie?" Damian asked.

"Between eleven-thirty and midnight," Cassie informed him. "That's why it struck us as odd. On our first night here, Mrs. Muggoch had told us an absurd tale about a monk's ghost haunting the Chapel. She seemed to believe it, but we didn't. Still, we couldn't imagine why anyone would be out there at such a late hour."

Damian peered at Cassie with a curious intensity. "Did you mention the lights to Mrs. Muggoch?"

"Certainly not," she said. "Peter and I don't want to draw attention to ourselves. And after a good night's sleep, it dawned on us that the same might be true for whoever was on Cieran's Chapel."

"Cassie thinks it must have been drug smugglers," said Peter, "dropping off a load or picking one up. And I agree with her."

"Drug smugglers!" I exclaimed. "You can't be serious."

"We're perfectly serious," said Peter. "The Western Isles are a hotbed for drug smuggling. I've read stories about it in all the newspapers. Dealers drop shipments off in remote locations, and locals take the shipments to the mainland for distribution. You have to admit that Cieran's Chapel would be a useful transit point."

"Quite useful," Damian murmured.

I looked from one face to another in disbelief. "You think the *locals* are involved?"

"I'm afraid we do," said Cassie. "No outsider could use the Chapel without their full knowledge and cooperation."

I opened my mouth to protest but closed it again. I didn't want to believe that the illicit drug trade had sullied Sir Percy's little corner of paradise, but it might be true. I recalled the revelation I'd had the night before and realized with a sinking heart that my newborn suspicions dovetailed rather neatly with Cassie's.

Aunt Dimity's words came back to me so clearly that I could

almost see them written in the air: *If you want to keep people from visiting a place, you scare them off.* Erinskil was all but inaccessible to casual visitors, and the few tourists who found their way to the island could theoretically be kept away from Cieran's Chapel by the spooky mythology the islanders had built up around Brother Cieran. It was entirely possible that the islanders' antitourism campaign had been designed to protect their drug-trafficking operation.

"You needn't look so shocked, Lori," said Peter. "Smuggling is a traditional source of revenue in the islands. Drugs are simply the latest—and most lucrative—cargo."

"But they don't need drug money," I said feebly. "Percy told us that the islanders are part of a tweed-making cooperative. They make a good living selling high-quality tweed."

"*Tweed?*" Peter said incredulously. He and Cassie exchanged glances, got to their feet, and slung their day packs over their shoulders. "Come with us, Lori. There are a few things we'd like to show you."

Twelve

*D*amian and I scrambled after Peter and Cassie as they climbed the boulder-strewn hill above the overlook. It wasn't a long climb, but the hill was steep, and I was overheated by the time we reached the crest. I paused to unsnap and unzip my rain jacket, then jogged to catch up with the others. They'd made their way across the rounded summit and stood just below the hilltop, looking east.

The hill's inland slope didn't end in precipitous cliffs but fell gently to the wide valley below in a series of broad, deep terraces. On the highest terrace, commanding a sweeping view of Erinskil's sheep-dotted fields, lay the monastery's skeletal remains.

"There's not much left," said Peter, gazing down at the ruins. "But Mrs. Muggoch told us that there wasn't much there in the first place. It was never a wealthy priory, like Lindesfarne in Northumberland. It didn't last long enough to become well endowed and powerful. It was an outpost that failed."

Wandering sheep acted as the ruins' groundskeepers, cropping the grass as neatly and far more quietly than any lawnmower. The short grass made it easy to see the layout of the little community, outlined in crumbling stone. Six nave pillars and a few paving slabs were all that remained of the church, and the cloister was marked by the stumps of broken arches.

A dark stream cut a trough in the turf as it tumbled downhill from a spring some twenty yards south of the monastery, and the terraces below might once have been divided into garden plots. The monks, it seemed to me, had chosen their site wisely. It offered them fresh water, arable land, and protection from the winter gales that blew in from the west. It had not, however, saved them from the Vikings.

I looked to my left and saw the distant specks of Stoneywell's tidy houses gleaming white in the morning sun. The marauding Norsemen had swept through the village like flames. They'd poured into the valley to plunder the farms, then moved up the terraced hillside to slaughter the monks, loot the monastery of its humble treasures, and burn it to the ground. From the Vikings' point of view, it had been a good day.

"The monks must have seen what was coming," I said, half to myself. "Why didn't they run and hide?"

"We'll never know," said Damian. "The answers to some questions are buried too deeply in the past. We can never resurrect them."

"On the other hand," Peter piped up, "some answers are buried mere inches beneath the surface. It takes only a bit of scratching to uncover them. I'll show you. Come along."

We zigzagged down the slope to the highest terrace, then headed for its southernmost edge, stopping on the way to look into the ruined church. The cracked and pitted paving slabs led to an oblong block of stone that lay near the church's east end, the spot where the altar had stood.

The block of stone appeared to be a memorial tablet, similar to the one marking the old laird's grave on Cieran's Chapel, but far older. The passage of time had long since erased the name of the man who'd been buried there, but the tablet's incised decoration could still be discerned—a diamond-patterned border, bold in its simplicity.

"Only the head of the order would have been buried so near the altar," Peter commented, nodding at the tablet.

"Poor man," I said. "I wonder if he screams along with his fellow monks?"

"Screaming monks?" Peter's face came alive with interest. "Mrs. Muggoch hasn't mentioned a word to us about screaming monks. Are you making it up?"

"No, but Sir Percy might have been," Damian answered dryly. "He likes to embellish legends."

I smiled, then turned to Peter. "Sir Percy told us that if you stand inside the monastery ruins on certain nights, when the moon and stars are just so, you can hear the screams of the massacred monks."

"Fantastic," said Peter, gazing eagerly at the tablet. "I wonder if Mrs. Muggoch can give me the proper coordinates for the moon and stars?"

"Peter," Cassie scolded, "you're being revoltingly insensitive, *and* you're allowing yourself to be distracted. Shall we move on?"

We moved on, jumping over the tumbling stream and walking to the edge of the terrace, where a half-buried boulder served as a convenient bench. When we'd taken our seats, Peter pointed toward a cluster of farm buildings not far from the foot of the hill. A long, graveled drive connected them to the road that crossed the valley from north to south.

"MacAllen's croft," he said. "Look at it through your binoculars and tell me what you see."

I raised the binoculars to my eyes and focused them on the farmhouse. After a short time, I moved on to the outbuildings, the pens, and the walled fields. I could tell by Damian's movements that he was subjecting the croft to an examination that was far more minute than mine. Finally I lowered the binoculars.

"It's a farm," I said. "Or, as they say in Scotland, a croft. It has a farmhouse and farm buildings and farmyards filled with sheep, which qualify as farm animals." I shrugged. "It's a farm."

Damian, who had yet to lower his binoculars, said thoughtfully, "It's rather a nice farm, though."

"Exactly." Peter nodded enthusiastically, as though Damian were his star pupil.

"Look again, Lori," Cassie said, taking note of my perplexity. "The MacAllens have a satellite dish. They've roofed their house with costly tiles and fitted it with insulated windows. They've added at least six rooms to the original four-room structure."

"The sheep interest me," said Damian.

"They should," said Peter, unable to restrain himself. "Those are North Ronaldsay sheep. They're an endangered breed. At last count there were fewer than three hundred ewes on the mainland."

"How on earth do you know that?" I asked, staring at him.

"I rang an informative lady at the Cotswold Farm Park," he answered. "Miss Henson is an expert on endangered domestic animals. I described Mr. MacAllen's sheep to her, and she told me all about them. The rest of Erinskil's sheep are fine animals that produce high-quality wool, but they're not rare. Mr. MacAllen is an ovine connoisseur."

"I still don't understand what you and Cassie are getting at," I said, peering down at the sheep with my binoculars. "Mr. MacAllen's croft is in good shape, and he owns some unusual sheep. So what?"

"The croft isn't in good shape, Lori," said Cassie. "It's flawless. We've seen it up close. There's not a fleck of peeling paint or a tile out of place. The MacAllens have central heating. They have a *sauna* and a *hot tub*. Those aren't the sorts of things you find on your average farm."

"But they're not completely unexpected," I objected. "If you live on an island, you have to make your own fun."

"If MacAllen's croft were the exception, I'd agree with you," said Cassie.

"Ladies and gentleman," said Peter, through cupped hands, "I hope you've enjoyed Exhibit A. Please follow me to Exhibits B through . . . F, would you say, Cassie?"

"Possibly G," said Cassie. "We have been rather busy."

"We have," said Peter, grinning.

Peter left the half-buried boulder and headed south again, descending from the terrace until he reached a faint trail that wound up and down the sides of the adjoining hills. I was certain that the trail had been made by and for sheep rather than human beings, but Peter was as sure-footed as a mountain goat. As I clambered after him, I sent a silent word of thanks to Rob and Will for keeping me in fairly good condition. The hours I'd spent chasing cricket balls for them had not been entirely wasted.

Peter motioned for us to join him on a slight promontory that jutted out over the valley, and he pointed down to a cluster of long, tin-roofed structures behind another complex of farm buildings.

"The shearing sheds," he said, "are managed by the Mackinnon brothers, Neil and Norman. The Mackinnons travel with their wives and children to Australia and New Zealand every year to participate in sheepshearing competitions. They've won quite a few."

"Family holidays Down Under are not cheap," Cassie pointed out, "nor is the equipment they use to shear Erinskil's sheep. It's mod cons all the way for the Mackinnon brothers. On we go."

"Wait a minute." I spoke up in order to catch my breath before we tackled the sheep track again, but also because a memory had stirred. "I saw a woman hanging laundry on a line when the boys and I flew over the island with Sir Percy. If everything's so up-to-date on Erinskil, why wasn't she using an automatic clothes dryer?"

"That would be Siobhan Ferguson," said Peter. "Mick Ferguson's daughter-in-law. She doesn't like gadgets. She owns a tumble dryer, Lori, but she uses it only when the weather forces her to." He hopped back onto the sheep track. "Let us proceed."

The next leg of the tour took us all the way to the Sleeping Dragon, the spiky ridge Sir Percy had pointed out to me from the helicopter. I managed to keep up with Peter for a while, but his long strides ate up ground much faster than my short ones, and I was soon lagging behind. Cassie chose to hang back with me, and Damian, of course, was never more than a few feet away from me. I rapidly developed a deep antipathy toward both of them. It was, I felt, cruel, inconsiderate, and possibly unnatural of them to hold a casual conversation when all I could do was pant and puff.

"How did you find out so much about the islanders?" Damian asked the young woman. "You've been here less than a week, and they're reputed to be extremely tight-lipped."

"It's Peter." Cassie gazed at Peter's distant back and smiled. "Peter could chat up a stone statue. Everyone—simply *everyone*— talks to him. It's because he's so enthusiastic, so authentically sincere. He's truly interested in every subject under the sun— sheepshearing, family history, *everything*."

"Why isn't he at university?" Damian asked.

Cassie laughed and I gave a gasping chuckle as we attacked the Sleeping Dragon's nearly vertical northern flank. We knew something Damian didn't.

"Peter took his degree when he was seventeen," Cassie kindly explained. "He took three, in fact, in natural history, anthropology, and business management."

"What business does he intend to manage?" asked Damian.

"The family business," Cassie replied. "Peter will inherit the Hailesham estate when his grandfather dies. He intends to keep it intact for his children and his grandchildren."

"Britain's future is in good hands, it seems," said Damian, nodding.

"Peter's a smarty-pants," I agreed, between huffs.

Peter was waiting for us when we finally clambered to the top of the spiky ridge. I insisted on a ten-minute break and gulped a bottle of water before following him to the ridge's inland tip and the best view of the island I'd seen since I'd flown over it. The small lake shone like quicksilver below us, the windmill farm whirred away to our right, and the castle looked like a toy fort atop its headland far to the north.

Peter immediately made it clear that he hadn't brought Damian and me there to enjoy the scenery. His pointing finger moved from one croft to the next, up and down the valley, as he reeled off the information he and Cassie had gathered about each of them.

One crofting family coddled a collection of rare orchids in a custom-built greenhouse. Another raised champion sheepdogs. A third made an exquisite single-malt whiskey that was available only on Erinskil. All of the croft buildings had been expanded and improved, using the finest materials, and each was extraordinarily well maintained.

When he'd finished his litany, Peter turned with a sweep of his arm toward the windmill farm.

"I've visited all of the islands in the Inner and Outer Hebrides," he said, "and I've never seen anything like *that*."

"Sir Percy told us that the islanders installed the original system twenty years ago," I said.

"It seems a curious thing to do, don't you think?" said Peter. "Why would the islanders spend a fortune to generate power for their own use, yet invest not one penny in improving the harbor? The lake, by the way, isn't a lake," he added, peering downward. "It's a man-made reservoir that supplies the islanders with fresh water." He gave me a sidelong glance and turned to pick his way back along the ridge. "One more stop and our tour is finished."

I looked at my watch and saw to my dismay that it was already past noon.

"Is it a long way?" I asked, hoping I didn't sound as pathetic as I felt.

"Yes," said Peter, over his shoulder, "but there's a marvelous picnic spot at the end of it."

The promise of lunch was the only thing that got me through the last and by far the longest leg of the tour. When we arrived at the spot Peter had in mind—a shallow cave that overlooked the village—he spread a groundsheet for us and I laid out the many delectable treats Cook had prepared. For the next hour or so, *I* didn't know the meaning of the word "moderation."

The day packs were much lighter by the time we finished. We even polished off the caviar.

Thirteen

F've seldom enjoyed a meal more. The fact that we were sitting down was a huge plus, but the pleasant company, the beautiful setting, the exquisite weather, and the superior quality of the food helped a lot, too. Even so, I couldn't keep myself from casting a suspicious glance at the sky every now and then. The previous day's deluge was still fresh in my memory. I didn't relish the thought of being ambushed by another one.

"It's not like that, Lori," Peter said after I'd craned my neck a half dozen times. "The weather doesn't follow a schedule on Erinskil. Rain comes when it will."

"It doesn't look as if it will anytime soon," said Cassie, scanning the cloud-free horizon. "Our luck with the weather seems to be holding."

While Damian and I packed away the picnic things, Cassie unpacked her maps and field guides and scattered them on the groundsheet—for verisimilitude, I assumed. When the stage was set, we sat four abreast among the thrift and quivering sea grasses at the mouth of the cave and looked down at the village. I expected Peter to ask us to raise our binoculars again, but instead he took his story out to sea.

"As you know," he began, "Cassie and I came to Erinskil on the interisland ferry. It's a long trip from the mainland, because the ferry stops at other islands on the way. Cassie and I had plenty of time to explore."

"When we went down to the hold," Cassie continued, "we discovered that shipments bound for Erinskil were packed in containers that were different from the others. We wondered why until we arrived in the harbor and watched the crane swing Erinskil's cargo onto the jetty."

"I asked the ferry captain about the shipping containers," said Peter. "He told me they'd been designed and built to order by a firm in Glasgow, exclusively for Erinskil. He also mentioned that the crane is always in tip-top condition. He'd never known it to malfunction."

"The boats inside the breakwater piqued our interest, too," said Cassie. "There are only two fishing boats registered on Erinskil, and both belong to the Murdoch family." She gave me a meaningful glance. "Erinskil doesn't support itself with its fishing fleet."

"Alasdair Murdoch's catch of the day doesn't end up in an Edinburgh restaurant," Peter added, driving the point home. "It ends up on the islanders' plates or in Alasdair's cold-storage locker for future use—by the locals."

"Lucky locals," I murmured.

"Stunningly lucky," said Peter. His eyes roved over the village. "We come at last to Stoneywell. I won't ask you to examine it through your binoculars, because we're supposed to be studying birds, not buildings. In fact, it would be a good idea for you to point your binoculars toward the sky occasionally, in case a villager happens to see us up here."

"In keeping with our cover story," Damian put in. He picked up a field guide and thumbed through it.

"I wish our expedition could include a stroll through the village." Faint worry lines furrowed Peter's smooth brow. "But I think we should continue to maintain a low profile there. We want the islanders to go on believing that we're harmless bird-watchers. It's a matter of personal safety as much as anything else."

"Are you afraid of the paparazzi?" I asked.

"Not particularly," Peter answered, "but I have a healthy fear of drug dealers. They're not known for their gentle ways. If they suspect us of prying into their business, they might turn ugly." He lifted a hand to the sky. "So please raise your binoculars while I point to the flock of kittiwakes that happens to be flying by."

Apprehension made my hands tremble as I followed the flock.

"Peter," I said from the corner of my mouth, "maybe you and Cassie should move into the castle with me and the boys. Sir Percy won't mind, and if you're right about the islanders, you may already be in danger. You've been awfully inquisitive."

"We've also been endearingly naive," Peter said with a light-hearted laugh. "No one suspects us of anything but youthful curiosity—yet. We don't intend to push it any further."

"A wise plan," Damian said quietly. "But keep Lori's invitation in mind. If you feel threatened in any way, come to Dundrillin."

"Thanks," said Cassie.

"Now, about Stoneywell . . ." Peter bent over his map, as though he were consulting it. "Did you notice anything about the village when you were there yesterday, Lori?"

"I noticed that it was wet," I replied. "Very, very wet."

"It wasn't the best day for sightseeing," Peter conceded. "If it had been, you might have seen some rather unusual sights. . . ."

If I hadn't lived in Finch for seven years, Peter's "unusual" sights might not have struck me as unusual. But the longer he talked, the clearer it became to me that Stoneywell was not an ordinary village.

Finch's village shop was well stocked by small-town standards, but its gourmet-food department was limited to a few dusty tins of fish paste. Stoneywell's shop, by contrast, supplied the islanders with basic staples as well as freshly ground coffees, a broad range of cheeses and pâtés, and an interesting selection of foreign and domestic wines. Mr. Muggoch, who with his wife ran the small bakery as well as the pub, produced croissants and brioches along with traditional Scottish breads and pastries.

"Finch doesn't even have a bakery," I grumbled.

"No, it doesn't," said Peter. "Nor does it have a resident doctor with a fully equipped, modern surgery. But Stoneywell does. Dr. Gordon Tighe was born and raised in Stoneywell. He opened his practice here as soon as he'd qualified."

"The other islands we've visited have nothing like Stoneywell's surgery," said Cassie. "Dr. Tighe can take care of almost any medical emergency. Only the most desperate cases have to be evacuated to the mainland."

Peter passed the map to me and picked up a field guide. "Then there's the school. . . ."

Finch's two-room village school had been shut down in the 1950s, but according to Peter, Stoneywell's was still alive and kicking. It had a staff of one full-time teacher, aided, it seemed, by the entire adult population of Erinskil.

"They give talks on sheep rearing, dye making, fishing, baking, brewing, medicine—whatever profession or trade they know best," Peter informed us. "The children go to a boarding school on the mainland when they've finished here, and most of them go on to university. A staggeringly high percentage return to Erinskil after earning their degrees."

"I don't blame them for coming back," I said, shaking my head. "The outside world must seem pretty shabby compared to Erinskil. Is there a church?"

"Church of Scotland," Peter answered. "There's nothing remarkable about it, except that the pastor is yet another Erinskil native. Reverend Lachlan Ferguson is Mick Ferguson's brother."

"What about law and order?" I asked. "Are there policemen on Erinskil?"

"Not one," said Peter. "But since there doesn't seem to be any crime—apart from the rather notable one of drug trafficking—there's no pressing need for a police force." He reared back as a flock of birds swung into view around the headland. "Look! Fulmars!"

I raised my binoculars and focused on a fulmar. It was indistinguishable from every other seagull I'd ever seen.

"Last but not least," Peter continued, as if the passing flock of fulmars hadn't interrupted his narrative, "we come to Erinskil's tweed mill. The wool comes from the island's own sheep. Most of the spinning is done by various islanders in their homes. A few have looms at home, too, but most of the weaving is done on the looms in the mill."

"I hope you're not going to disillusion me by saying that the looms are computerized," I said, lowering the binoculars. "Sir Percy told us that the islanders use traditional tools and techniques to make the tweed."

"They do," said Peter. "They use hand looms and natural dyes and spinning wheels, which is why the tweed is so valuable and why it couldn't possibly support the kinds of lives these people lead." He raised his hands in a helpless gesture. "I don't care if they've learned how to spin wool into gold, Lori. They'd have to produce *miles* of the stuff *each year* to pay for their hobbies and their houses, not to mention the school, the surgery, the windmill farm, and the custom-built shipping containers. It isn't physically possible to manufacture that much tweed using traditional tools and techniques. We think they're using the tweed mill to launder the drug money."

"Don't you see, Lori?" asked Cassie. "There's no tourist trade, no fishing fleet, no research center, like our observatory, and the tweed mill can't produce an adequate amount of tweed—there's nothing tangible to explain the island's prosperity. How, then, do the residents supplement their incomes?"

My mind was reeling with the information the two young friends had collected since they'd come to Erinskil. They had, it seemed, subjected the island's residents to the same intense scrutiny they were accustomed to using on migrating seals. I couldn't, of course, dispute any of their observations.

The island's houses were in pristine condition—Sir Percy himself had told me that he hadn't had to repair so much as a dripping tap since he'd become laird—and the amenities were plentiful. There did seem to be a concerted effort by the islanders to repel rather than attract tourists. Every investment they'd made—in the windmill farm, the reservoir, the shipping containers, the modern surgery—had been made with their own comfort and well-being in mind, not the comfort and well-being of visitors. Why?

Because, according to Peter and Cassie, visitors might turn into unwanted witnesses. Even if they didn't see mysterious lights on Cieran's Chapel, they'd see the wines in the shop and the brioches in the bakery. If they were curious and intelligent, they might ask the same questions Peter and Cassie were asking—and draw the same conclusion.

No matter how hard I tried, I couldn't bring myself to agree with the conclusion. The drug trade was a filthy business. I hated to think that the islanders' rich, fulfilling lives were financed by filth, so I searched for an alternate explanation.

"Maybe they all inherited money," I proposed, "and maybe they invested it wisely, as a group. And maybe they don't want tourists to come to the island because some of the tourists would want to stay. Housing prices would skyrocket, the place would become overcrowded, and their way of life would be ruined."

Peter stared at me openmouthed for a long moment, then leaned over and flung an arm around me, chuckling. "You see why I love her, Cassie? She refuses to think ill of anyone."

"He's lying," I said darkly, squirming out of Peter's hold. "I think ill of lots of people. I just don't believe in conspiracies. They ask too much of human nature. I mean, think about it. Everyone on the island would have to agree to participate in a major criminal activity and then keep mum about it for decades, because none of the stuff you've pointed out happened overnight." I folded my arms and regarded Peter stubbornly. "You know as well as I do, Peter, that no one in Finch can keep a secret for more than ten seconds. I don't believe the islanders could keep one for ten years or more."

"All right, Lori," Peter said, smiling indulgently, "have it your way. The islanders aren't buying comfort with tainted cash. They're the innocent beneficiaries of a massive inheritance and wise financial planning."

Cassie leaned her chin on her hand and sighed. "You make me feel quite jaded, Lori. Since we can't prove anything one way or the other, I choose to believe your story. It's much nicer than ours."

"I'd rather you believe it because of its impeccable logic," I said, "but I won't ask for the moon. What do you think, Damian?"

"I think," he said, looking at his watch, "that we should return to the castle soon. It's nearly teatime in the nursery."

I checked my own watch and yelped. I hadn't realized how late it was. "Sorry, guys, but Damian's right. I should be getting back. Will and Rob will want to tell me about their day."

Cassie and Peter went to work clearing the cave mouth,

Cassie collecting the maps and the field guides, Peter folding the groundsheet and tucking it into his pack. They worked well together, smoothly and efficiently, like dance partners who understood each other's rhythms and could predict each other's moves. They'd told their long, complicated story the same way—cooperatively rather than competitively. They were so clearly on the same wavelength, and so filled with admiration for each other, that I couldn't help thinking that the despicable, truth-twisting tabloids had gotten at least one thing right. Something closely resembling love was in the air.

Peter lifted his day pack from the ground and and looked at me uncertainly.

"It's been nearly a year since I've seen Will and Rob," he said. "I don't suppose we could cadge an invitation to the castle, could we?" He frowned anxiously. "Or would it be too great a risk? The twins are sure to recognize me, and someone from the castle might spread the news to the rest of Erinskil."

"I wouldn't worry too much about the rest of Erinskil," said Damian. "I doubt that the islanders will alert the media when they discover your true identities. If you're right about them, they'll be even less willing than you to face a rabble of reporters. They'll guard your privacy, if only to protect their own."

"What about Sir Percy?" Cassie asked.

"Your secret will be safe with him," I assured her. "He despises the gutter press, as do all right-thinking people. Come to the castle tonight, around six. You can spend time with Rob and Will and stay for dinner. But please, keep your suspicions to yourselves, will you? Sir Percy loves this place. He'll think you're either crazy or rude if you tell him he's laird of a drug cartel."

"We won't say a word," Peter promised.

"In that case," I said, "Sir Percy will be delighted to meet you."

"Good," said Cassie with a decisive nod, "because *I* want to meet Sir Percy."

"Why?" I asked.

Cassie closed her pack and stood. "My father owns a rather large estate, with a number of tenant farmers. They do nothing but grumble and whine—replace this, repair that, and do it *now*. It's understandable—there's almost always a streak of resentment between tenant and landlord—but I have yet to hear anyone on Erinskil say a word against their new laird. Sir Percy must be a remarkable man."

"He's one of a kind," I said. "We'll see you tonight, then?"

"Oh, yes," said Peter, his face brightening. He reached out to lay a hand on my day pack. "If this is Cook's idea of a picnic, I can't wait to see how she defines dinner."

Fourteen

*D*amian called Mrs. Gammidge as we made our way back to the castle, to let her know that two guests would be joining us for dinner. When I took the cell phone and informed her that our guests would be young and hungry, she replied loftily that Cook, who was accustomed to presiding over banquets, could safely be relied upon to provide adequate nourishment for two young people, however hearty their appetites.

Damian and I stopped in the Cornflower Suite long enough to wash the dust from our brows and change into clean clothes, then headed up to the nursery, where tea was already in progress. Andrew called down to the kitchen for extra cups and cakes, and Will and Rob entertained us while we waited.

Sir William and Lord Robert had spent an active day on the battlements with their valiant esquire, Andrew the Red, fending off everything from pirates to sea monsters. I was particularly impressed by their duel with the well-armed giant squid, but my stomach twisted painfully when they recounted their greatest triumph: capturing the Bad Man. Until that moment I hadn't realized that Abaddon had invaded my sons' imaginations.

"Lord Robert and I caught him," Will said, "and Andrew the Red put him in the dungeon."

"In chains," Rob added firmly.

Before I could react, Damian's cell phone rang. It was Bill, so I took the telephone into the foyer, to keep little ears from overhearing words that might darken their fantasies further.

Bill's morale was at an all-time low. While he continued

searching his client files for anyone who might fit Abaddon's profile, Chief Superintendent Yarborough's team of detectives had begun interviewing current as well as former clients. Bill believed that the interviews were necessary but suspected that they wouldn't be especially good for business.

"Can you imagine the impression it will make?" he asked. "How would you react if a policeman knocked on your door and asked to speak with the family psychopath?"

"I'd introduce myself," I said brightly, but my husband was in no mood for jokes.

"Ha," he said bleakly.

"I'm sure the detectives will be consummate professionals," I said, throwing all attempts at humor overboard, "and I know that everyone will understand and be eager to do whatever they can to help. You've spent years building solid relationships with your clients, Bill. They think you're wonderful."

"One of them doesn't," Bill muttered gloomily.

At which point I carried Damian's cell phone back into the nursery and turned it over to the twins, in hopes that a father-sons chat would lift Bill's spirits. Thankfully, Will and Rob became so involved in describing their complex battle with the squid that they forgot to mention the Bad Man.

The battery should have been dead by the time the boys gave the phone back to me, but the medicine had worked. When I returned to the foyer to continue our conversation, Bill sounded more cheerful than he had in days.

"You haven't told me about Peter yet," he said. "Did you find out why he's on Erinskil?"

I gave him the highlights of Peter's story, carefully editing out the colorful history of the Slaughter Stone and Cassie's preposterous allegations regarding illegal drugs. Tales involving smugglers and human sacrifice, I decided, would only put a damper on Bill's newly happy mood.

"Poor old Peter," Bill said, when I'd finished. "Hunted like a rat for being decent. He and his friend chose a good place to go to ground, at any rate. Erinskil sounds fantastic."

"It's amazingly beautiful," I said. "We'll come back here for a family vacation when . . . when Chief Superintendent Yarborough's detectives finally knock on the right door."

"When Abaddon's caught and put away." A note of gloom reentered Bill's voice, but he shook it off. "Yes. We *will* go to Erinskil as a family, and we'll hike the coastal path and tour the tweed mill and fight squids together on Percy's battlements. I can't wait. I *really* can't wait." He promised to call again the next day and then went back to the seemingly hopeless chore of finding the hidden psychopath in his roster of staid and eminently civilized clients.

Mrs. Gammidge called a short time later to announce the arrival of our guests. Damian asked her to send them up and went with me to meet them at the elevator. Although their wardrobes were probably even more limited than Damian's, Peter and Cassie had done what they could to spruce themselves up. They'd exchanged their bird-watchers' costumes for freshly laundered jeans and crewneck sweaters and swapped their grubby hiking boots for fairly clean sneakers. Peter's dark hair was neatly combed, and Cassie had bundled hers into a sophisticated chignon.

They also came bearing gifts: a pair of adorable stuffed animals—seal pups—for the twins.

"We sell them to raise funds for the trust," Peter explained. "Cassie and I always have a few in our packs."

"The boys will love them," I said.

"I'm sorry we're so late," Cassie added. "Mrs. Muggoch wanted to hear about each and every bird we'd spotted."

"Kittiwakes and fulmars," I chanted. "I'm pretty sure I saw a pigeon, too, but I don't suppose it would interest Mrs. Muggoch. And don't worry about being late. I'm letting the boys stay up past their bedtime anyway, in honor of your visit."

Rob and Will nearly came unglued when they saw Peter. He was one of their great heroes, a man *they knew* who'd not only paddled down the Amazon but explored the smoking craters of active volcanoes. They accepted their baby seals with unconcealed delight, introduced Peter to their little knights, and gave him an exhaustive tour of the nursery before pulling him into an arm-chair and perching on its arms while he regaled them with seal stories. It took them a long time to notice Cassie.

"Is Cassie your girlfriend?" Rob asked, out of the blue.

"She's a chum," replied Peter, blushing.

Will wasn't buying it. He studied Cassie for a moment before saying matter-of-factly, "You and Peter could get married at the castle if you like. Sir Percy won't mind."

"Thank you, Will," said Cassie, flushing crimson. "But Peter hasn't asked me to marry him."

"You should," said Rob, focusing his relentless gaze on Peter's beet-red face. "Cassie likes you."

Dinner's timely arrival spared my friends further torture at the hands of my insightful sons, and we distracted them afterward with games, but they returned to the subject after they'd had their baths, when Peter was helping me to settle them—and their seal pups—in their beds.

"When you and Cassie have babies," said Will, as though he'd given the subject serious consideration, "you can leave them at Anscombe Manor with me and Rob."

"We'll teach them how to ride," said Rob, yawning.

Will nestled his head sleepily into his pillow. "When they get bigger, we'll let them ride our ponies."

"I'll tell Cassie," Peter promised.

"G'night, Peter," the twins chorused, and fell asleep without even asking for a bedtime story.

Peter sat on the edge of the bed, gazing down at Will's tousled head. "They've got it all worked out," he said softly.

"Have you?" I asked.

Peter looked up at me with a crooked smile. "As a matter of fact, I do. She's a wonderful girl, Lori—fearless and kind and wise. I think she'd say yes if I asked her." He ducked his head shyly. "I'm just waiting for the right moment, I suppose."

"You'll find it," I told him, and bent low to kiss my brilliant baby boys good night.

Andrew came in to take the night shift, and the rest of us went down to the dining room for what promised to be a truly memorable dinner.

Sir Percy greeted Peter and Cassie with his customary ebullience and listened avidly while Cassie told him of their travails with the press. Cassie was forced to do all the talking, because the smoked-haddock chowder and the crabmeat-stuffed ravioli commanded every particle of Peter's attention. When the roasted rack of venison appeared, surrounded by roasted potatoes, carrots, and onions, I half expected him to forsake his true love, run from the dining room, and propose marriage to Cook instead.

Sir Percy knew Cassie's father and Peter's grandfather.

"Festhubert and I were at school together," he told Cassie while Mrs. Gammidge served the venison. "He was a pompous ass as a boy, and I'm sorry to say that he hasn't changed much since then, though I'm sure he's a fine father."

"He is," said Cassie. She seemed slightly taken aback but mostly amused by Sir Percy's frankness.

"And you," Sir Percy went on, turning to Peter, "you're Elstyn's grandson, eh? I know your grandfather, of course, the stiff-necked old buzzard, and I saw his letter in the *Times*. It's a pity he landed you in it by trumpeting your virtues in public, but hardly surprising. Pride was ever his downfall."

Peter was too familiar with his grandfather's foibles to be offended by Sir Percy's unflattering observations.

"Grandfather hasn't quite come to terms with the twenty-first century," he explained, with a wry smile. "He much prefers the eighteenth, when gentlemen were gentlemen, ladies were ladies, and everyone else was obligingly invisible."

"He's been more than generous to the Seal Conservation Trust," Cassie put in, casting a swift glance in Peter's direction.

Peter caught the glance, put down his knife and fork—with some reluctance—and turned to gaze attentively at Sir Percy. I watched, ate, and waited. I had a feeling that the pair were about to solicit a donation from their wealthy host.

"Grandfather has been generous," Peter agreed. "Thanks to him we'll be able to open a second observatory this year."

"Glad to hear it," Sir Percy boomed. "Fascinating creatures, seals. Erinskil has its own colony, you know. They breed on the rocks near the Devil's Teeth—the stacks off the western shore."

"I'm aware of the Devil's Teeth colony." Peter stared down at his folded hands for a moment, then looked again at Sir Percy. "If you find Erinskil's seals fascinating, sir, why won't you allow the trust to study them?"

Sir Percy responded with a faintly puzzled smile. "Sorry, old man, you've lost me. I've nothing to do with the trust."

"But you're Erinskil's laird," Peter countered. "Dr. Withers, the project director, has written to you several times, asking for permission to build our new observatory on Erinskil. He has yet to receive a reply."

"I haven't replied to your project director," said Sir Percy, "because none of his letters have reached me."

"He sent them, I assure you," said Peter. "Three or four of them."

"Has he, by God?" Sir Percy's mouth tightened, and he beckoned to Mrs. Gammidge. "Would you please ask Elliot to join us? My personal assistant," he explained to Peter and Cassie. "Elliot handles all my correspondence. We'll soon get to the bottom of this."

Sir Percy was, for once, being overly optimistic. Elliot Southmore had never seen the letters written by Jocelyn Withers.

"Did Dr. Withers write to Sir Percy's corporate address?" Elliot inquired.

"No," Peter answered. "He wrote last summer, when Sir Percy was in residence on Erinskil. He thought the proposals would have a greater impact if Sir Percy was on the island when he received them. He sent the letters to Dundrillin Castle."

"They must have gone through the Stoneywell post office, sir," Elliot said promptly, turning to his employer. "Rather, they *didn't* go through the post office. It appears that they were . . . diverted."

Sir Percy drummed his fingers on the table. "Someone's been playing silly buggers with my post. How very interesting."

"Shall I investigate, sir?" Elliot asked.

"Leave it with me," said Sir Percy, and reached for his wineglass. "Sorry to interrupt your evening, Elliot."

"Not at all, sir." Elliot nodded to each of us and left the dining room.

Damian's features were inscrutable, but I could tell at a glance what Peter and Cassie were thinking: *The drug smugglers strike again!* Erinskil's wicked residents didn't want an observatory in their midst because they didn't wish to be observed, so they'd intercepted Sir Percy's mail and disposed of Jocelyn Withers's applications. My young friends must have been sorely tempted to speak out, but they were true to their word. Although their covert glances spoke volumes, they kept their suspicions to themselves.

"I owe you an apology, Sir Percy," said Peter. "I feel as though I've abused your hospitality. I had an ulterior motive for coming here tonight—and I assure you that Lori knew nothing about it. She invited us here in complete innocence." He gave me an apologetic nod before turning back to his host. "I wanted to know why you'd turned down our request, but I'd no idea that my question would lead to such a disturbing revelation. You must be distressed."

"Must I?" Sir Percy pursed his lips and peered at the Waterford chandelier, then shook his head. "I don't think so. I'm sure there's been a miscue somewhere, a simple misunderstanding that will be easily resolved. Elspeth MacAllen—Erinskil's esteemed postmistress—is a woman of unimpeachable integrity. If she waylaid my post, I'm certain she did so with the best of intentions. And your apology, by the way, is unnecessary. If I were in your shoes, I'd have done the same—gone to the source to find the answer. Nothing wrong with that, my boy."

Peter's eyes began to twinkle. "I understand now why you and Lori get on so well, sir. You both like to think the best of people."

"I'm afraid you'll think the worst of me in a minute," Sir Percy cautioned. "Because I have to tell you that, as Erinskil's laird, I would have withheld my permission to build your observatory even if your applications *had* reached me."

Peter's eyebrows rose. "May I ask why, sir?"

Sir Percy rested his elbows on the table and tented his fingers. "Erinskil is a perfect jewel. To add or subtract anything would diminish its brilliance. I'll contact your director and explain the matter to him. If he wishes, my people will help him to find another location that meets his requirements."

"We've already found another location," Peter informed him, "but thanks all the same."

"If you don't mind my asking, Sir Percy," said Cassie, looking up from her plate, "didn't your refurbishment of Dundrillin Castle add an awful lot to Erinskil?"

"Dundrillin is occupied only during the summer months," Sir Percy told her, "and my guests do not intrude on island life. They come here to conduct business and to enjoy the castle's many pleasant features, one of which is its fine cuisine." He picked up his fork and waved it at Cassie. "Eat up, eat up. I don't want Festhubert to accuse me of starving you."

"There's no danger of that." Cassie laughed and renewed her assault upon the venison.

Peter needed no encouragement.

Sir Percy told travel tales throughout the rest of the meal and coaxed Peter and Cassie into telling some of their own. By the time Mrs. Gammidge served the sticky lemon cake—with strawberries this time, and enough clotted cream to clog every artery on the island—he'd formed a high opinion of the two. When he invited them to stay for an after-dinner film followed by a midnight swim in the heated pool, however, they begged off.

"We're usually asleep by ten," Peter confessed, stifling a yawn.

"Youth is wasted on the young." Sir Percy sighed. "A word in your ear before you go, chaps. I run a tight ship at Dundrillin, but leaks are inevitable. I have little doubt that news of your persecution by the paparazzi will be common knowledge in Stoneywell by tomorrow morning. I don't think the islanders will mind in the least—in fact, I'm sure they'll sympathize—but if you feel uncomfortable, please feel free to come here and stay for as long as you like. I've plenty of room, as you can see, and I enjoy your company. Elstyn and Festhubert may be a pair of old fossils, but you're not."

Sir Percy offered to have Elliot Southmore drive them back to the village, but Peter and Cassie refused, saying that they'd sleep better if they had a chance to walk off some of Cook's magnificent meal. They promised to return the next day for dinner, and Sir Percy, Damian, and I accompanied them to the entrance hall to wave them on their way.

"A fine young couple," Sir Percy commented after they'd left. "They're weathering their first storm like seasoned sailors. It'll take more than a few pesky photojournalists to knock them off course."

I couldn't have put it better myself.

"Sir Percy," Damian said quietly, as we climbed the gray stone staircase, "would you like me to look into the situation at the post office?"

"Don't be ridiculous, old man," Sir Percy boomed. "You've got a job to do, and it's a damned sight more important than tracing the whereabouts of a few piffling letters. You leave the mystery of the missing post to me." He clapped his hands together and rubbed them vigorously. "Anyone for a swim? Or we could jog up to the observatory and have a peep at the stars. The sky's on fire tonight."

I sagged against the balustrade and groaned.

Damian almost smiled. "I believe Lori is telling you, in her own subtle fashion, that she's tired, Sir Percy."

"I couldn't jog from here to the top of the stairs," I conceded, "much less to the top of the southwest tower. We walked from one end of Erinskil to the other today, Percy. If I don't get to bed soon, Damian will have to carry me there."

"One end of Erinskil to the other, eh?" Sir Percy glanced at me shrewdly. "It seems a long way to go to convince the islanders of your passion for bird-watching. You could have spent the day sitting comfortably on the Slaughter Stone and created the same impression."

"I wanted to stretch my legs," I said quickly. "And, believe me, they're stretched."

"Hobble off to your suite and rest them, then," said Sir Percy. "I'll see you in the morning."

We parted at the red-carpeted corridor, but not before Sir Percy had nailed me with another penetrating glance. I ignored it. I was determined to avoid telling him the true reason for our extended tour of the island. Erinskil was, in his mind, a perfect jewel. I didn't want to be the one who diminished its brilliance.

Fifteen

*F*kicked off my shoes the moment I reached the Cornflower Suite, where lamps had been lit, a fresh fire laid, and the bed turned down. Reginald had evidently won the chambermaid's heart, because a small upholstered armchair had been appropriated from the nursery for his use. My pink flannel rabbit sat serenely near the fireplace in the bedroom, looking for all the world like a country squire awaiting his pipe and slippers.

I touched a match to the blocks of dried turf in the hearth and sank with a grateful sigh into the standard-size armchair in the bedroom. After greeting Reg, I put my weary stockinged feet up on the hassock, propped Aunt Dimity's journal on my knees, opened it, and launched with hardly a pause for breath into a rapid-fire account of Erinskil's alleged criminal activity. Dimity, however, proved true to her gossip-laden upbringing in Finch by interrupting me and asking first and foremost to be informed about the "nature of the relationship" between Peter and his dark-haired companion. I told her what I knew.

Fearless, kind, and wise—what splendid qualities to praise! They're far more practical than mere prettiness, and more durable as well. Dimity's fine copperplate acquired so many extra curlicues that the journal page began to resemble a Victorian valentine. She was extremely fond of Peter. *I do hope Peter won't spend too much time searching for the right moment, or that Cassie will be fearless enough to choose the moment herself. She sounds a perfect match for the dear boy— so clever of her to dye her hair!—and he deserves nothing less. Emma and Derek will be so pleased.*

"I expect they will be, if the paparazzi ever leave them alone," I said.

Paparazzi are like midges, my dear. They swarm from one warm body to the next, seeking fresh blood. When the story goes stale, which it inevitably will, they'll move on to their next victim. Now, what's all this about a conspiracy?

I curled my legs beneath me and shifted the journal to my lap. I was eager to review Cassie's outrageous explanation for the islanders' prosperity and to find out what Dimity thought of my sensible theory.

She didn't think much of it.

A group inheritance could happen, I suppose, and clever investments might endow a community on an ongoing basis, but I'm afraid that the rest of your argument is weak. It doesn't explain why the islanders have gone to such lengths to discourage visitors.

I felt a prickle of frustration. My hypothesis seemed sound to me. Why did it strike everyone else as preposterous?

"I've told you, Dimity," I said patiently. "The islanders don't want to share what they have. They don't want crowds of newcomers to move in and spoil their beautiful island."

You're laboring under a misapprehension, my dear. The islanders could build a covered bridge to the mainland and they still wouldn't attract crowds of permanent, full-time residents. Erinskil may seem like paradise at the moment, but its winters are brutal. The days are short, the nights are long, and the gales are nothing less than ferocious. It takes a special breed to endure such trying conditions for months on end. I'm sorry, Lori, but I can't imagine rows of condominiums springing up on Erinskil, despite its fine school and modern medical facilities. One winter would be enough to send the vast majority of newcomers packing.

"But you can't agree with Cassie," I protested. "She's being cynical and jaded, and you're neither."

One needn't be cynical or jaded to accept Cassie's explanation as the more likely of the two. One may simply be logical. I'll grant that such a community-wide conspiracy would be difficult to maintain in a place like Finch, but we're not dealing with Finch. As Peter pointed out, smuggling is a traditional pastime in the islands. It's reasonable to assume that the islanders, unlike your neighbors, are good at keeping secrets.

"How admirable of them," I muttered, but Dimity took no notice.

Furthermore, a drug-smuggling operation, using Cieran's Chapel as a transfer point, would account for the mysterious lights you, Peter, and Cassie witnessed, as well as for the islanders' zealous efforts to keep strangers away. Finally, I can think of no other commodity that would bring in enough supplementary income to pay for the luxuries you've described.

"But it's so . . . unpleasant," I murmured dejectedly.

If only we could build a wall to keep unpleasant things at bay. . . . We'd have to keep rebuilding it, of course, because unpleasant things have a way of chipping through brick and mortar. I agree with you, Lori, of course I do, though I would put it a good deal more strongly. The drug trade is immoral, corrupt, murderous, and altogether evil, and I hope most sincerely that Cassie is mistaken. What does Damian think of her allegations?

"Search me," I said with a shrug. "He didn't sneer at them, but he didn't stand up and salute them either. He didn't say much of anything about it."

A pity. I'd be very interested to know his thoughts on the matter. Damian is a man of the world, after all—a man of the underworld, one might say, considering his profession. I'd value his opinion. Perhaps you could ask him tomorrow.

"I'll ask," I said, "but I can't guarantee that he'll answer. Damian's as tight-lipped as an unshucked oyster, Dimity. I'll be lucky if he—" I gasped and looked up from the journal. The lights in the suite had gone out all at once, as if someone had flipped a master switch. "Dimity? I think we've had another power failure. Do you mind if I leave you for the moment?"

Not at all. Run along and find Damian. He'll know what's going on.

I closed the journal and placed it on the ottoman. The bedroom wasn't as dark as the dining room had been the last time the power had failed, but it was almost as spooky. The firelight created a host of queer, quivering shadows, and the moonlight streaming through the arched windows gave a cold, blue edge to the darkness. I rose from the armchair and made my way into the sitting room, pausing there to take the poker from its stand.

The foyer door opened a crack, and I raised the poker. Damian put his head into the sitting room, saw me, and stepped inside.

"No need to panic," he said. "It's a castlewide outage. Mrs. Gammidge is taking care of the problem as we speak."

"Good," I said, releasing a pent breath. "That's good."

Damian came forward and gently removed the poker from my grasp. "I approve of the sentiment, Lori, but it would be better if you left the heavy work to me. I'm sorry you were frightened."

I ducked my head ruefully, remembering my pitiful reaction to the previous power failure. "You must think I'm a big baby."

"Babies don't usually defend themselves with pokers," Damian pointed out.

"Nor do I," I admitted. "I just picked it up because it's the sort of thing people do in movies. I don't think I could actually hit anyone with it."

"You can't know what you're capable of, until you're put to the test." Damian regarded me gravely. "I hope you never have to find out."

"Me, too." I glanced back into the bedroom and caught sight of the nearly full moon's reflection in the gilt-framed mirror—it looked like a pale, misshapen face peering out of a dark shroud. I gulped and sidled a step closer to my bodyguard. "What happens to the alarm system when the electricity quits?"

"A backup generator takes over," he replied. "It would be foolish to be without one in a place where the power supply is so unreliable." He returned the poker to its stand. "Why aren't you asleep, Lori? I thought you were exhausted."

"Too much to think about," I said, and decided on the spot to make use of the opportunity afforded me by the power failure. Damian was wide-awake, and he seemed to be in a sympathetic mood—why wait until morning to discuss Cassie's theory with him? I motioned for him to take a seat before the fire. "Would you be willing to hang out with me for a while? I've got so much on my mind. It would help if I could talk it over with someone."

· "As you wish." He closed the foyer door and sat on the edge of the armchair I'd indicated, his back ramrod straight, his face wooden, his eyes focused on the fire. The sympathetic moment had evidently passed.

I sat in the armchair facing his across the hearth and studied his profile. I was at a loss to explain his abrupt mood swing until an amusing suspicion began to take shape in a wicked corner of my mind. I'd invited him to stay with me, in the dead of night, in a firelit room, with my husband far, far away and a king-size bed close at hand. . . .

"Relax, Damian," I said. "I'm not planning to seduce you."

He jumped as if I'd stung him.

"I . . . I never thought you were," he stammered.

"I expect it's the sort of thing that happens to you all the time," I observed conversationally. "You're not bad-looking, and you're nicely put together, and you've got an intriguing scar on your temple. You're a strong, silent, manly man—women must throw themselves at you."

"Could we please change the subject?" he asked tersely.

"I don't blame them," I continued, as if he hadn't spoken, "but I want to assure you that I'm not throwing myself anywhere near you. Even if I were playing the field, which I'm not, you wouldn't be in the running. The strong, silent type has never appealed to me. In my experience, still waters run stagnant. Not that you're *completely* stagnant, but—"

"Lori!" he exclaimed, turning at last to face me. "You really are the most *infuriating* woman. If you don't change the subject this instant, I'll—"

"I was just trying to get you to look at me," I interrupted, with an air of injured innocence. "I didn't want to spend the night talking to your left nostril. But admit it, you were a little worried about my intentions, weren't you?"

Damian sat stock-still, staring at me, until a slow, slightly exasperated smile crept across his face.

"Yes," he said, "I was a little worried about your intentions." He eased back into his chair with a sigh. "It's an occupational hazard. Fear makes some people needy. All too often they expect me to provide them with a variety of comforts not included in the contract."

"You could add a subclause," I suggested.

"No I couldn't," he responded sternly. "Emotional entanglements endanger me as well as my clients. In order to do my job properly, I have to maintain a certain level of detachment. Apart from that, it would be unscrupulous to take advantage of a client's temporary dependence on me."

"You're a man of principle," I said, bestowing upon him one of my highest accolades.

"I'm a businessman," he countered, deftly deflecting the compliment. "Sleeping with frightened clients is not only distasteful and dangerous, it's bad for business. It opens the door to endless recriminations as well as potential legal difficulties. When the danger's passed, when my clients have recovered themselves, they are invariably grateful to me for refusing their invitations and readily recommend me to others."

"Have it your way," I said, folding my arms, "but I still think you're a decent guy."

"And I think we've talked about me long enough." Damian cleared his throat peremptorily. "What's keeping you awake, Lori?"

"Peter and Cassie," I replied, and leaned toward him on the overstuffed arm of my chair. "What do you make of their crazy story? Do you think Erinskil's a haven for drug kingpins?"

"I think . . ." Damian turned his gaze to the fire. "I think something's not right."

"But you can't put your finger on it," I said in a sudden burst of recollection. "That's what you told me after we had lunch with Percy, when I asked if anything was bothering you. You said something's not right, but you couldn't put your finger on what was wrong. But that was *yesterday*." My eyebrows shot up. "Are you telling me you knew that the islanders were up to no good before we ever spoke with Peter and Cassie?"

"I knew that the islanders were up to something as soon as we landed on Cieran's Chapel." Damian's head swiveled as the lights came back on. "Well done, Mrs. Gammidge."

I waved off the distraction. "Never mind Mrs. Gammidge. What did you see on Cieran's Chapel?"

"Several things." He paused, as if to gather his thoughts. "Mick Ferguson and Mrs. Muggoch have gone out of their way to convince us that the Chapel's off-limits. It's cursed, haunted, tainted, and so forth. They would have us believe that few people ever go there."

"And those who do are rewarded with bad luck," I said, recalling Percy's story about the friend with the broken leg.

"If so few people visit the islet," Damian went on, "why would anyone go the trouble of driving a ringbolt into the rock? The ring's only purpose is to anchor boats. If boats rarely land there, why bother?" He pursed his lips. "The condition of the ringbolt is suggestive as well."

I remembered Damian reaching out to tug on the iron ring before turning with Mick Ferguson to help me hop from Mick's dinghy onto the islet's slippery stone shelf.

"Suggestive of what?" I asked.

"The ring's exposed constantly to seawater," he said. "It's either submerged by high tides or deluged with spray when the tides are low. Since it's made of iron, it should be heavily corroded, but it isn't. I can think of only one explanation: The ringbolt must be replaced at regular intervals and kept well oiled between replacements. Why take such good care of it if it's so rarely used?"

Damian's powers of observation were transcendently superior to mine. I'd been too busy keeping my balance to notice whether or not the iron ring was rusted, and it hadn't for a moment occurred to me to wonder what it was doing there in the first place.

"Then there's the matter of the old laird's grave." Damian rested his elbows on the arms of his chair and tented his fingers. "As you will recall, it lies at the bottom of a large, bowl-shaped depression. The depression isn't natural—it doesn't fit in with the rest of the Chapel's topography. I believe it was created when the old laird's grave was dug."

I visualized the oblong stone slab with its Celtic lettering and realized that Damian was right. The islet's surface was rough and uneven, but it held only one bowl-shaped hollow.

"The soil is quite shallow on the Chapel," Damian continued. "In order to dig the laird's grave, the islanders would have had to cut through solid rock—a time-consuming, laborious task. Why, then, did they dig such a large grave? Unless the laird was laid to rest in an enormous sarcophagus—which seems unlikely, given the size and simplicity of the grave marker—the hole could have been much smaller. Why didn't the gravediggers spare themselves the extra work?"

The list of rhetorical questions I couldn't answer was growing by leaps and bounds, but I didn't mind. I was looking forward to the thrilling conclusion, when Damian would sweep aside the veil of mystery and reveal all.

"The old laird died in 1937," he said. "It seems safe to assume that he was buried soon after the grave had been prepared for him on Cieran's Chapel. In other words, the laird's grave was closed and the marker put into place many years ago." Damian's silvery eyes glinted in the firelight as he turned his head to face me. "But I'm willing to swear that the ground around the grave has been disturbed much more recently. As recently, perhaps, as two days ago, when you, Peter, and Cassie, saw the strange lights on Cieran's Chapel."

I tried to look intelligent, even though I was totally at sea. Damian had clearly given me a monumental clue, but I had no idea what to do with it. My best guess was so far-fetched that I could scarcely bring myself to voice it, but he sat there expecting a response, so I tamped down my misgivings and offered one.

"You don't think someone was out there . . . digging up the old laird, do you?" I asked.

"Oh, no," he replied. "I think they dug him up years ago."

My jaw dropped. "I was *kidding*, Damian."

"I'm not," he said, and shifted his gaze back to the fire. "I suspect that the islanders exhumed the old laird's remains some time ago and reinterred them on Erinskil. The tomb could then be expanded and used for the temporary storage of contraband. I suspect that couriers come and go fairly frequently—hence the installation and meticulous maintenance of the ringbolt. When visitors are on the island, the couriers move by night." His eyes found mine again. "Your light wasn't made by Brother Cieran's ghost, Lori, but by someone picking up or delivering illegal goods stored in the old laird's grave."

"Drugs?" I whispered.

"Possibly." Damian cocked his head to one side. "A consignment of cocaine, for example, would fit easily in the expanded tomb, where it would be stored until called for. Mick's dinghy could be used to bring the shipment from the Chapel to Alasdair Murdoch's fishing boats, and Mr. Murdoch would take it to the mainland for distribution. I suspect that the islanders use the tweed mill to launder the dirty money." He nodded. "Drug transport is a lucrative business, Lori. It would pay for many of the things Peter and Cassie pointed out to us today."

"Your theory is worse than theirs!" I cried, sitting upright. "And I refuse to believe it. Mick wasn't faking his affection for the old laird, nor was Mrs. Muggoch. The islanders loved him. They'd never desecrate his grave. They wouldn't betray him for the sake of a few creature comforts. It's . . . it's *sacrilegious*."

"I won't argue the point, Lori," said Damian. "You asked my opinion, and I've given it."

"But what are you going to *do* about it?" I demanded. "If you honestly believe what you've just told me, Damian, shouldn't you do *something*? Shouldn't you tell Percy?"

"Tell him what?" Damian retorted. "My opinion is just that—an opinion. It's based on suspicions and suppositions, nothing more. I've no real evidence of wrongdoing, and I don't intend to seek it out. I'm not a policeman, Lori. I'm a bodyguard." He got to his feet. "And now, if you'll excuse me, I'll get back to work."

I wrapped my arms around myself and stared unhappily into the fire. As Damian passed my chair, he paused briefly to put a hand on my shoulder.

"You're not a policeman, either, Lori," he said. "You came here to protect yourself and your sons. Remember that. Don't let yourself be distracted."

The hand was removed, and a moment later I heard the foyer door open and close. I slowly uncoiled myself from my chair, went to the bedroom, and picked up Aunt Dimity's journal.

"I spoke with Damian," I said, standing with the journal open in my hands. "He thinks the islanders dug up the old laird's body and replaced it with shipments of cocaine. The world's gone mad, Dimity."

I'm afraid you won't restore it to sanity tonight, my dear. Try to get some sleep. Who knows? A new fact may come to light tomorrow that will sustain your faith in human nature and prove the doubters wrong.

I smiled wanly, bade Aunt Dimity good night, and went to bed, where my agitated thoughts gave way to agitated dreams involving gangs of sinister fishermen who looked like Mick Ferguson and sounded like Mrs. Muggoch.

Sixteen

The next day's schedule of events could have been torn from the calendar of a child-friendly resort—if the resort offered live-in bodyguards as an optional extra. Damian and I rose early, breakfasted with Andrew and the twins in the nursery, and descended with them to Sir Percy's sheltered cove armed with the usual cricket gear as well as a bucketful of knights-in-armor to man the sand castles. When the sky began to cloud over, we retired to Dundrillin for a splash in the heated swimming pool, from which Damian abstained. Andrew took his midday meal in the nursery with Will and Rob, and Damian and I had ours in the dining room with Sir Percy.

A misty drizzle settled in after lunch, so we spent the afternoon in the nursery. The twins and I created unsung masterpieces with finger paints and modeling clay until teatime, then whiled away the hours before dinner building a complicated complex of sea caves for their seal pups, using blankets, tables, model cars, knights in armor, plastic dinosaurs, and a variety of other items seldom observed in the wild by the Seal Conservation Trust but which my sons deemed essential to a baby seal's happiness. After dinner came bath time, story time, bedtime, the elevator ride to the Cornflower Suite, and then, as we stepped out of the elevator, a joyfully breathless telephone call from Bill.

"Yarborough's men have come up with a lead," he crowed. "I can't stay on the phone—too much to do—but Yarborough's convinced that we're on the right track. With any luck we'll capture our man within the next day or two."

"But who is he?" I demanded. "Who is Abaddon?"

"It's too complicated to explain right now," said Bill. "I'll give you the whole story when I see you, and I'll see you very soon. Thank heavens Yarborough did those interviews, Lori. I'm sorry, love. I've got to go. Kiss the boys for me. I'll see you soon!"

Bill rang off. I stood in the foyer, staring at the cell phone, dazed and a bit weak-kneed with relief, until Damian took the phone from me and offered a quiet word of caution.

"I'm aware of recent developments," he said. "They sound promising, but—"

"Stop right there," I said, warding him off with an outstretched palm. "I'm not letting you rain on my parade. Bill's not like me, Damian. He doesn't exaggerate for dramatic effect. If he says something is so, it's so."

"But he hasn't said—"

"I'm not listening," I broke in. "It's half past six. Please call Percy and tell him that I *will* join him and Kate and Elliot in the library for cocktails before dinner." I clapped my hands and danced into the sitting room, closing the door behind me. When I reached the bedroom, I grabbed the blue journal and flung it open, saying, "Dimity! Great news!"

You've had word from Bill, I take it?

"The best of best words," I said. "Abaddon's as good as caught!"

I don't wish to seem pessimistic, my dear, but I must point out that "as good as caught" isn't nearly good enough.

I frowned. "You're as depressing as Damian. The detectives have a *lead,* Dimity. They're hot on Abaddon's trail. Bill's sure they'll catch him *soon.*"

Until they have him in custody, Lori, I would urge you to remain vigilant.

"Of course I'll remain vigilant," I retorted, "but I'm going to be happy, too, no matter how much cold water you and Damian throw on me. I'll talk to you later, all right? I have so much to tell you!"

I hope you'll be able to tell me by then that Abaddon is well and truly caught.

"He will be," I vowed, and closed the journal.

I quickly changed into a blouse of crimson silk and an elegant, long black skirt and joined Damian, who'd donned his trusty blue blazer. Together we made our way to the library, where we met up with Sir Percy and his assistants.

It was easy to see why Kate and Elliot preferred Dundrillin's library to the pub in Stoneywell. The oak-paneled room was a softly lit, restful retreat filled with leather-bound books, hung with fine oil portraits of Sir Percy's ancestors, and warmed by a handsome fireplace of Portland stone. Reading tables and racks of magazines occupied the center of the room, and traditional, masculine leather furniture—a sofa and four armchairs—clustered companionably around the hearth, with polished walnut occasional tables placed conveniently nearby, to receive a discarded book or a Waterford tumbler. An assortment of silver candelabras was also in evidence—insurance, no doubt, against the next power outage.

Kate and Elliot had already claimed the chairs nearest the hearth, so I sat in the corner of the sofa, facing the fire. Damian, who preferred to keep an eye on the door, took the chair next to Kate's, and Sir Percy took charge of the liquor cabinet, busily dispensing gin-and-tonics that contained far more gin than tonic. He poured a glass of sherry for himself and sat with it at the other end of the sofa. I waited until everyone was seated to announce Bill's spectacular news.

"Bravo!" boomed Sir Percy, and raised his glass to toast my brilliant husband, the brilliant chief superintendent, and the general brilliance of Scotland Yard. "Knew they'd nab the villain. Couldn't be happier for you, my dear."

Kate and Elliot added their congratulations, and Sir Percy proceeded to entertain us with wildly comic speculations about Abaddon's true identity ("The prime minister's been looking rather shifty-eyed lately. . . ."). Damian alone took no part in the general merriment. Although he smiled dutifully at Sir Percy's antics, he maintained an air of sobriety that told the rest of us quite plainly that our giddiness was premature. We paid no attention to him.

"I don't envy Peter and Cassie their walk to Dundrillin," Elliot ventured, after Sir Percy had settled down. "It's a miserably damp, foggy evening."

"It'll get worse before it gets better," Sir Percy said. "I've had a peep at the radar. A storm's brewing to the west. It'll be here before dawn." A sunny smile lit his face. "I love a good storm. Thunder, lightning, rollicking surf—you'll feel the headland quake like a cowardly puppy, Lori." He sipped his sherry, then added, as an aside to me, "Wouldn't advise stepping out on your balcony in the thick of it, though. You might find yourself airborne."

I was about to tell him that I fully intended to enjoy the storm from the safety and comfort of my bed when Damian's cell phone rang. I held out my hand, hoping against hope for news of Abaddon's capture, but Damian didn't pass the phone to me. He kept it pressed to his ear, and I could tell by his taut expression that he didn't like what he was hearing.

"You've confirmed his identification?" he asked. "And the hire agreement? What about the boat? Have you searched it? Good.

It's unfortunate, of course, but there's not much we can do about it. Keep me informed." He ended the call and returned the cell phone to the inside breast pocket of his blazer.

"Well?" said Sir Percy.

"That was Cal Maconinch, the harbormaster," Damian announced. "It's bad news for Peter and Cassie, I'm afraid. A journalist from the *Morning Mirror*—a chap called Jack Nunen—has dropped anchor in Stoneywell Harbor, in a powerboat he hired on the mainland. The good news is that his ID checks out—Jack Nunen is who he claims to be—and he came alone. Cal searched the boat from stem to stern and found nothing to indicate that our stalker hitched a ride to Erinskil."

The good news should have cheered me, but I was too sorry for Peter and Cassie to think of myself.

"Bloody *Morning Mirror*," Sir Percy fumed. "If they've sniffed out the trail, the rest of the pack won't be far behind. Mark my words, the wolves will be circling en masse by tomorrow night."

"Didn't Mr. Nunen object when Mr. Maconinch searched his boat?" Kate inquired. "I would have expected him to kick up a fuss."

"He probably would have, had he been aware of the search," Damian acknowledged. "Cal elected not to trouble him. He boarded the boat after Mr. Nunen had gone to the pub to book a room."

"Excellent!" Sir Percy roared. "The *Mirror*'s maggots have no respect for anyone else's privacy. Why should we respect theirs?"

"You're Erinskil's laird, Percy," I said. "Can't you ban reporters?"

"I can, but I won't. It would only add fuel to the fire." Sir Percy spelled an imaginary headline in the air as he spoke: "'Feudal

Laird Shields Lurking Lovers.'" He dropped his hand. "I assure you, Lori, interference from me would only make matters worse for our young celebrities. They should have come to Dundrillin when I asked them to. Mrs. Gammidge is an expert in pest control."

"We can warn them, at least," I said desperately. "You've got Peter's phone number, Damian. Call him. Tell him the jig is up."

"I expect he knows it already," Sir Percy murmured.

"Even so . . ." I looked beseechingly at Damian.

He took out his cell phone and dialed, but there was no answer.

"Peter must have turned off his mobile," he said, returning the phone to his pocket. "We could send someone down to the pub with a message, Sir Percy."

"Don't be daft, Damian. They'll be here in less than an hour. We'll break the news to them when they arrive." Sir Percy heaved himself to his feet, returned to the liquor cabinet, and busied himself with topping up our drinks. "If they change their minds about moving into the castle, Kate and Elliot can fetch their things from the pub."

The clock on the mantelpiece ticked ponderously as we sat brooding over our drinks. Sir Percy expressed his feelings by stabbing the fire viciously with the poker, but Elliot was the first to speak.

"I've been meaning to ask, Sir Percy," he said. "Have you had a word with the postmistress about the missing mail?"

"A misunderstanding," said Sir Percy, "just as I predicted. Mrs. Gammidge asked Elspeth MacAllen to dispose of junk mail addressed to me through the Stoneywell post office. Elspeth decided that letters from something called the Seal Conservation Trust had to be junk mail and disposed of them." He tossed more turf onto the fire. "It won't happen again. Elspeth will deliver *all* of my mail to Dundrillin from now on. You and Kate will decide what to discard."

"A safer system for all concerned, sir," said Elliot. "I was also wondering—"

We never found out what Elliot was wondering, because at that moment Mrs. Gammidge appeared in the doorway, with a bedraggled and breathless Cassie on her heels.

"Miss Thorpe-Lynton to see you, sir," she said to Sir Percy. "She seems quite agitated."

I hastily set my glass aside and ran to Cassie. She wore no hat or gloves, and her anorak was wide-open. Her hair was disheveled, her jeans and crewneck sweater were wet, and she was shivering.

"Your jacket, Damian," I said. "She's freezing."

"Blankets, Mrs. Gammidge, if you please!" roared Sir Percy as he headed for the liquor cabinet.

I stripped off Cassie's anorak, and Damian wrapped his blazer around her. Kate and Elliot shoved a chair closer to the fire, Cassie sank into it, and Sir Percy thrust a glass into her shaking hands.

"Brandy," he said. "Get it down you."

Cassie gulped a mouthful, sputtered, and tried to speak, but before she could get a word out, Mrs. Gammidge returned to cocoon her in an armful of woolen blankets.

"Shall I ring Dr. Tighe, sir?" the housekeeper asked.

"No!" cried Cassie, finding her voice. "I don't need a doctor."

"Not at present, thank you, Mrs. Gammidge," said Sir Percy. "I'll ring if I need you."

"Very good, sir," said Mrs. Gammidge, and withdrew.

I sat on the arm of Cassie's chair. "What's happened? Is it the reporter? Has he come after you already?"

"Reporter?" Cassie said blankly, then shook her head. "No, it's nothing to do with him. Mrs. Muggoch told him that her rooms were full up. He's spending the night on his boat."

"Bravo, Mrs. Muggoch," Sir Percy boomed. "She knows a rat when she sees one. It'll be a rough night, too. Ha!" He raised his glass, grinning gleefully. "Serves him right!"

"What is it, then?" I said to Cassie. "What's wrong?"

"It's Peter." The young woman's voice broke. "He hasn't come back. Anything could have happened to him."

My stomach clenched with fear as the reason for Cassie's distress struck home. Had Peter asked one question too many? I wondered. Had the islanders decided to rid themselves of their meddlesome guest? I looked anxiously at Damian, who shook his head minutely, knelt before the frantic girl, and clasped her free hand in both of his. When he spoke, his deep voice was as kindly as a priest's.

"Where did Peter go, Cassie?"

"To the monastery," she answered shakily, and twisted her head to look up at me. "He wanted to hear the monks you told us about, Lori, the ones who'd been killed by the Vikings."

"When did he leave?" Damian asked, drawing her attention back to him.

"Around four o'clock," she replied. "He wanted me to come with him, but I didn't fancy a hike in the fog, so I stayed at the pub. He said he wouldn't be long, but he's been gone for nearly four hours."

Damian chafed her hand. "What route did Peter take to the monastery?"

"The coastal path. It's the only route we've ever taken." Cassie's pretty face crumpled, and tears rolled down her cheeks. "If only I'd gone with him . . ."

"Then we'd be searching for both of you." Damian pulled a white handkerchief from his trouser pocket and handed it to her.

Cassie mopped her cheeks and blew her nose. At Sir Percy's urging, she took another gulp of brandy and tried to collect herself.

"I've rung him a dozen times," she said. "No answer. I thought of going to look for him on my own, but—"

"You did the right thing by coming to us," Damian interrupted. "We'll find Peter. In the meantime I want you to go back to the pub."

"I want to look for Peter," she protested.

"I know you do," said Damian soothingly, "but someone has to stay at the pub, in case Peter turns up there. Otherwise we could find ourselves running in circles all night. Kate and Elliot will go with you. You can wait with them in your room." He pressed her hand. "Please, Cassie, for Peter's sake . . ."

"All right," she said, with great reluctance. "I'll go." She wiped her eyes, returned her glass to Sir Percy, and began unwrapping the cocoon.

"Take the blankets with you," said Sir Percy. "And take the car, Elliot."

Elliot rushed ahead to bring the electric car to the main entrance. Kate put her arm around Cassie's blanket-draped shoulders and guided her out of the library. When the door had closed behind them, Sir Percy turned to Damian.

"Young scamp's sprained an ankle, I'll wager, or wandered off the path," he said. "Shall I raise the alarm? Form a search party? I can have twenty local men here in a twinkling."

It suddenly dawned on me that Damian was in an impossibly awkward position. Sir Percy assumed that Peter was injured or lost in the fog. He had no reason to suspect foul play. No one had explained to him that his island was inhabited by a species of lowlife that made paparazzi look like cuddly kittens. How would Damian find the words to tell him that a search party made up of islanders would be more likely to lead us *away* from Peter than toward him? Even if he wished to acquaint Sir Percy with our suspicions, he couldn't hope to do so without wasting precious time.

"I'd rather not complicate matters, sir," Damian said smoothly. "Visibility is poor tonight. I don't want a search for one man to turn into a search for twenty. I'll look for Peter on my own."

"Oh, no you won't," I said. "I'm coming with you."

"I don't think you are," said Damian, frowning.

"Think again," I stated firmly.

Damian squared his shoulders. "Lori, you are not—"

"I'd save my breath if I were you, old boy," Sir Percy interjected. "I've known Lori longer than you have."

I squared my own shoulders and calmly explained the situation to Damian. "Peter's parents aren't just my neighbors. They're my best friends. They'd dodge bullets to help my sons, and if you think I'm going to sit around wringing my hands while *their* son is in trouble, you're *incredibly* mistaken."

"Don't waste time arguing with her," advised Sir Percy. "She's as stubborn as a stoat."

I lifted my chin defiantly. "You'll have to chain me up and lock me in the dungeon to keep me here."

"Don't tempt me," Damian growled. His jaw hardened ominously, but he evidently knew when he was beaten, because after a moment's bristling hesitation, he relented. "You'll have to change into something dark-colored and warm."

"Give me five minutes," I said, and dashed past him into the corridor.

He caught up with me at the elevator, and we both rode it to the suite, where I swapped my elegant evening clothes for a pair of tweed trousers, a heavy, dark brown wool sweater, wool socks, and hiking boots. I grabbed a stocking cap and my rain jacket from the wardrobe, ran through the sitting room, flung the foyer door wide, and stopped short.

I'd caught Damian in the midst of pulling his black crewneck sweater over his head. He must have heard the door open, because he hurriedly yanked the sweater down to conceal his naked torso, but it was too late. I'd already seen the scars—puckering the skin above his collarbone, below his ribs, on his chest, curving like a snake over his shoulder.

I'd also seen the gun. The deadly looking automatic was tucked into a holster on his belt.

"You told me you were unarmed," I said, trying not to think about the scars.

"I was, when you asked." He turned away from me, put on his rain jacket and a black watch cap, and squatted to rummage through his duffel bag. When he stood, he was holding two black-handled, hooded flashlights on black lanyards, but he didn't offer one to me. Instead he spoke quietly, urgently, as if he still thought he could persuade me to change my mind. "Peter may have twisted an ankle or broken a leg. He may simply have lost track of time. It's not hard to imagine him perched on a boulder on one of the hills, watching the fog move in over Erinskil. But we don't believe he's been delayed for any of those reasons, do we, Lori?"

I shook my head.

"We believe he's in trouble," Damian went on. "We believe he's been waylaid by people who will stop at nothing to protect their business ventures. We're not going on a picnic, Lori. This is a serious affair. You're taking a great risk by coming with me. I wish you wouldn't. You can stay here with Andrew. No one will think less of you."

"*I* will." I took one of the flashlights from him and slung the black lanyard around my neck. "Besides, you're my bodyguard. You're not allowed to leave me behind."

His lips twitched into a grudging smile that crinkled the corners of his eyes, then vanished. He gripped his own flashlight tightly, punched the elevator button, and we were on our way.

Seventeen

We stepped out of the tower's side entrance into a world changed beyond recognition. The headland's breathtaking views had been transformed. Shifting banks of fog blanketed the island's central valley and mantled the ocean in a heavy shroud, deadening the surf's thunder. The cliff path and the hills bordering it stood above the mist, like an island chain rising from a sea of cotton wool.

"Don't use your torch," Damian instructed. "I'd rather we didn't advertise our movements."

I agreed with him about the flashlights—we didn't need them to find our way. The full moon bathed the sunken track in silver light, and the path's waist-high banks would not allow us to totter over a cliff or wander off into the hills by accident.

There was hardly a breath of wind stirring, and the evening air was heavy and damp. As I jogged along behind Damian, clammy droplets gathered on my hands and face, clung to my trousers, and trickled like icy fingers down the back of my neck, until I thought to pull my jacket's hood over my stocking cap. I quickly yanked it down again when I heard Damian muttering to himself up ahead.

"Fool," he said under his breath. "Thoughtless, stupid, selfish young fool."

"I hope you're referring to Peter," I murmured, catching up with him.

"Why did he go off on his own?" he demanded, keeping his voice low. "The boy's convinced that Erinskil's riddled with murderous thugs, but he goes off on his own regardless. When I think of the state Cassie's in . . . of the danger Peter may be in . . . of the rules I've broken by allowing you to come with me . . ." Damian ground his teeth. "If the islanders haven't wrung his neck already, I may do it for them."

"I know you're worried about him, Damian," I said. "I am, too, but I'm not really sure why we should be. Peter shared his suspicions with us, but I'm certain he didn't share them with anyone else on Erinskil. How do you think the islanders found out?"

"Mrs. Muggoch," Damian replied shortly. "She's his landlady, and it's a landlady's duty to listen at keyholes. If she overheard his conversations with Cassie, you can be sure that she wouldn't keep the information to herself."

"She could have heard them talking about the monastery, too," I said anxiously. "She must have told someone he was going to the ruins."

"I suspect she alerted more than one someone." Damian consulted his wristwatch and began to jog faster. "They may simply want to chat with him, Lori, to get him in a corner and frighten him into keeping his mouth shut. Threatening to harm Cassie would do the trick, and he's certainly made it easy for them, going off by himself and leaving her with no protection. How could he be so *stupid?*"

"He's young," I offered.

"He's an idiot," Damian muttered, and charged onward through the fog.

We came to a halt a short time later. While I caught my breath, Damian peered into the murk, as if to confirm his bearings. He nodded once, then swung around and put his mouth close to my ear.

"Here's the plan, Lori," he whispered. "We're going to leave the path here, in case they have a lookout posted at the Slaughter Stone. We'll cut around the side of the hill until we reach the monastery terrace—it's the highest of the three, remember? Then we'll see what's what. Keep close to me and don't use your torch until I tell you to. No more talking—not even in whispers—from this point on. Understood?"

I demonstrated my understanding by nodding.

We boosted ourselves over the edge of the sunken path and began to climb. The hill was steep and the long grass was infuriatingly slick, but although I slipped and slid and bashed my knees repeatedly on half-buried rocks, I managed to keep my vow of silence. More important, I managed to keep up with Damian, who was as goat-footed as Peter.

I was greatly relieved when we came across a sheep track, where the grass was sparse and the footing a trifle less treacherous. We followed the faint trail as it curved around the side of the hill, until our boots hit close-cropped grass and level ground. We'd reached the outer edge of the highest terrace.

Damian motioned for me to crouch beside him while he surveyed the ruins. They gave me the willies. The plundered monastery's skeletal remains loomed before us in the moonlight. Shreds of mist drifted like ghosts between the stunted pillars and clung like cobwebs to the broken arches. Shallow pools of vapor swirled sinuously along the ground, obscuring the foundation stones and curling like smoke around the crumbling walls. The only element missing from the magnificently haunting scene was the soul-rending scream of a massacred monk.

Fortunately, the only sound to reach my straining ears was the muted gurgle of the spring-fed brook tumbling merrily downhill, and though I stared long and hard at our surroundings, I couldn't see so much as a flicker of light glimmering in the gloom. It seemed to me that if a gang of thuggish islanders were grilling Peter in the ruins, they were being extraordinarily stealthy about it. The monastery appeared to be deserted.

Damian evidently agreed with my assessment, because he put his lips close to my ear and whispered, "They may have taken him somewhere else, but we'll have a look round, just in case."

We crawled from the edge of the terrace to the heap of stones that was all that remained of the church's north wall. Damian stepped over the stones, bent low, and turned on his hooded flashlight. Tendrils of fog wrapped the narrow beam in a gossamer veil as he swung it from side to side, scanning the ground for clues. I moved beside him, my eyes trained on the cracked and pitted slabs that paved the church's central aisle until he flung an arm across me and knocked me flat onto my bottom.

I swallowed an indignant croak and stayed where I was, wondering what had set him off. Rolling onto my knees, I followed the ghostly thread of light from his flashlight as he inched toward the church's eastern end, where an incised memorial tablet marked the burial site of a long-forgotten churchman. I raised myself higher, to get a better view, and clapped a hand over my mouth to suppress a gasp.

The tablet had been moved. The great stone slab had been raised like a door on hinges, and in its place a chasm yawned, a passage hewn from solid rock, with steep steps plunging into utter blackness.

I sat back on my heels, stunned by the chilling realization that Damian had very probably saved my life. If he hadn't seen the peril in time and knocked me flat, I would almost certainly have crawled into the hole and tumbled headlong down the precarious stone stairs. I instantly forgave him for manhandling me and crept forward until I reached the lip of the yawning cavity. Coils of fog wafted down a staircase that was so steep it was nearly vertical.

Not one fiber in my being wanted to find out where the staircase led, but fond thoughts of Peter and his parents enabled me to override every particle of my common sense and a significant percentage of my terror. I pointed first at Damian, then at myself, and finally at the chasm, insistently.

He understood, although he didn't approve. He tried to convince me, through mime, to wait in the church while he explored the dark passage, but the notion of huddling alone in the ruins while he descended to his doom must have ignited lightning bolts of dread in my eyes, because he soon gave up. I could go with him, he gestured, but only if he went first. I nodded my heartfelt assent.

Damian slung his lanyard around his neck and threaded it through the snaps on his rain jacket, until only the tip of the hooded flashlight protruded, pointing downward. The staircase was so steep at any rate that he had to descend it facing inward, as if it were a ladder, so the light was further shielded by his body.

I quickly arranged my flashlight in the same fashion, turned it on, and followed him onto the staircase. It was like climbing into a coffin-shaped manhole, though the passage became rounder and more constricted as we descended. A fat man would have had great difficulty following us—he would have gotten stuck like a cork in a bottle less than halfway down.

The stone steps were deep, evenly spaced, and smoothly carved, but there were a lot of them. My knees were complaining, and I was beginning to think we'd end up treading the seabed when Damian tapped my boot to signal that he'd reached the bottom.

I descended the last few steps, and he caught me around the

waist as my feet touched the ground, as if he expected my knees to buckle. When they did, he eased me into a sitting position on what felt like a soft mound of sand.

I could hear the far-off boom of crashing surf and smell a mingled scent of brine and seaweed, but I couldn't see a thing beyond the small circle of light in my lap, where my flashlight was pointing. My hands were so cold that I had difficulty disentangling the lanyard from the snaps on my rain jacket, but Damian retrieved his light easily and proceeded to check out our surroundings.

"We seem to have the place to ourselves. There's no sign of—" He stopped short on a swift intake of breath.

"See something?" I whispered, still tugging on the lanyard.

"Oh," he said softly. "Oh, dear."

An odd note in his voice made me look up.

"What is it?" I asked.

He said nothing. His light was traveling in a wide arc around the floor, sliding slowly over a group of curious rock formations that seemed strangely familiar to me. I stared at them intently, turning my head to follow the path of the circling beam, until my brain finally caught up with my widening eyes.

Goose bumps rippled all up and down my arms. If my hair hadn't been tucked into a stocking cap, it would have stood on end. My aching knees twitched, as though willing me to flee back up the stairs, but my legs refused to move. I uttered a quavering moan, released the tangled lanyard, and pressed both of my hands to my mouth.

The staircase had deposited us in what appeared to be a natural cavern, roughly circular in shape, with a sand-covered floor and a vaulted roof. There were three low, irregular openings in the chamber's jagged walls, leading to further passages or perhaps to other caves. I didn't particularly care where they went. My mind was wholly focused on the skeletons.

They lay on their backs with their heads to the walls and their feet pointing inward, as if stretched out for a communal snooze—hollow-eyed skulls, knobbly vertebrae, the diminutive bones of fingers and toes, all in their proper order and tidily arranged, as if awaiting the arrival of an anatomist. By the time Damian had finished turning a complete circle, the beam of light had played over the grisly remains of some forty human beings.

While I sat rigid with horror, Damian squatted to inspect a set of bones. He rolled a skull onto its side, touched a finger to a rib, a femur, a scapula. He did the same thing with the next skeleton and the next, until he'd worked his way around the charnel house. Then he stood and shone his light in my direction.

"You were right, Lori," he remarked mildly. "The monks did run and hide."

"It's the *monks?*" I exclaimed, sending echoes reverberating through the cavern. "Oh, thank *heavens.*" I breathed a shuddering sigh of relief and leaned my forehead on my hand. "I mean, it's dreadful and I feel sorry for the poor guys, may they rest in peace, but they died a long time ago. I was afraid we'd found evidence of a . . . a more recent mass murder. Are you *sure* it's the monks?"

Damian came to sit beside me on the sandy mound, as if to reassure me with his presence.

"The monks were living in turbulent times," he said. "They knew that their monastery was a likely target for Viking raids. They must have made an escape route for themselves, carving a passage from their church to the caves below and concealing the entrance with the false memorial tablet. Unfortunately, their hiding place was discovered. Perhaps the raiders had encountered the same sort of thing in other monasteries and knew where to look." Damian reached over to untangle the mess I'd made of my lanyard. "Do you remember what Sir Percy told us about the skull your sons found in the cove?"

"He could tell by its color that it was old," I replied. "He also mentioned, in his colorful way, that it was cracked like a softboiled egg."

"These bones are similarly discolored," said Damian, jutting his chin toward our silent companions, "and they show telltale signs of traumatic injuries. The raiders may have found the monks trying to escape and hurled them down the staircase."

"Clever of them to land in a circle," I remarked dubiously.

"Do you think we're the first people to set eyes on this place since the eighth century?" Damian asked. "I expect an islander discovered the monks' mortal remains many years ago—perhaps hundreds of years ago—and rearranged them, as a sign of respect. I find it rather touching."

"I find it unspeakably creepy," I said, with feeling. "Can we leave now? The monks, God rest their souls, won't help us to find Peter."

"I'm going to look into the side passage first," said Damian. "I want to find out where they—"

A faint, grinding thud sounded overhead, rumbled down the stone staircase, and echoed hollowly in the cavern. Damian swore under his breath, pushed himself to his feet, and leapt up the staircase, taking two steps at a time. I stood at the bottom, peering upward, and several long minutes later heard Damian pounding his fist against stone and shouting. After a few more minutes had passed, he began to climb down again. As soon as his hiking boots hit the sand, he reached for my flashlight and turned it off.

"We'd better conserve the batteries," he said.

"Why?" I asked, though my sinking heart told me that I already knew the answer.

"Because we may be here for some time. Someone closed the memorial tablet, and it's too heavy for me to lift. I'd no right to call Peter an idiot," he added, his voice edged with self-reproach. "*I'm* the idiot. I've led you straight into a trap."

"Percy will rescue us," I said promptly. "Call him."

"I can't." Damian cleared his throat, as if preparing himself to administer another dose of unpleasant news. "My mobile is at the pub, with Cassie."

"*What?*" I cried.

"My mobile was in the pocket of my blazer," he explained. "The blazer I wrapped around Cassie. The blazer she was wearing when she returned to the pub with Kate and Elliot. If Mrs. Gammidge hadn't swaddled her in blankets, I might have remembered it, but . . ." He bowed his head. "I'm sorry."

"Yeah," I said limply. "So am I."

"I doubt that we could have gotten a signal." He tilted his head back to look at the cavern's roof. "Too much rock between us and the outside."

"That's a comfort," I murmured.

"We'll be all right," he said bracingly. "I've been in tighter spots than this, and I've always found a way out. I just need a moment to think. I'm going to turn off my torch, so have a seat. You'll be less likely to stumble over . . . things."

We sat side by side on the sandy mound near the bottom of the stairs. When Damian's flashlight went out, we were enclosed in a kind of darkness I'd never before experienced. It was like being buried alive. I waggled my hand in front of my face, but I might as well have been blind. I could see absolutely nothing, but I could feel the hollow-eyed stares of Brother Cieran's unfortunate brethren. I pulled my knees to my chest and swallowed the surge of panic that threatened to choke me. Damian and I were trapped in a bone-littered cavern, with no means of calling for help.

"Well," I said to the darkness, "at least we're dry."

Eighteen

*W*hen Damian failed to respond to my plucky comment, yet another ghastly image rose in my fear-racked brain.

"We're going to *stay* dry, aren't we?" I asked tremulously. "The ocean isn't going to rush in here and *drown* us, is it?"

"It seems unlikely," said Damian. "The sand's bone-dry, if you'll pardon the expression, and the monks have been here rather longer than we have. Since they haven't been washed out to sea, it seems safe to assume that we won't be either."

"But one of them *was* washed out to sea," I reminded him. "The skull Will and Rob found must have come from here. Percy said it was *ancient*."

"It may have been separated from the rest of the bones," said Damian. "A few of the monks may have . . ." His words trailed off.

Five seconds later he switched on his flashlight, stood, and strode purposefully around the cavern, pausing at each of the three low openings in the walls. When I asked what he was doing, he hushed me and kept going. When he reached the third portal, he cocked an ear toward it and inhaled deeply through his nostrils.

"Yes, this is the one," he said. "Come with me."

I didn't need to be told twice. I scrambled to my feet and ran after him, into the opening.

Damian went forward easily at first but was soon obliged to duck his head to avoid hitting it on the roof. I was, for once, pleased with my notable lack of height. I had no trouble whatsoever walking upright, though I still had to walk attentively—the tunnel's floor was sprinkled with loose, ankle-turning stones.

Damian finished his thought as we walked on. "Some of the monks may have gone farther into the caves than the others. They may have tried to escape to the sea. The skull we found in the cove may have belonged to one of them. If I'm right, then we're following in their footsteps."

"Why do we want to follow in their footsteps?" I asked.

"If this tunnel led them to the sea," said Damian, "it'll lead us there, too. It can serve as *our* escape route."

The passage curved abruptly to the right, and the sound of the throbbing surf intensified. A chill breeze began to blow steadily against us. After perhaps thirty yards of downward progress, the passage leveled off and opened out into a much larger chamber. Damian's light picked out knots of driftwood and tangles of seaweed scattered on the rocky, sand-strewn floor. Ten more strides took us across the chamber to a low archway in the opposite wall. We ducked under the archway and found ourselves looking down on a wondrous sight.

We were standing on a ledge at the back of a cavern that opened onto the sea. The dense fog had apparently dissipated, because silver flashes of moonlight streaked the foaming waves that surged and crashed against the cave's glistening walls. The sound was deafening, the tumult stupefying, and we kept well back from the ledge's slick edge. Damian studied the unearthly scene until spray began to run in rivulets down our rain jackets, then turned around and led the way back through the tunnel to the relative peace and quiet of the monks' cave.

"The ledge leads around the wall to the cavern's mouth," he informed me upon our arrival. "But it's no good to us now. The tide is too high. We should be able to get through in a few hours, though."

"Get through to what?" I asked, eyeing him warily. "The cliffs out there are pretty perpendicular."

"I can climb them," Damian said confidently. "You can wait here while I go for help."

"I'll come with you," I said flatly. "And don't even *try* to talk me out of it. I'd rather break my neck falling from a cliff than sit here wondering if you've broken yours. Percy knows that we came to the monastery, Damian, but he might not know about the movable tablet or the hidden staircase. If—God forbid—you had an accident on your way to the castle, I could be *trapped* down here *forever*. And I simply will *not* allow you to do *any* sort of climbing until it's light out. If you take one step toward that tunnel before sunrise, I'll knock you senseless, I *swear* I will."

I started crying about halfway through my tirade and kept crying until I reached the end, when I began to sob. It had been a stressful night, and I was temporarily out of pluck. Damian reached toward his trouser pocket and cursed lustily.

"Damn and blast," he blustered. "Cassie has my *handkerchief* as well!"

It was too much. My fearless bodyguard had been able to contain his temper while a band of murderous thugs kidnapped Peter and sealed us into a secret subterranean tomb, but when it came to a *missing handkerchief* . . . My sobs turned into a strangled giggle. I pulled a handkerchief out of my jacket pocket, buried my face in it, and sank onto the sand, shaking with laughter.

"Are you hysterical?" Damian inquired, squatting in front of me. "Should I slap you?"

"No, thanks," I said, gasping. "I'll stop in a minute. I'm

s-s-sorry about your hanky." It was an unwise comment, because it set me off again, but after a few more unsuccessful tries, I managed to regain my composure. "Forgive me, Damian, but you pick the strangest things to get angry about."

Damian sat beside me, with his shoulder touching mine, and turned off his flashlight. Darkness swallowed us, but it didn't bother me as much as it had before. I'd purged my fear with laughter and tears. I could face whatever happened next with still-imperfect but much-improved equanimity.

"I'm angry with myself," Damian confessed. "I've behaved like the rankest amateur."

"You haven't done so badly." I groped for his knee and patted it reassuringly. "You kept Percy from saddling us with a posse that would have led us astray. You made sure Cassie would be safe by sending her back to the pub with Kate and Elliot as an escort. And let's not forget that you saved my bacon upstairs in the church. I would have fallen into the hole if you hadn't knocked me over in the nick of time. Take credit where credit is due."

Damian grunted disparagingly.

"I don't understand why the islanders shut us up in here," I mused aloud. "We're the laird's special guests. They must know we'll be missed."

"It may be another scare tactic," Damian reasoned. "Or they may hope that we'll kill ourselves attempting to climb the cliffs. There'd be no way to prove that we hadn't lost our way in the fog and fallen from the coastal path." He sighed explosively. "I've been playing this game too long to make so many basic mistakes. I should never have allowed myself to be caught up in an affair that has nothing to do with my assignment."

"I'm glad you did," I told him. "Otherwise I'd be sitting here with only the monks for company."

"Yes," he retorted, with considerable asperity. "I can easily imagine you chasing after Peter on your own. I should have locked you in the suite when I had the chance."

"I would have tied my sheets together and swung down from the balcony," I responded airily.

"Lori," he snapped, his temper flaring. "You still don't understand, do you?" He swung sideways and leaned in close to me. *"My mistakes get people killed."*

His words hit me like heat from a blast furnace. My frivolous mood evaporated, and I lapsed into a pensive silence.

"I'm sorry," he said after a few moments had passed. "I didn't mean to hurt your feelings."

"You haven't." I hesitated, then asked, in a voice that was barely above a whisper, "Damian . . . how did you get those scars?"

He sat unmoving for several minutes. Then, without speaking, he reached across my body for my right arm, found my hand, and guided my fingers to his left shoulder.

"Knife," he said, and moved my hand to his collarbone, his chest, his ribs, saying in turn, "Gun, gun, knife again. A round from a Kalashnikov grazed my right buttock as I was pushing Sir Percy to the ground one memorable evening, but since I'm sitting on the souvenir, we'll pass that one by." Finally he pressed my fingertips lightly to the scar on his temple and said, "A reminder of the bullet that killed me."

He released my hand, but my fingers stayed at his temple. As I grappled with a thousand churning thoughts, one sentence came back to me, something he'd said the night before, after he'd removed the poker from my shaking hand: *You can't know what you're capable of, until you're put to the test.*

Here was a man who'd been tested, who knew precisely what he was capable of doing and enduring. The warmth of his skin beneath my cold fingertips brought home to me as nothing had before the magnitude of the sacrifice he was willing to make. Damian Hunter, a man I'd known for less than a week, would, without hesitation, lay down his life for me. I felt like a child beside him.

I drew my hand back. "What happened, Damian? How did you . . . die?"

"I was assigned to guard the teenage daughter of a government official in a part of the world where kidnapping is common." He spoke casually, as if he were recounting an ordinary incident in a routine day. "She gave me the slip one night, for a lark. By the time I caught up with her, two men were forcing her into the boot of a car at gunpoint. I took out one, but the other took me out. Luckily, my partner arrived in time to pick off the shooter, rescue the girl, and get me to hospital. I was dead on arrival, but they revived me. The girl and my partner told me later what had happened. I have no memory of the event."

"I'm sorry," I mumbled. "I shouldn't have asked."

"I've been waiting for you to ask," he said. "You're not the sort of person to let questions go unanswered."

"I'm the kind of person who should have her mouth stapled shut," I said bitterly. "My God, Damian, I *teased* you about your scar. I said you were *stagnant*."

"You said I wasn't *completely* stagnant," he corrected.

"I called you an *action hero*. I made *fun* of you." I covered my face with my hands, distraught. "I've said so many asinine things to you I've lost count. I haven't taken you seriously. I've treated you with appalling disrespect. I'm surprised you haven't pushed me off the balcony."

"I'd prefer to keep you *on* the balcony," he said.

"Why?" I asked brokenly. "Why would you risk your neck to save a fool like me?"

"Because you're worth saving," he replied.

"The pay must be *awfully* good," I muttered.

"Do you know why you haven't taken me seriously?" Damian asked. "It's because, as Peter said, you like to think the best of people. You have faith in the essential goodness of human nature. You don't really believe, deep down, that anyone would wish to harm you. You're not naive. You're aware of evil, but you're convinced that goodness will conquer it every time. I'd almost forgotten that people like you exist. You're an endangered species, Lori, and I will not allow you to become extinct. The world would be a much poorer place without you. And, of course, the pay is *awfully* good."

I elbowed him in the ribs but smiled ruefully through my tears and put my handkerchief to work again. When I'd finished with it, I wrapped my arms around my knees and asked, "Is that why you didn't come swimming with us this morning? Because you didn't want us to see your scars?"

"I didn't want to frighten the children," he admitted.

"Those little ghouls?" I snorted. "You wouldn't have frightened them. They would have thought you were the coolest guy on earth." I hugged my knees more tightly. "Speaking of cool—is it my imagination, or is it getting colder down here?"

"You're getting colder because you're sitting still," said Damian. "We'll stay warmer if we keep moving. Time to explore the other passages, I think. Close your eyes. I'm going to turn on my torch."

When our eyes had adjusted to the dazzling brightness of Damian's flashlight, we stepped through the opening to the left of the one that had taken us to the sea. It led to a passage so low that

I had to duck my head to avoid concussing myself. Poor Damian was forced to bend almost double. I think we were both relieved when we came to a rockfall that filled the tunnel from floor to ceiling and forced us to turn back.

The last passage went on for twenty yards or so before it, too, was blocked by a rockfall. I started to turn around, but Damian stayed put. He ran the light across the piled stones, then reached for the topmost one, pulled it out, and passed it back to me.

"I thought so," he murmured, leaning forward to peer into the hole. "It's too neat. Nature didn't bring these rocks down. Someone stacked them here to seal off the tunnel. The wall's no more than six inches thick. Let's find out what's behind it."

He carefully dismantled the man-made rockfall until he'd opened a doorway large enough for us to walk through. A short passage beyond the doorway took us to a sandy-floored cavern similar in size and shape to the monks' cave. Damian strode ahead of me, making a circuit of the walls, looking for openings that might lead to still more caverns.

"No fissures, cracks, or crevices," he announced. "I think we've reached a dead——" He broke off abruptly as he stumbled over some obstacle and fell to his knees. The flashlight flew from his hand, but the lanyard kept it from flying too far, and he was soon in possession of it again.

"Damian?" I said, walking cautiously to his side. "Are you all right?"

"No damage done," he answered, but he didn't stand. He stayed on his knees and trained his light on the object that had tripped him up.

The oblong container was the size of a steamer trunk and made of opaque black plastic. Two hefty latches held its hinged lid shut. Eleven identical containers sat beside it, ranged end to end along the cavern's wall.

"Well, well, well," Damian murmured. "What have we here?"

"Buried treasure," I said. "What else?"

"Let's find out, shall we?" He slipped the lanyard over his head and handed his flashlight to me, saying, "Keep it steady."

He pressed his thumbs to the latches. They popped open, and with some effort he lifted the lid.

"Oh . . . my," I murmured, when I could speak.

The container was packed to the brim with clear-plastic food-storage bags, and each bag held a banded bundle of English currency. Hundred-pound notes predominated, though packets of fifties, twenties, and even a few stray bundles of lowly tens helped to break up the monotony. Damian dug down to the bottom of the container, but there was nothing in it besides money.

"As I told you last night, Lori, drug transport is a lucrative business." He ran his hands across the bags. "There must be half a million pounds here."

"A m-million dollars," I managed. I was breathing rather rapidly. "That's a lot of cash to leave lying around."

"Drug dealers deal in cash, which can be awkward for those on the receiving end. A red flag would go up at the Inland Revenue if such large sums were to appear suddenly in a private bank account." Damian pointed to strips of rubber that ran along the inside edges of the container's lid and rim. "The gaskets form an airtight seal—that's why the box was hard to open. Designed to keep out moisture, I imagine. Custom-made by the same firm that builds their shipping containers, no doubt."

He didn't need to explain who "they" were. No one but the islanders could have used the hidden cavern as a bank vault.

"Please note the conspicuous absence of locks," he went on.

"I don't suppose burglars get down here too often," I commented.

"Let's open the rest," he suggested.

I followed Damian with the light—which was none too steady—as he crawled from one chest to the next, popping latches and lifting lids. Ten of the remaining containers were filled to the brim with cash, but the eleventh fulfilled my prophecy.

It was filled with treasure.

In truth, the container was only half full, but the half that remained was enough to make my eyes start from their sockets. Goblets, coins, candlesticks, and many pieces of jewelry lay jumbled together in a gleaming gold-and-silver heap. Some of the objects were enameled, some were encrusted with gems, and some were decorated with interlaced patterns of birds and beasts and leaves. Each was exquisitely wrought and appeared to be of great antiquity. I sank to my knees beside Damian and held my hand out to the glittering hoard, half expecting to warm myself by its glow.

"Sir Percy was quite correct when he described his people as resourceful," Damian said sardonically. "They're smuggling antiques as well as drugs. Don't touch," he added, gripping my wrist as I reached for a golden goblet. "We don't want to leave more fingerprints than we have to."

A pang of disappointment shot through me when he closed the box, and I followed somewhat reluctantly as he retraced his steps, closing each of the containers in turn.

"Well," I said sadly, "we've found the evidence you wanted."

"We have indeed," he agreed. "I'll speak with Sir Percy when we get back to Dundrillin. I'll leave it to him to contact the authorities." He closed the last container and stood. "It would be best to leave everything as it was when we found it. Come along. We have a wall to mend."

We rebuilt the man-made rockfall and returned to the monks' cave, but we didn't have much to say once we got there. I was depressed by our discovery because of the pain it would cause Sir Percy. Damian was no doubt envisioning the route he would take when he attacked the cliffs at sunrise. We both nearly jumped out of our skins when a grinding creak sounded overhead and a voice floated down the staircase.

"Lori? Damian? Are you there? Can you hear me?"

"It's Elliot," I said, thunderstruck. "What's Elliot doing here?"

"Rescuing us, apparently." Damian turned on his light and ran to the bottom of the stairs, calling, "Yes, we're here! Stay where you are! We'll be right up!"

My heart was so light as I climbed to freedom that my knees didn't dare complain. Elliot Southmore had the good sense to keep his powerful flashlight pointed away from us as we emerged from the black hole, but even the cloud-crowded moon seemed too bright to my light-sensitive eyes. Squinting against the glare, I watched in amazement as Elliot single-handedly lowered the memorial tablet back into place.

"You're stronger than you look," I said.

"It's lighter than it looks," he said in return, brushing grit from his palms. "You won't have to walk back to the castle. I parked the car at MacAllen's croft."

"I don't care about the car," Damian said impatiently. "How did you know where to find us? How did you open the tomb? I couldn't budge the blasted slab."

"You didn't know how to work the latches," Elliot told him.

"Latches?" said Damian, bending toward the slab. "What latches?"

"Sir Percy will explain everything," said Elliot. "Let's get down to the car, shall we? The storm Sir Percy predicted is moving in, and I'd rather not be caught out in it."

"Elliot!" I cried, stamping my foot out of sheer exasperation. "You have to tell us—"

"Sir Percy will explain everything," he repeated doggedly, and headed downhill, toward MacAllen's croft.

Nineteen

lliot Southmore delivered us to the castle before the first drops of rain fell, but a threatening gust of wind chased us across the courtyard and heavy clouds swallowed the moon as we gained the entrance hall.

"Sir Percy is waiting for you in the library," Elliot informed us. "If you'd care to change first——"

Damian and I were halfway up the main staircase before he finished his sentence. We weren't interested in fresh clothes. We wanted explanations.

Sir Percy was standing before the fire when we reached the library, but he wasn't the only one waiting for us. Cassie sat in the chair Kate had occupied earlier, looking far more serene than she had the last time I'd seen her. The reason for her composure wasn't hard to understand. In the chair next to hers, clad in red silk pajamas, a paisley dressing gown, and deerskin bedroom slippers that were slightly too large for him—and sipping what I assumed to be an extremely large brandy—was the long-lost Peter.

He set his glass aside and crossed hurriedly to meet us in the doorway, his slippers flapping against his bare feet.

"I'm so sorry," he said. "It's my fault, my fault entirely. If I'd known——"

"All in good time, young man. First things first." Sir Percy intercepted Peter before he reached the doorway and guided him back to the chair, then turned to beam amiably at us. "Quite an adventurous night for all concerned. Off with your jackets, you two. You won't be going out again. Can I get you a drink?"

"Yes," I said, and moved closer to the fire. "I want a great big pot of hot cocoa and a huge pile of sandwiches, because if I don't eat something, I'll get drowsy as soon as I thaw out. Damian and I have been stuck in a freezer for the past—" I turned to Damian. "How long were we down there?"

He consulted his watch. "Almost two hours."

"Is that *all?*" I stared at him, nonplussed. "It seemed like *ages.*"

"How time drags when you're not having fun," boomed Sir Percy, chuckling.

Mrs. Gammidge entered the library in our wake, as if summoned telepathically. She placed a pile of woolen blankets on the couch, looked askance at our sandy boots, relieved us of our jackets and caps, took Sir Percy's order for cocoa and sandwiches, and departed.

"Are you sure you don't want to change into something more comfortable?" Sir Percy asked solicitously. "You seem rather rumpled."

I subjected him to a glare that should have scorched his eyebrows. "I am perfectly comfortable, thank you, but if you don't tell us what's going on, Percy, I am going to *scream.*"

"Now, now . . ." Sir Percy clucked his tongue like a disapproving nanny, led me to the sofa, and tucked a blanket around my lap. "We've all had a bite to eat, but you missed dinner, my poor poppet. You'll feel better when you have some food in you. At ease, Damian," he added over his shoulder. "You're among friends."

Damian took a seat at the other end of the sofa and declined Sir Percy's offer of a blanket. He crossed one leg over the other and regarded Peter speculatively. He seemed thoughtful rather than incensed.

"We'll wait for the comestibles, I think," said Sir Percy, taking a seat in the chair on my right. "It's a wonderful story—you'll laugh about it in years to come, I promise you—and it would be a pity to spoil it with interruptions."

Fortunately for Sir Percy, Mrs. Gammidge's efficient household was clicking on all cylinders, and we didn't have long to wait. In less than twenty minutes, she returned with a selection of Cook's hearty sandwiches, an insulated pot of hot cocoa, and thick slices of moist chocolate cake topped with whipped cream. While Sir Percy helped himself to a piece of cake, I swooped down on the sandwiches like a ravening vulture and proved him right. I felt much better with food in my stomach.

When the worst pangs of our hunger had been assuaged, Sir Percy gave Peter an encouraging nod.

"The floor is yours, you young noodle," he said. "Tell Lori and Damian all about it."

Peter gave us a profoundly apologetic look, fortified himself with a drop of brandy, cradled the glass in his hands, and began to tell his tale.

"It's my damnable curiosity," he said. "I couldn't resist investigating the legend of the screaming monks. As you know, most legends are founded in fact, so I went up to the ruins to see if a natural phenomenon created the noise people mistook for screaming." He paused for another sip of brandy, then went on. "I was there for only a few minutes when I heard the most god-awful howls. They made my skin crawl, I can tell you, particularly since they seemed to be coming from beneath the old memorial tablet. It sounded like a dozen souls crying out to be released."

I shivered involuntarily and fortified myself with a swig of cocoa.

"I knew there had to be a rational explanation for the howls," Peter went on, "so I went over the tablet inch by inch, and what do you think I found?"

"Latches," Damian replied laconically. "Elliot told us. How many did you find?"

"Two," Peter replied. "They were designed to blend in with the deep carving around the edge of the tablet. They were so cleverly concealed, in fact, that I passed over them three times before I realized what they were. Once I'd found them, what else could I do but try them?"

"Of course you had to try them," roared Sir Percy. "Only possible thing to do. Tell 'em what happened *next*."

"The tablet popped open," Peter said. "I couldn't believe my eyes. I released the latches, and one side of the tablet rose an inch or two from the ground. I examined the opposite edge and discovered that it was *hinged*. But the most remarkable thing about the tablet was its weight. The stone slab should have weighed a ton, but it was no heavier than a packed suitcase. As soon as it was open, the howling stopped. The wind, you see, was streaming up the staircase and leaking out around the tablet, making a—"

"Yes," Sir Percy intervened, "I think we can work the trick out for ourselves, dear boy. Skip ahead to the staircase."

"Well," said Peter, "when I saw the staircase, I had to find out where it went."

"Naturally," said Damian, a bit sourly.

Peter's face reddened and he ducked his head, but he carried on despite his embarrassment. "You know what I found down in the cave, so I needn't describe it. Did you explore the three tunnels?"

"We did," Damian answered.

"Then you know about the two dead ends," said Peter. "What you don't know is that I followed the tunnel to the sea and . . . well . . . I decided to have a go at climbing the cliffs."

Cassie calmly reached across the space between their chairs and punched him, hard, on the shoulder. Peter flinched and grimaced but uttered no word of complaint. He must have agreed with me that he was getting off lightly. If Bill had ever tried such a harebrained stunt, I would have rewarded him with more than a punch on the shoulder.

"It was an imbecilic thing to do," Peter acknowledged, glancing timidly at Cassie. "But the tide wasn't high enough yet to reach the ledge and it wasn't completely dark out, so it didn't seem all that risky at the time. Once I reached the mouth of the cavern, I found that a staircase had been carved into the cliff. The steps were badly eroded, but there were enough of them to get me up to the coastal path."

A rumbling chuckle sounded from Sir Percy.

"You'll love the next part," he said, waggling his eyebrows at me and Damian. "Go on, Peter, tell them what you did next."

Peter looked as though he would have given anything to *avoid* telling us what he did next, but he drank another drop of brandy and soldiered on.

"I didn't want anyone to fall down the staircase by accident," he said, carefully avoiding our eyes, "so I went back to the ruins and closed the tablet."

The moment of stunned silence that followed was shattered by Sir Percy's robust guffaws.

"Told you it was a wonderful story, didn't I?" he said happily. "You run off to rescue the lad, and he seals you up all right and tight in a cave filled with skeletons! Simply marvelous! Haven't enjoyed anything so much since Tufty Wiggins dropped a water balloon on the bishop."

I waited stoically while Sir Percy quaked with mirth. Damian ate another sandwich and refilled our cups with cocoa. Cassie smiled vaguely, as though her mind was on other things. Peter studied the floor.

"Ah," Sir Percy sighed, mopping his streaming eyes. "Forgive me. I promised that there would be no interruptions, but I couldn't help myself. Pray continue, young Peter."

"The fog was beginning to shift when I reached the coastal path," said Peter, still staring at the floor, "so I climbed a hill and watched it for a while before walking back to the pub. When I got there, Mrs. Muggoch collared me to warn me about the journalist. She seemed to know all about our troubles with the press."

"I imagine everyone does," said Sir Percy, with a complacent nod. "Newspapers do reach Erinskil, and your disguises weren't impenetrable."

"She was very sympathetic," Peter said.

"Of course she was," said Sir Percy. "She's a good-hearted woman. She wouldn't want to see you and Cassie persecuted."

"That's exactly what she told me," said Peter, "at great length. I was so grateful to her for getting rid of the journalist that I just let her go on and on."

"We understand," said Sir Percy. "We're familiar with Mrs. Muggoch's wagging tongue."

Peter smiled wanly. "I eventually managed to extricate myself and go upstairs, where I found Cassie, Kate, and Elliot. Cassie became hyster—" He glanced cautiously at her and promptly rephrased his statement. "Cassie was justifiably upset with me, and it wasn't until we'd calmed her down that Kate was able to explain that you two had gone looking for me."

"I tried to ring you, Damian," said Cassie, "until I found your mobile in the pocket of your blazer."

Damian accepted the cell phone from Cassie's outstretched hand and gallantly refrained from mentioning his handkerchief.

"I wouldn't have been able to reach you even if you'd had your mobile with you," said Cassie. "My earlier calls didn't go through to Peter because his mobile didn't work down in the cavern."

"Too much solid rock," said Damian.

"Blocked the signal," Peter confirmed. "We rang Sir Percy, though, to find out if you'd returned. When he told us you hadn't, I admitted to him that if you'd followed me into the cavern, I *might* have closed the memorial tablet on top of you. When he finished laughing, he ordered Elliot to go and get you."

"I also convinced our young celebrities to move into Dundrillin," Sir Percy interposed. "Though it would be more accurate to say that Mr. Nunen's unwelcome arrival convinced them. Mrs. Gammidge put them in the Daffodil Suite, in the northeast tower, where they'll be safe from prying eyes and lenses."

"Mrs. Gammidge also decided that my entire wardrobe required laundering." Peter smoothed the lapel of his paisley dressing gown. "Sir Percy very kindly allowed me to borrow some of his son's night attire."

Cassie uttered a stifled croak of laughter, which she disguised—unconvincingly—as a cough. Peter's blush outshone his red pajamas.

Damian stirred. "About the memorial tablet . . ."

"Sir Percy told us about it," Peter said eagerly. "It's absolutely fascinating."

"Feel free to share your knowledge with us," I coaxed, looking from him to Sir Percy.

"The original tablet was damaged by shrapnel," said Sir Percy, "when the Royal Navy was using Erinskil for target practice.

When the islanders returned after the war, they replaced the original with a convincing fake."

"Why?" I asked.

"They intended to use the caverns as a bomb shelter, if the occasion ever arose," Sir Percy explained. "We'd entered the atomic age, remember. Bomb shelters were all the rage."

"But why replace the original tablet with a fake?" I persisted. "The original would have given them access to the caves. The monks were able to lift it."

"It took six strong men to lift it," Sir Percy informed me. "The replacement is made of a composite material that a healthy child can shift. The islanders wanted everyone on Erinskil to be able to seek shelter there."

"I believe we're the first outsiders to enter the caverns," Peter said with a touch of pride.

"Apart from the Vikings," Damian murmured.

"Here endeth the lesson," droned Sir Percy. He studied Peter and Cassie for a moment, then clapped his hands commandingly. "Off to your suite, my children. It's well past your bedtime. Don't lose any sleep over the journalist. Mrs. Gammidge will sort him out."

Peter drained his glass, placed it on a table at his elbow, and flapped over to stand before me and Damian.

"I'm more sorry than I can possibly say," he said. "If I'd known the amount of bother I'd cause, I wouldn't have gone to the ruins."

"It's okay." I pushed the blanket aside and stood to give him a hug. "You can't help being curious. You were raised in Finch."

"Damian?" said Peter anxiously, when I'd released him.

"No harm done," said Damian. "But if Mrs. Gammidge suggests barricading you in the northeast tower, I won't argue with her."

Peter smiled gratefully and turned a tentative eye toward Cassie. After a brief hesitation, he held his hand out to her. She gripped it as if she'd never let it go and graciously permitted her contrite young swain to escort her from the library. I resumed my seat on the couch and pulled the blanket over my lap, hoping they'd take Will's advice and hold the wedding at Dundrillin.

"Well, that's settled," said Sir Percy, after they'd gone. "She's been glowering at him all evening. I was afraid I'd have to put them in separate towers. But all's well that ends well." He glanced at the clock on the mantelpiece. "Half past eleven. I expect you're both ready for bed."

"Not quite, Sir Percy," Damian said quietly. "There are a few points we'd like to discuss with you before we retire."

"No time like the present." Sir Percy sat back in his chair and folded his hands across his waistcoat. "Fire away, old man."

Damian regarded him steadily. "The security dossier you prepared for me and Andrew fails to mention the false memorial tablet, the staircase, and the caves below the monastery ruins. Why were those items left out of the report?"

"They're not relevant," Sir Percy replied. "The caves wouldn't help your quarry to sneak into Dundrillin even if he did manage to discover them, which is hardly likely. Besides, the islanders hold the caverns to be something of a sacred site. They don't like outsiders knowing about them, and I didn't care to betray their confidence."

"I'm afraid that the people of Erinskil have other reasons for concealing the caverns," said Damian. "Peter failed to explore the tunnels thoroughly, Sir Percy, but Lori and I did not. I believe that what we found there will be of interest to you."

"Do tell," said Sir Percy.

"We discovered twelve airtight chests," said Damian, in a calm, dispassionate voice. "Eleven were filled with currency adding up to millions of pounds. The twelfth held valuable antiquities."

"Millions of pounds, do you say?" Sir Percy's eyebrows shot up. "My goodness, but the islanders are thrifty. Can't blame them for avoiding banks. The fees are outrageous. And who's to say that the caverns aren't just the place to store Granny's gewgaws?"

"Sir Percy," Damian said patiently, "the objects we found can't possibly be described as gewgaws. They should be in the British Museum. As for the cash . . ." He pursed his lips. "It grieves me to tell you this, but I strongly doubt that the money Lori and I found was earned through any legitimate enterprise. If you'll permit me to explain . . ."

"I'm all ears, old man," said Sir Percy, leaning forward in his chair.

For the next half hour, Damian walked Sir Percy through the long list of clues we'd accumulated, from the light on Cieran's Chapel to the well-maintained ringbolt and the old laird's over-large grave; from the antitourist campaign's myriad manifestations to the man-made rockfall that blocked the third tunnel.

"The islanders have invested heavily in their own comfort," said Damian, "but they've virtually ignored tourist accommodations. In fact, they've made it quite difficult for tourists to visit Erinskil. Why?"

"I'm sure you'll tell me," said Sir Percy encouragingly.

"I believe that they don't want *anyone* to visit Erinskil," said Damian. "I believe that Elspeth MacAllen diverted your post, sir, in order to prevent the Seal Conservation Trust from building a research facility on the island, because a research facility would bring strangers to the island—something the islanders have gone to great lengths to avoid."

"You make my people sound positively antisocial," Sir Percy protested.

"When it comes to outsiders, sir," Damian stated, "your people *are* antisocial. The lack of a tourist trade hasn't hurt them, however. On the contrary, they live lives of relative splendor."

"The tweed business has been very kind to them," said Sir Percy.

"It must be clear to you, as a businessman, that the tweed mill can't produce enough income to pay for the luxuries the islanders enjoy." Damian tented his fingers. "It is my belief, Sir Percy, that the islanders are supplementing their incomes by trafficking in drugs. Drug shipments are deposited by major dealers on Cieran's Chapel, transferred from there to Alasdair Murdoch's fishing boats, and taken by boat to the mainland. The islanders store their cash profits in the cavern temporarily, until they can launder them by means of the tweed mill. As a side business, they sell or fence stolen antiquities on the black market. Such enterprises function best away from the public eye. It is, therefore, in the islanders' best interest to discourage tourism."

"Fascinating," marveled Sir Percy, leaning his chin on his hand. "I hope you haven't troubled our young friends with your disturbing revelations. I wouldn't want their stay on Erinskil to be spoiled."

"Cassie started the ball rolling," I told him. "She's convinced that everyone on Erinskil is involved in a criminal conspiracy. That's why she didn't want Mrs. Gammidge to call for Dr. Tighe. That's why she was so frightened when Peter went missing. She thought Peter had been abducted, possibly murdered, because he'd gotten too close to the truth."

Sir Percy drew such a sorrowful breath that I almost wished we hadn't ventured beyond the man-made rockfall. He rose from his chair, shook his head, and walked slowly to stand before the fire. His shoulders drooped as he contemplated the flames, as if a heavy weight had fallen on them, but his expression was oddly quizzical when he turned to face us.

"I never realized you had such a vivid imagination, Damian," he said. "I thought you were all business, all the time, but clearly I was mistaken. I am, I confess, somewhat taken aback by your portrait of my people. Thieves? Kidnappers? Murderers? What else, I wonder?" His eyes sought mine. "I knew you were inquisitive, Lori, but I'd rather hoped that concern for your own safety, and that of your sons, would override any desire you might have to nose about Erinskil. I should have known better."

Damian uncrossed his legs. "You're not as shocked as I expected you to be, Sir Percy."

"Why should I be shocked?" Sir Percy hooked his thumbs in his waistcoat and threw out his chest. "My dear fellow, I'm the laird. Do you seriously imagine that anything takes place on this island without my knowledge?"

Grinning like a mad magician, he unhooked a thumb, flung a hand out with a flourish, and pressed a button on the Portland-stone mantelpiece. An oak panel to the left of the fireplace slid back soundlessly, and six grim-faced, tweed-jacketed men marched forth to stand like a wall in front of Damian and me. I recognized the hostile eyes of Mick Ferguson glaring down at us and gripped the blanket, confused and a little shaken.

Damian reached for his gun.

Twenty

*D*amian's hand hovered perilously near his concealed holster but retreated when Sir Percy stepped forward, his blue eyes twinkling with mirth.

"Lori, Damian," he said, flinging his arms around the shoulders of the men nearest to him, "please allow me the great pleasure of presenting to you the elders of Erinskil. You know Mick Ferguson, of course—he took you to Cieran's Chapel. Mick, would you be so kind as to see to the drinks? I'm sure no one will refuse a wee dram on such a devil of a night."

"Yes, sir, your lairdship," said Mick, and he moved with alacrity toward the liquor cabinet.

"The elders are charged with the awesome responsibility of governing Erinskil," Sir Percy explained, beaming down at me and Damian. "I hope you won't be too put out with me when I confess that I invited them here to listen in on our riveting conversation. I thought it might contain information of interest to them."

"They've been *eavesdropping?*" I said, scandalized.

"*Such* a time-saver," said Sir Percy with unimpaired good humor. "Completely eliminates the need to rehash your side of the story."

"What made you think that our side of the story would be of interest to these gentlemen?" asked Damian.

"With you and Peter wandering through the caverns, there was no telling what you might have discovered," Sir Percy replied. "I summoned the elders because they have a right—indeed, a duty—to know if you stumbled upon the airtight chests."

"I'd like to question them about those chests," said Damian.

"No doubt you would." Sir Percy rubbed his palms together energetically. "The first order of business, however, must be introductions. Damian has met the elders already, though he was unaware of their governmental roles at the time. I will, therefore, direct the introductions to you, Lori. From left to right, we have Cal Maconinch, harbormaster; Alasdair Murdoch, fisherman; Neil MacAllen, crofter and mill manager; George Muggoch, publican and baker; and Lachlan Ferguson, pastor."

The men appeared to be in their sixties and seventies, though Pastor Ferguson's flowing white hair and deeply creased face made me suspect that he was the eldest elder. George Muggoch was as round as his wife—unsurprising in a man who ran both a pub *and* a bakery—but the others were fit and trim. Alasdair Murdoch was broad-shouldered and burly, as befitted a man who spent his days hauling fishing nets, and Neil MacAllen had the long, lean build of a shepherd. Cal Maconinch's auburn hair was scarcely touched by gray, which led me to believe that he was the youngest of the six. All of the men wore shirts and ties beneath exquisite tweed jackets—examples, no doubt, of the mill's fine wares.

As they were introduced, each man touched a hand to his forehead in a brief salute, murmured a polite "How do you do?" and took a seat. Three chairs had to be carried from other parts of the library to accommodate the new arrivals, but in the end we formed a snug circle before the fire. The elders sat, wee drams in hand, gazing expectantly at Sir Percy, who lounged back in his great leather armchair, looking uncharacteristically reflective.

"Strangest thing," he mused aloud, gazing at the ceiling. "Boring old sticks-in-the-mud like Cassie's father are credited with brains because they never smile. I, on the other hand, have gained the reputation of being a fool simply because I enjoy life. I've never quite understood the equation."

"No one here thinks you're a fool, your lairdship," Mick assured him.

"Lori and Damian do," said Sir Percy, eyeing us shrewdly. "They wanted to shield me from an awful truth I was too simple-minded to perceive. I should sack you, Damian, for poking your nose where it doesn't belong, but it wouldn't do the least amount of good. You're the sort of chap who won't let go of a bone once he's begun to worry it." He let his gaze travel over the elders' attentive faces. "I'm very much afraid, gentlemen, that we shall have to explain ourselves, and throw ourselves on the mercy of the court."

"Is it absolutely necessary, your lairdship?" asked Pastor Ferguson, his brow knitting.

"My dear pastor," said Sir Percy, "my friends are convinced that Erinskil is a den of iniquity inhabited by ruthless felons. Surely it is better for them to learn the truth than to cling to such a grievous misapprehension. Consider the difficulties that would arise if they took their spurious accusations to the police."

"What about the youngsters?" growled Mick.

"They're harmless," Damian said quickly. "They don't know about the money. They may have suspicions, but they have no proof."

"Will they go looking for it?" Mick pressed.

"With Fleet Street nipping at their heels and Cupid harassing their hearts?" Sir Percy tossed his head derisively. "I sincerely doubt it."

Pastor Ferguson turned to us. "I would like it to be understood that what is said within these walls stays within these walls."

"I'll tell my husband," I confessed, with a sheepish shrug. I knew I'd tell Aunt Dimity as well, but I had no intention of trying to explain *her* to the elders. "I can't help it. I tell Bill everything."

"We'll make an exception for Lori's husband," Sir Percy pronounced. "I will vouch for Bill Willis, gentlemen, for he is the rarest of hybrids—a lawyer and an honorable man. He won't betray us."

The elders exchanged grave glances, then nodded, one by one. Pastor Ferguson, who seemed to be the chief elder, was the last to nod. He turned to Cal Maconinch.

"Cal?" he said. "Will you begin?"

"Only right that I should," said the harbormaster, "since it began with my father." He shifted slightly in his chair, as if settling down to tell a story he'd told a hundred times before. "My father was for thirty years the sexton at St. Andrew's."

"The church in Stoneywell," Damian put in, for my benefit.

"Aye," said Cal. "A sexton has many jobs, but the only one that need concern us is the job of gravedigger. When the tenth earl died, my father rowed out to Cieran's Chapel to dig the grave. He brought his sturdiest picks with him, because he knew he'd be doing more rock-breaking than digging, and he set to work at the spot James Robert had chosen. When he'd finished clearing away the thin layer of topsoil, he brought his pick down on the bare rock. The next thing he knew," Cal continued, "he was lying at the bottom of a crater, all bruised and battered and wondering if there'd been an earthquake, because the ground had given way beneath his feet."

"*Had* there been an earthquake?" I inquired, enthralled.

"Only the one my father started." Cal smiled wryly. "He was a big man, and he swung a heavy pick."

Pastor Ferguson took up the story. "Once the dust had settled, old Mr. Maconinch noticed a gold gleam among the rocks that had come down with him. The gleam came from a chalice, as fine and rich as anything he'd ever seen, and there was more to come—gold plates, reliquaries, jewelry, coins—"

"The sort of thing Damian and I found in the twelfth container," I put in.

Pastor Ferguson nodded. "Old Mr. Maconinch realized at once that he had, purely by chance, discovered a treasure trove."

"Whose treasure was it?" I asked.

Neil MacAllen cleared his throat. "Since all of the objects date back to the eighth century or earlier, and since most are religious in nature, we believe that they belonged to the monks of Erinskil."

The elders had obviously had plenty of time to analyze the find. Each contributed a segment to the fantastic story that followed.

"During the course of the monastery's existence," Pastor Ferguson theorized, "Erinskil's monks must have acquired a hoard of valuable objects."

"Wealthy patrons may have sought to buy indulgences with gold," said George Muggoch, "or a monk from a well-to-do family may have donated priceless personal possessions upon taking holy orders."

"Either way," said Alasdair Murdoch, "the monks ended up with a problem to solve: How would they keep their precious treasures safe when Vikings came to call?"

"Cieran's Chapel was the logical solution," Neil MacAllen offered. "They chose the islet as their hiding place and with pick and shovel created a cache they hoped would fool the Viking raiders. At the first sign of an invasion, a monk would load the church's treasures into a boat and row it out to the islet for safekeeping. The rest would seek shelter in the caves below the monastery."

"How long have you known about the caves beneath the

monastery?" Damian asked. "The entrance was pretty cleverly hidden."

George Muggoch shrugged. "Our families have lived on Erinskil from time out of mind. It's impossible to say who discovered what, when. It's just something we've always known."

"And always kept to ourselves," Mick added, with a hint of resentment.

"Tragically," said Pastor Ferguson, returning to the main drift of the story, "the monks' plan backfired. When the Vikings found nothing to plunder in the church, they vented their fury and frustration on the poor brethren."

"It may be a romantic notion," George Muggoch inserted, "but we believe it was Brother Cieran's job to hide the treasure. After the last raid, when Brother Cieran realized that he was the sole survivor, he went back to his post and stood guard over the hoard until he died."

"He was a bit mad," Alasdair Murdoch observed, tilting his head sympathetically.

"He was barking mad," Mick Ferguson said gruffly. "Not that anyone blames him, mind you. He'd had a bit of a shock."

Since the understatement was spoken in all sincerity, I fought down a desire to smile and carefully avoided making eye contact with Sir Percy.

"We believe that Brother Cieran laid out the bodies in the cavern," Pastor Ferguson went on. "One man could hardly be expected to carry so many mangled corpses up the stone staircase and go on to dig forty graves or more. He did what he could to show his respect for his brothers in Christ, then went back to the islet to do his duty."

The elders paused to sip their drinks in silence, as if according Brother Cieran the same respect he'd shown his fellow monks, then brought the story forward to the day old Mr. Maconinch had discovered the hoard.

"In order to understand what my father did next," said Cal, "you have to understand the state Erinskil was in at the time."

"Erinskil was dying," said Pastor Ferguson bluntly. "James Robert—the tenth earl—had been the most recent in a long line of lairds who'd been good men but bad managers. Death duties and personal debt had reduced his income to the point where he couldn't afford to spend more than a pittance on Erinskil's up-keep. By the time he died, we were in such desperate straits that many of us were discussing emigration."

Alasdair Murdoch pursed his lips. "Everyone agreed that Erinskil would fare no better under James Robert's son—he could barely pay his own bills, let alone invest in the island's main-tenance. Old Mr. Maconinch decided, therefore, that it would be daylight madness to turn the hoard over to the new laird, to whom it rightfully belonged."

"He would have sold the treasure to pay his taxes," Cal de-clared, "and our families would have been forced to leave the is-land forever. My father couldn't let it happen."

"He couldn't leave the treasure where it was," said Neil MacAllen, "because the old laird's burial service was coming up, and he couldn't dig another hole for it on the Chapel because everyone would wonder what had been buried there. So he moved the hoard from Cieran's Chapel to the monks' cave and said noth-ing about it until after the tenth earl had been laid to rest."

"By then," said Alasdair Murdoch, "word had come down from on high that the island was to be evacuated for the duration of the coming war. When Cal's father convened a special meeting of the elders, to inform them of his find, they had many things to consider."

"The elders agreed that the hoard should be used to benefit the islanders rather than the laird," said George Muggoch, "but that nothing should be done hastily. They'd hide the treasure in the cavern behind the artificial rockfall until the war was over and the islanders returned from the mainland."

"While in exile they'd learn everything they could about the antiquities trade," Pastor Ferguson explained. "They'd identify a trustworthy dealer who would be willing to sell individual pieces over an extended period of time to private collectors worldwide. In this way they hoped to avoid drawing undue attention to their find."

"They planned to sell the hoard off piece by piece," said Cal Maconinch, "and keep the profits to rebuild Erinskil."

Since it looked as though the profits would be considerable, the elders had to find a way to explain the island's prosperity. Their solution was to study businesses while they were on the mainland and choose one that would work well on Erinskil. It didn't take them long to conclude that a tweed mill would suit the island setting as well as the interests and abilities of the vast majority of islanders. Creative bookkeeping would allow them to disguise profits from the antiquities' sales as earnings from the mill.

"Finally," said George Muggoch, "the elders called together every adult on Erinskil. They asked the assembled men and women if they would choose to stay on Erinskil if the island had a good school, a resident doctor, a reliable supply of fresh water, and steady employment. If they were given a chance to rebuild their homes and maintain them properly, would they remain on the island? If they could live a civilized life on Erinskil, would they still prefer to emigrate?"

"Everyone laughed," said Pastor Ferguson. "I was a wee lad at the time, but I still remember the grim laughter. No one believed that Erinskil's problems could be solved. It took some time for the elders to convince them that they were in earnest, but once they had, the show of hands was unanimous—if life on Erinskil became less of a struggle, no one would leave."

"The elders then laid out their plan of action," Alasdair Murdoch went on. "They explained that it would come to nothing unless everyone on the island participated in it. Each family had to agree to make subtle, gradual changes in their manner of living, rather than extravagant, sudden changes, or the plan wouldn't work. Capital improvements, they argued, would be made for the welfare of residents, not transients. The elders weren't interested in creating a tourist mecca. If outsiders wanted to visit Erinskil, they would have to earn the privilege, because a privilege it would be."

"If the plan failed," said George Muggoch, "Erinskil would become another nature preserve, with a few scenic ruins thrown in for tourists to photograph. If the plan succeeded, Erinskil would be reborn as a living community with hope for the future."

"The people voted to succeed," Pastor Ferguson concluded simply.

"There was no dissension?" Damian asked.

"Why would there be?" I retorted. "*I'd* like to live here."

George Muggoch took Damian's question seriously. "Agreements are easier to reach when you're dealing with a small, homogeneous population. Most of us can trace our roots on Erinskil back for hundreds of years. We've always had to depend on each other. It was natural for us to go on doing so."

"We wanted to have a say in our own destiny," Alasdair Murdoch added. "If my children choose to stay on Erinskil, fine. If not, that's fine, too. But I want it to be their choice. I don't want some bureaucrat in Edinburgh or London to make their decisions for them."

"It was too good a deal to pass up," said Mick with finality. "Our fathers saw a chance for independence, and they grabbed it."

"They plundered an archaeological site of great historical value." Damian spoke with a candor that bordered, in my opinion, on the foolhardy. "They sold off their country's heritage."

"Our country drove us off our island," Cal responded bitterly. "Our country filled our fields with shell holes and unexploded bombs."

"As for heritage . . ." Neil MacAllen gave a short, mirthless laugh. "Our country has more heritage than it knows what to do with. You can find museums full of heritage all over Scotland. We're not depriving anyone of anything they can't find somewhere else."

"The way we see it," said Mick Ferguson, "the old laird was too fretted by debt to help us while he lived, but he gave us the means to help ourselves when he died. We think he would've been proud of what we've done with his gift."

I recalled the inscription on the old laird's tomb. " 'The heart benevolent and kind,' " I quoted, " 'The most resembles God.' "

"Aye," the men chorused.

They raised their glasses, as if they wished to make a silent toast to their unwitting benefactor, but their wish for silence was foiled. Several glasses were still on their way up when an earsplitting crack of thunder rattled the bottles in the liquor cabinet, and a torrent of rain buffeted the draped windows. A moment later the lights went out.

"Ah," said Sir Percy. "My storm has arrived." He heaved himself up from his chair and bustled from one candelabra to the next, striking matches and lighting candles. "It's going to be a stinker, I'm afraid. Gentlemen, you are, of course, welcome to stay the night—what remains of it, at any rate—or to use my fleet of cars to wend your way home."

"I'd rather no one leave just yet," Damian objected. "There are a few details I'd like to clear up."

"Still worrying the bone, eh? Good man." Sir Percy tossed the spent matches into the fire, returned to his chair, and smiled good-naturedly as a blast of thunder shook the windows. "Speak, Damian. We are at your service."

Damian turned to Pastor Ferguson. "Why is there so much cash in the cavern? Why haven't you moved it through the tweed mill's account books?"

"We were saving up for a special purchase," answered Pastor Ferguson. "We wanted to buy Erinskil. We were extremely disappointed when Sir Percy snatched the island out from under us, but our pockets will never be as deep as his."

"And he's not such a bad laird," Mick allowed, "as lairds go."

Mick's comment provoked a ripple of appreciative chuckles, in which Sir Percy joined wholeheartedly. Damian waited for the laughter to die before continuing his interrogation.

"Did you really intend to use the caverns as a bomb shelter?" he asked.

Alasdair Murdoch cast a pitying look in Sir Percy's direction and raised his voice slightly, to be heard over the driving rain.

"The laird was being inventive," he said generously. "The original stone tablet was damaged by the Royal Navy, but we would have replaced it in any case. We needed easy access to the hoard, and the original tablet was simply too heavy. Cal's father could move it because he was a giant of a man, but most of us aren't. And we weren't worried about thieves. No one comes and goes on Erinskil without our knowledge."

Damian nodded, but he hadn't finished yet. "If you're using the cavern as a storeroom, there seems little need for frequent trips to Cieran's Chapel. Why, then, do you maintain the ringbolt in such pristine condition? Why was the soil around the old laird's grave disturbed?"

"We still go out to the Chapel to check on the grave," Alasdair Murdoch explained. "It's sunken a bit over time. We don't want visitors wondering why the hole is so big, so we open the tomb from time to time, to replace the braces and keep it from caving in."

"We were doing just that," said Cal Maconinch, "when Sir Percy arrived in his helicopter five days ago with his unexpected guests. We had to close the grave in a hurry, in case one of you took it into your head to visit the Chapel."

"Which we discourage," Neil MacAllen interjected, "by putting out the story about Brother Cieran's ghost and backing it up with mysterious lights."

"That's me," Alasdair Murdoch confessed, grinning.

"You're Brother Cieran's ghost?" I said, my eyes widening.

"Only when Sir Percy has guests," said Mr. Murdoch modestly.

George Muggoch joined in. "If they come to the pub, my wife talks a blue streak about the ghost, the curse, and the haunted monastery. If that doesn't rattle them, she puts in a bit about the Slaughter Stone and human sacrifices as well. She gave our friendly journalist an earful tonight, I can tell you, drove him right back onto his boat. There's no one like my wife for spinning a yarn."

"She's a wonder," agreed Neil MacAllen. "And the curse works more often than not. When people believe they're jinxed, they get nervous, and nervous people tend to have accidents."

"Like the guy who broke his leg," I said, nodding.

"The rest of Sir Percy's guests avoided the Chapel after that," said Mr. Murdoch, with satisfaction.

"Is there anything else we can tell you, Mr. Hunter?" asked Pastor Ferguson.

"Yes," said Damian. "I'd like to know the truth about Sir Percy's missing mail."

Neil MacAllen's tanned face reddened as the other elders cast baleful looks his way. "My wife was overzealous in her efforts to keep the conservation group away from Erinskil. She's apologized to his lairdship. It won't happen again."

"I should think not," said Pastor Ferguson, a bit huffily. "Anything else, Mr. Hunter?"

"No," Damian replied. "Thank you for clarifying the situation."

"You've certainly put my mind at ease," I chimed in cheerfully. "I can't tell you how glad I am that you're not a horrible gang of drug smugglers. I never really thought you were. It just didn't seem right. Not on Erinskil."

"Certainly not," Pastor Ferguson declared, straightening his tie. "But we must ask you, we must ask *both* of you: Will you keep our secrets? We are aware that our endeavors entail a certain amount of illegality. Are you going to turn us in? If you do, you'll have to turn in every adult on Erinskil."

"Including me." Sir Percy had been silent for so long that his hearty voice made everyone jump, but he addressed his words directly to me and Damian. "Do you remember asking me about a laird's responsibilities, Lori? There's one responsibility I didn't mention at the time. A laird is duty-bound to protect his people. The modern world offers threats every bit as dire as those offered by marauding Norsemen. I don't know what your intentions may be, but I intend to defend my island from all pillagers—including and most especially the barbarians from the Inland Revenue."

"As far as I'm concerned," I said, looking around the circle of questioning faces, "you've saved your country more than you've taken from it. You're doing what government is supposed to do but so seldom does—you're keeping people healthy, well educated, and employed. All I have to say is, keep up the good work."

"I'll tell no one," said Damian. "As Sir Percy pointed out earlier, your affairs are irrelevant to my assignment. I apologize for intruding." He turned to Sir Percy. "I would like to know one more thing, however."

"Only one?" said Sir Percy, raising an eyebrow.

Damian acknowledged the barb with a slight tilt of the head but went on, undaunted. "How did *you* find out about the treasure, sir? The elders refused to share their secret with the previous laird. Why did they share it with you?"

A mischievous gleam lit Sir Percy's blue eyes.

"They didn't share their secret with me," he replied. "They shared it with Mr. Shuttleworth. Mr. Shuttleworth was a soft-spoken, amiable chap who spent two weeks on Erinskil four years ago. Mr. Shuttleworth was a keen walker and a huge fan of kitti-wakes and puffins. He was an excellent listener, too."

"Why are you talking about him in the past tense?" I asked. "Has he passed away?"

"You see him before you, my dear." Sir Percy stood to take a sweeping bow. "I never consider a purchase until I know exactly what I'm buying. When I first laid eyes on Erinskil, I knew it was too good to be true, so I returned as Mr. Shuttleworth to carry out some reconnaissance work. Mr. Shuttleworth could give our young celebrities a lesson or two in the art and science of disguise."

"I'll be damned," Damian muttered.

"I'm truly not as daft as I look," Sir Percy said with mock earnestness. "Mr. Shuttleworth was every bit as affable as Peter and a hundred times more cynical than Cassie. It took him less than ten days to put two and two together. As you've told me so often, Lori, there are no secrets in a village, and what is Erinskil but a seagirt village?"

I gazed at him with unrestrained admiration. "You're amazing, Percy."

"Not I, my dear," he responded. "The people of Erinskil are amazing."

"Yes, they are," I agreed, on a gurgle of laughter. "They've learned to spin gold into wool!"

Twenty-one

S ir Percy stood to survey the elders. "I believe our meeting has reached its natural conclusion, gentlemen. There's nothing more to say."

The elders murmured their assent. Chairs were returned to their original positions, and glasses were left for Mrs. Gammidge to clear away. Although the elders treated Damian and me politely, they continued to regard us with a faint air of disquiet, which was understandable. We were unknown quantities. There was no reason for them to trust us.

They did, however, trust Sir Percy. They were prepared to believe him when he promised yet again that Damian and I would never breathe a word of what we'd heard to anyone—except Bill, who, Sir Percy vowed once more, was unimpeachable. With that, and a last wee dram of single-malt, they had to rest content.

The storm raged unabated, and the lights flickered, then came back on while the elders were taking their leave of Sir Percy.

"I'm sure the castle's beds are comfortable, your lairdship," said Pastor Ferguson, "but we'd like to get back to our own. We'll make use of the cars, though, if the offer's still open."

"Of course it is," said Sir Percy. "Think I'd send you home on foot on such a filthy night?"

"We'll be off, then," said the pastor. "Thank you for a most . . . er, *unusual* evening, your lairdship. We know the way out."

Sir Percy, Damian, and I shook hands with each of the elders as they filed from the library, as if we were in a receiving line at a wedding. I was afraid that Sir Percy would invite us to put the seal on our unusual evening by joining him in yet another nip of whiskey, but he had mercy on us.

"Time for bed," he announced as thunder sounded overhead. "Past time, if truth be told. I hope my storm doesn't keep you awake."

"Nothing will keep me awake," I asserted.

"Sir Percy," said Damian, with a preoccupied air, "I'd like to know——"

"Enough," Sir Percy interrupted in a magisterial rumble. He grasped us each by an elbow and hustled us toward the doorway. "It's two o'clock in the morning, Damian. Quench your insatiable curiosity until after you've had some rest. Run along, now. I'll snuff the candles."

"Yes, sir," said Damian.

As I stepped across the threshold, I paused, turned, and went up on tiptoe to kiss Sir Percy on the cheek.

"Good night, your lairdship," I said. "Your people are lucky to have you. You're a good man *and* a good manager."

"I'm an all-around good fellow," Sir Percy acknowledged buoyantly, and closed the door in our faces.

The sound of the storm dropped instantly to a distant rumor. The corridor's thick, windowless walls insulated us from the sound-and-light show that seemed set to continue until dawn. Although I was beginning to droop with fatigue, I strode toward the elevator in high spirits. I was looking forward to sharing every detail of the night's adventure with Aunt Dimity, who would be as delighted as I was to learn that Cassie's suspicions could be tossed out with the trash. I was also looking forward with great anticipation to swapping my hiking boots for a pair of soft and supple bedroom slippers.

"We were wrong, wrong, wrong!" I crowed. "Ain't it great?"

"I'm sorry to disagree with you," Damian commented, "but *you* weren't wrong. You've insisted from the beginning that the islanders were innocent. The rest of us were too cynical to listen to you."

"Goody Two-Shoes triumphs again," I said, with a wry chuckle. "Except that the islanders aren't innocent. They're thieves and liars and tax-dodgers." I thumped my chest. "My kind of people."

Damian allowed himself a brief smile but remained silent. The elevator doors opened, and we stepped inside.

"I'm proud of you, you know," I said as the doors closed.

"Are you?" Damian pressed the button for the third level. "I can't imagine why. I've made such a hash of this assignment that I believe I'll retire when it's over. I'll buy a cottage in a small village and open a flower shop. Much safer for everyone."

The elevator had by now reached the Cornflower Suite. I gave Damian a narrow, sidelong glance as we stepped into the foyer and stood eyeing him severely until the elevator doors slid shut.

"You can wallow in self-pity if you like," I scolded, "but you won't keep me from being proud of you. Sure, you broke a few rules, but you did it because you thought a young man was in danger. You were willing to take on a whole gang of bad guys single-handed in order to rescue him. It was a *heroic* thing to do."

"You already know my opinion of heroes," he returned disdainfully. "And, as I said before, I shouldn't have taken you with me."

I shook my head. "You had no choice. You're used to dealing with powerful men and women, Damian, but there's no fiercer creature on earth than a mother defending her young. Peter Harris is like a son to me. No one could have kept me from going after him."

"Stubborn as a stoat," he murmured.

"Try messing with a stoat's babies," I retorted. "She'll bite your fingers off." I reached over to squeeze his arm. "I won't argue with you about early retirement—I don't want you to die again, my friend, not even for a little while—but if you think life in a small village is peaceful, you're in for a huge disappointment."

"Even in a flower shop?" he asked.

"Especially in a flower shop," I confirmed. "I've seen wars break out over bridal bouquets."

"I'll bear that in mind." He put his hand on mine. "Thanks, Lori."

"My pleasure," I said, and spoiled the sweet moment by pulling my hand back to cover a cavernous yawn. "Sorry, Damian. It's way past my bedtime."

"It's past everyone's bedtime on Erinskil," he said, "with the possible exception of Sir Percy. Sleep well."

"At last!" I declared, opening the door to the suite. "An order I can obey!"

Damian rolled his eyes heavenward, but when I glanced over my shoulder at him from the doorway, he favored me with a smile that warmed me to the core.

Sir Percy's storm reasserted itself the moment I closed the door. Wind roared, lightning flared, and rain hammered the balcony door. Needless to say, I had no desire to step outside for a closer view.

Although lamps had been lit in the sitting room, the fire hadn't. The suite was colder and draftier than it had ever been before. The wind, I thought, was finding its way through chinks I hadn't noticed. Shivering, I strode toward the bedroom, intent on lighting a fire, changing into my warmest flannel nightie, and snuggling under the down comforter with Reginald. I was contemplating the advantages of postponing my tête-à-tête with Aunt Dimity until much later in the morning when I noticed several things in quick succession, like snapshots flashed before my darting eyes.

The gilt mirror that guarded the emergency staircase was ajar. Reginald was sitting on the threshold, facing me. Beside him, as if dropped there by accident, lay a colorful toy knight.

I experienced a moment of utter disorientation. Had Andrew treated the twins to an adventure by bringing them to my room via the emergency stairs? If so, why hadn't he closed the mirror behind him when he'd taken the boys back to the nursery? And why hadn't the alarm sounded? I moved forward to investigate.

The mirror opened onto a spiral staircase. Wall-mounted lightbulbs encased in little cages provided the staircase with dim but adequate lighting. Cobwebs draped the low ceiling and hung in shreds from the iron handrail that ran along the curving wall, and the stairs were coated with a fine layer of gray dust.

The air smelled stale, but someone had used the stairs recently, in both directions, leaving a trail of scuffed footprints in the dust. I was about to follow the footprints upward, toward the nursery, when I heard a muffled cry that stopped my heart.

"Mummy!"

It was Will's voice, coming from somewhere down below, and he was frightened.

There was no time to think or call for help. A flood of adrenaline released my frozen limbs, and I flew down the spiral stairs, caroming off the stone walls and clinging to the handrail to keep myself from falling. When a gust of cold air rushed up to meet me, I gave a panicked gasp and redoubled my pace. The cold air had to mean that the door to the coastal path had been opened—*someone was taking Will into the storm.*

I leapt down the final few stairs, skidded on the rain-covered floor, and made for the open door. The wind was so strong that I staggered sideways as I dashed outside, and the lashing rain made it difficult to see. I curled an arm around my forehead to protect my eyes and glimpsed, in a searing blaze of lightning, a tall, thin figure striding far ahead of me, toward the overlook. He was dragging Will and Rob behind him.

His strength was terrifying. My boys were big for their age, but he pulled them along as if they were rag dolls. When they stumbled, he yanked them up without stopping and moved on.

Abaddon, I thought, and the thought transformed my fear into cold fury. I bowed my head against the driving rain and pounded after him.

The sunken path had become a shallow, rushing stream, but I kept running in spite of the treacherous footing, peering ahead as best I could each time a lightning bolt ripped through the darkness, until I saw the shadowy figure come to a halt. He'd reached the overlook.

With one flick of his wrist, he could have thrown Will and Rob over the cliff, but instead he hauled them up and dumped them on the Slaughter Stone. There they lay, stunned and panting, while Abaddon made the sign of the cross over them. He stared down at them briefly, then spun on his heel, strode to the cliff's edge, and raised his arms, as if in supplication to the sea.

I flung myself behind the boulders bordering the path and clambered over them until I was crouching on a bed of rocky debris a few feet above the Slaughter Stone. My questing hand soon closed over a smooth stone. It was the same size as a cricket ball. When Abaddon swung about to face my sons, I stood and hurled the stone at him with all my might.

Abaddon's head jerked. He dropped to the ground as if his bones had turned to dust.

I slid down onto the Slaughter Stone and pulled Will and Rob to me. They were barefoot and wearing their pajamas.

"I'm here, my babies," I gasped. "Mummy's here." A sob silenced me as their arms tightened around my neck, but I blinked away my tears, lowered the boys gently onto the overlook, and climbed down after them. A quick inspection told me they were shaken but unscathed.

"He hurt Andrew!" cried Will.

"He's a bad man!" Rob shouted angrily.

"I know he is," I said, kissing them all over their beautiful, outraged faces.

"Did you kill him?" Rob asked, craning his neck to peer at the motionless body.

"I don't know," I replied. "That's why you have to run back to the castle as fast as you can. Don't stop for anything. Run to the castle and get Damian. Can you do that for Mummy?"

Before the boys could answer, I saw Abaddon stir.

"Go!" I screamed, and pushed them toward the castle. *"Run!"*

They took off, the soles of their bare feet flashing white as they splashed down the path, lit by chains and forks and ghostly sheets of lightning. I prayed that the path's high banks would keep them safe until they reached the castle, then picked up another rock, larger and more jagged than the first, and stepped toward Abaddon. He could have me if he could take me, but he would not touch my sons.

I was less than five yards away from him when he slowly raised one arm to point at me. There was a brief, bright pop of light, and something smacked into my shoulder, spun me around, and knocked me off my feet.

Time seemed to stop, and my senses seemed to sharpen. As I lay facedown and trembling, I could hear each separate raindrop, each shifting pebble, each curling wave that crashed against the cliffs. I could also hear the slow tread of approaching footsteps.

I tried to push myself to my knees, but my left arm was useless, so I rolled onto my back to confront him. A face loomed above me, pale as milk against the lightning-slashed sky, with eyes as black and empty as holes in a coal seam. He raised his arm a second time, to point at me.

The very air seemed to shudder. A thunderbolt screamed from the heart of a cloud. There was a blinding burst of light and then a deafening explosion. Shards of rock peppered my face, a numbing grayness closed in around me, and all was silence.

Twenty-two

F was floating dreamlessly in deep clouds of sleep. Something was wrong with my left arm, but it was not of any great importance. The light annoyed me, though. It was too bright, too insistent. It tugged at the frayed edge of memory, reminding me of something that had happened—a blinding flash, a thunderclap, a pair of eyes as black as the pits of hell.

My heart clutched, and the deep clouds fell away.

"My babies," I whispered.

"They're here," said a low voice. "They wouldn't leave you."

I opened my eyes. The room wasn't as brightly lit as I'd thought, though I couldn't be sure if the haze blurring my vision was in the air or in my mind. A white ceiling gradually swam into view, then a stainless-steel pole, an IV bag. The bed was comfortable but unfamiliar. There was no telling what time it was.

"Lori?" the voice said.

With an effort I focused my eyes and recognized Damian. He stood at my bedside, gazing down at me and holding my right hand tightly in both of his.

"You're in Dr. Tighe's surgery," he said softly. "Will and Rob are here, too."

He stepped back, and I saw on the far side of the stark white room two small cots, two mounds of blankets, and two identical, tousled heads nestled on two pillows.

"They're not hurt," Damian assured me. "They insisted on spending the night with you."

"My brave boys . . ." I murmured.

"They also insisted that I bring you . . . this." One hand released mine and disappeared from my field of vision. When it reappeared, it was holding Reginald. "Will and Rob told me that this little fellow would help you to get well. I'll leave him on the bedside table, shall I?"

I smiled lazily while Damian set my pink flannel bunny aside and returned to his original position. It was considerate of him to stand, I thought. It kept me from having to strain my neck to look at him.

Another memory intruded. "Andrew?"

"Dr. Tighe is with him," Damian informed me. "He took a nasty blow to the head, but Dr. Tighe is confident that he'll make a full recovery."

"Thank heavens." I drifted for a moment, then frowned in concentration. "Why am *I* here?"

Damian's grave expression softened. He reached out to smooth the hair back from my forehead. "You were shot, Lori. You were shot just below your left collarbone. We'll have matching scars."

"Just what I've always wanted," I said, with a drugged giggle.

He clasped my hand again. "I knew you'd be pleased."

"My face?" I was dimly aware that something wasn't quite right there.

"Nicks and cuts," Damian explained. "From fragments of flying rock. They'll heal nicely."

"No scars?" I said, vaguely disappointed.

"Sorry." He shrugged apologetically. "You'll have to settle for the one. Rest now. Your husband is on his way. He'll be here as soon as the wind subsides. We'll talk more later."

"No," I protested, fighting to stay awake. "Abaddon, on the cliffs—what happened?"

"He was struck by lightning," Damian replied. "Or perhaps it was the wrath of God. He's dead in any case. You'll never have to worry about him again." A quiet sigh escaped him as he stroked my hand. "It's supposed to be the other way round, you know. I should be lying where you are, and you should be standing here."

"I'll get it right next time," I promised, and let the inexorable tides of drowsiness sweep me away.

I slipped in and out of sleep for the next twelve hours. Visiting hours at Dr. Tighe's surgery were apparently quite flexible, because every time I woke up, a different face was hovering over me—Sir Percy, Peter, Cassie, Kate, Elliot, and Pastor Ferguson each put in an appearance. Dr. Tighe, who looked too young to be a practicing physician, showed up at regular intervals to take my pulse and blood pressure, fiddle with my bandages, and hang fresh IV bags.

Rob and Will were always there, sitting cross-legged at the foot of my hospital bed or playing quietly near their cots with their seal pups and their knights. Damian was their constant companion, and Reginald, of course, stayed within arm's reach. If one or more of them ever left my room, I was unaware of it.

By the time Bill arrived on the island—five hours later, by helicopter—I was strong enough to sit up in bed. Since words couldn't convey the range or the intensity of our emotions, the first moments he and I spent together, with the boys, were devoted to purely tactile communication. The hugs, kisses, and caresses continued long after Will and Rob, confident in their father's ability to look after me, allowed Damian to take them back to the castle.

After they were gone, Bill settled himself on the foot of my bed, with his shoes off, a pillow tucked between him and the footrail, and his legs stretched parallel to mine. His gaze shifted restlessly from my face to my bandaged shoulder, as if he were debating with himself whether or not I was well enough to hear what he had to say.

"Bill," I said, guessing his thoughts, "if you *don't* tell me, I'll die of curiosity, so you may as well get it over with."

"Patience never was your strong suit." He smiled, but his eyes were shadowed with melancholy. "It's an ugly tale, Lori."

"I didn't expect light comedy," I said gently. "Go ahead. I promise not to swoon."

"Okay . . ." He held up a warning finger. "But if I see the faintest flush of fever, I reserve the right to continue the story at a later date."

"Agreed," I said promptly, and rested my head against my pillows, to demonstrate my willingness to remain calm.

"Our part in the story began nine months ago," said Bill. "Sir Rodney Spofford asked me to draw up his will. I'd never worked with Sir Rodney before, but he was referred to me by an old client, so I took him on. The will turned out to be absolutely straightforward. Sir Rodney was a widower. Upon his death, therefore, the vast bulk of his estate would go to his only child, Harold Spofford. It took me less than a week to complete the paperwork."

I wrinkled my nose in puzzlement. "Why did he come to you? You specialize in messy, complicated wills. Why would he pay you big bucks to do something any run-of-the-mill solicitor could do?"

"I asked Sir Rodney the same question," Bill answered. "He told me that my firm had acquired a certain cachet among his circle of friends, but he was lying through his teeth. I know now that he came to me because I was unacquainted with the Spofford family. I had no reason to disbelieve him when he told me that Harold was his only child. I didn't find out until two days ago that Sir Rodney had another son, an older son: Alfred."

"How strange," I said. "Why did Sir Rodney lie to you about Alfred?"

"Because twenty years ago," Bill replied, "at the tender age of fourteen, Alfred Spofford was incarcerated in a private asylum for the criminally insane."

My eyebrows shot up. "Why? What had he done?"

"He had a history of psychotic behavior," Bill answered evasively. "The family's nanny had a religious mania which she passed on to little Alfred, but he wasn't very stable to begin with. He had violent outbursts of temper. Whatever he wanted, he took. From an early age, he saw it as his duty to . . . punish . . . small animals as well as other children, for their sins."

I felt a sick sensation in the pit of my stomach but kept my expression neutral. I didn't want Bill to start worrying about my temperature.

"Needless to say," Bill went on, "the Spoffords couldn't send Alfred to school. They kept him at their country estate, under close supervision, until, finally, he set fire to the summerhouse in which his mother was napping. She burned to death."

"He murdered his mother?" I said weakly.

"Nothing could be proved conclusively," said Bill, "but Sir Rodney found a telling scrap of biblical verse half burnt among the ashes. He concealed the evidence from the police and clapped Alfred into Brook House—a high-security, private institution. He then proceeded to eliminate Alfred's name from the family records. Harold, the younger son, became his *only* son, as well as his heir."

"How old was Harold when Alfred disappeared?" I asked.

"Twelve," said Bill. "An impressionable age. He never forgot his older brother. When Harold was in his twenties, he began visiting Alfred, on the sly. He encouraged Alfred to take occupational therapy classes. Alfred studied electronics and computer technology and became a model inmate. Years passed without a single psychotic episode. Harold came to believe that his brother had been rehabilitated."

"Did he mention Alfred's progress to his father?" I asked.

"Sir Rodney refused to acknowledge Alfred's existence." Bill shook his head. "As far as he was concerned, Alfred had died in the same fire that had killed Lady Spofford."

"So Alfred became Harold's little secret," I said.

"Alfred became Harold's obsession," Bill corrected. "He believed that Alfred had been treated disgracefully and strongly disapproved of the will I'd drawn up."

"I'll bet Alfred wasn't too happy about the will either," I commented.

"He was outraged. *He* was the eldest son. *He* was the rightful heir. No one had the right to disinherit him." Bill put a hand to his breast. "In his twisted vision, I was the instrument that had robbed him of his patrimony. He saw it as his duty to punish me. Alfred became Abaddon."

"The king of the bottomless pit," I murmured. "Did Alfred send the creepy e-mail to you from Brook House?"

"He didn't have to," said Bill. "He escaped from Brook House three months ago, aided and abetted by his younger brother. Sir Rodney hired private detectives to find Alfred, but Harold helped Alfred to outmaneuver them. Harold gave Alfred money, hid him, rented a car for him, bought the laptops Alfred used to send the e-mail threats. He also provided Alfred with a gun taken from Sir Rodney's collection of firearms."

"I wondered where he got the gun," I muttered. "Where was Sir Rodney while all of this was happening?"

"He was going about his business," Bill said matter-of-factly. "He didn't know that Harold had been in contact with Alfred until he spoke with a nurse at Brook House, after Alfred's escape. Even then he had no reason to suspect that Alfred was threatening me."

"Of course," I said, nodding. "Sir Rodney couldn't have known about our situation until the Scotland Yard team showed up to interview him."

"It was just as you predicted it would be," Bill observed, patting my leg. "The team finally knocked on the right door. Their questions roused questions in Sir Rodney's mind, and he began to see a pattern. Alfred's escape took place after the new will had been drawn up. Only three people were aware of the will's contents—me, Sir Rodney, and Harold. Since neither Sir Rodney nor I had spoken with Alfred about the will, the finger of suspicion pointed at Harold."

"Did the detectives question Harold?" I asked.

"Chief Superintendent Yarborough questioned Harold," Bill replied, with a look of grim satisfaction. "It took less than an hour to get the truth out of him. Well, most of the truth. He didn't tell Yarborough about the gun."

"And that's when you called me," I concluded, "to let me know that Abaddon was as good as caught."

Bill sighed. "I thought he was."

Dr. Tighe interrupted the proceedings at that moment, to make sure that his patient wasn't being overtaxed. I took the opportunity to ask after Andrew.

"He's awake," Dr. Tighe informed me, "but he's still quite weak. It'll be some time before he's up and about." He slid the blood-pressure sleeve from my arm and nodded to Bill. "She'll do. Tough as a nut, your wife."

"I know," said Bill, with feeling. "Believe me, Doctor, I know."

Twenty-three

When Dr. Tighe had gone, Bill insisted on pouring a glass of water for me, fluffing my pillows, and making a clumsy attempt to feel my pulse. He'd just reached the alarming conclusion that my heart was no longer beating when a quiet knock sounded on the door.

Damian put his head into the room. "I hope you don't mind. Sir William and Lord Robert sent me to spy on you." He crossed to my bedside and snapped to attention. "I'm under direct orders from their lordships to discover all I can about you and Andrew and report back without delay."

"You shouldn't let the boys bully you," I said, smiling, "but I'm glad you came." I held my hand out to him. "Someone needs to find my pulse before Bill calls for a defibrillator."

Damian took hold of my wrist and peered judiciously at the ceiling. "Strong, steady, a bit of a Latin beat . . . Wait, I think it's Morse code. Possibly Irish step dancing." He released my wrist. "Medical history in the making."

I goggled at him. "You made a joke. You *never* make jokes."

"Blame your sons," he said. "They're a terrible influence. They keep making me laugh. It's extremely inappropriate."

"But extremely welcome," said Bill. "Have a seat."

Damian sat in the well-worn visitor's chair, and Bill stretched out on the bed again, so that we formed a conversational triangle.

"Rob and Will are making gingerbread men with Cook," Damian informed us. "And Sir Percy moved the nursery to his youngest son's private apartment. He didn't think the boys would sleep well in the tower."

"God bless Percy," I said.

"You and Bill are to have one of the other private apartments," Damian went on, "until you're well enough to travel."

"Good," I said. "I'm not too keen on tower rooms at the moment either."

"Thanks for taking the twins back to the castle," said Bill. "We've been discussing things they shouldn't hear."

"Ah," said Damian, half rising from the chair. "Perhaps I should . . . ?"

Bill motioned for him to resume his seat. "We'd appreciate it if you'd stay. Lori wants to know everything, and you know more about the closing chapters of the story than I do."

"How far have you gotten?" Damian asked.

"Abaddon's armed and stalking us," I said, and turned to Bill. "How did he find out we were on Erinskil?"

"Yarborough believes he spent a few days in the hills above the cottage, watching us," said Bill. "That's when he took the photographs of the twins." He eyed me hesitantly. "Ivan Anton found evidence of a campsite, Lori."

"Where?" I asked.

"Ivan found a tarp rigged up as a one-person tent," said Bill, watching me closely. "He found it inside the old hedgerow."

"*Inside* the old hedgerow?" I repeated, as my stomach curdled in horror. "In the hollow where Will and Rob play?" I inhaled slowly and willed myself to stay calm. "My God . . . He must have been there when Percy's helicopter landed."

"We think he was," said Bill. "We think he overheard Percy talking about Gretna Green and going north of the border, and he deduced that Percy would take you to Scotland."

"Unfortunately," Damian put in, "Sir Percy's purchase of Erins-kil Island was widely reported in the press. Alfred Spofford—or Abaddon, if you prefer—would have had no trouble locating Dundrillin Castle on the Internet."

"So he followed us north," I said. "But how did he get onto the island?"

"He bought a ticket on the ferry," said Bill, "but since the ferry didn't leave until the following morning, he spent the afternoon in the pub."

"Where he ran into Jack Nunen," Damian interjected.

"Jack . . . ?" I searched my memory until the name clicked. "The reporter from the *Morning Mirror*? The guy who was chasing after Peter and Cassie?"

"That's right," Damian confirmed. "Mr. Nunen was in the pub, attempting to ferret out information on Peter and Cassie. According to witnesses, Abaddon engaged Mr. Nunen in a low-voiced conversation. They left the pub together. Shortly there-after Mr. Nunen hired a powerboat. It was seen leaving the harbor at six o'clock, but Mr. Nunen wasn't on it."

I tensed, remembering the gun. "Where was he?"

"Abaddon knocked him out, tied him up, stole his wallet, and dumped him in a little-used shed in the marina," Damian replied. "Mr. Nunen wasn't found until early this morning. He's in hospi-tal on the mainland, with severe concussion."

I released a small sigh of relief but couldn't keep myself from asking, "Why didn't Abaddon shoot him?"

"You may as well ask why he didn't shoot Andrew," said Damian. "I think he was saving the bullets for . . ." His words trailed off, and he glanced uneasily at Bill.

"He was saving the bullets for me and the boys," I finished. I licked my lips, which had suddenly gone dry. "I understand. He wouldn't want to waste valuable ammunition on less-important targets."

Bill rubbed my leg. "Should we take a break?"

"Am I swooning?" I inquired politely.

"No, but you look awfully pale," Bill observed.

"You'd look pale, too, if you'd lost eight gallons of blood," I said brusquely, and raised my chin. "Please, go on."

My husband gave my bodyguard the age-old look of one helpless man to another. "I told her I'd stop if she showed signs of flagging."

"There's no stopping now," said Damian. "I've seen that determined glint in her eye before."

"So have I." Bill surveyed my lifted chin appraisingly. "We could ask Dr. Tighe to sedate her."

"Just you try," I growled, and decided to move the story along myself. "Abaddon arrived in Stoneywell Harbor, in Jack Nunen's boat, around seven o'clock the night Peter went missing. How did he get past Cal Maconinch, Damian? Didn't you ask Mr. Maconinch to check his ID?"

"Abaddon stole Jack Nunen's press pass and his driver's license," said Damian. "Both men were thin, clean-shaven, fair-skinned, and dark-haired, and Abaddon wore Mr. Nunen's wire-rimmed glasses. The resemblance was close enough to fool Cal." Damian sat back in his chair and stretched his legs in front of him. "Abaddon's visit to the pub in Stoneywell wasn't as cut-and-dried as Peter made it sound. He stayed there for quite some time before returning to his boat—long enough to confirm your presence on the island and to learn the location of your rooms. He also found out that the castle is equipped with an alarm system. Mrs. Muggoch, of course, told him about the Slaughter Stone."

Bill's lips tightened. "The stone's association with human sacrifice must have appealed to him."

"'I will strike your children dead,'" I murmured, "'and give your wife a like measure of torment and mourning.'"

"We don't know when he left the harbor," Damian went on, "but several circumstances made it absurdly easy for him to enter the castle." He held up one hand and ticked the points off on his fingers. "Cal left his post to join the elders in Dundrillin, so no one was keeping an eye on the boat. The storm obscured the cameras monitoring the side entrance. The power failure made it easier for him to override the alarm system."

"I thought the alarm system had a backup generator," I said.

"He'd studied electronics at Brook House," Bill reminded me, "and he'd brought a set of specialized tools with him. He would have disarmed the system without the storm's help, but there's no denying that the power outage took place at an opportune moment."

"While we were saying good night to the elders," Damian continued, "Abaddon let himself in through the side entrance and climbed the emergency stairs. No one can know for certain, but I believe he stopped first at the Cornflower Suite."

"When he found it vacant," said Bill, "he went on to the nursery."

"Andrew was asleep when the mirror opened," said Damian. "Abaddon brought a lamp down on the back of his head and grabbed the boys."

The mental image of my little ones being snatched from their beds sent a wave of nausea through me, but I fought it off and said, "They must have taken their knights to bed with them. When Abaddon carried them past my room, they dropped one by the open mirror. I remember wondering what it was doing there. Then I heard Will cry out for help."

"Why didn't you call for Damian?" Bill asked. "Why did you go after Abaddon on your own?"

I expected Damian to chime in with a gentle reproof, but he just smiled.

"No one could have stopped her, Bill," he said. "A wise woman once told me that there's no fiercer creature on earth than a mother defending her young. When Lori heard her son's voice, rational thought gave way to primal instinct."

"Which is a nice way of saying that I lost my head," I conceded. "I'm sorry, Damian. How long did it take you to realize that I was gone?"

"Too long." He waved his hand in a gesture of self-reproach. "When Andrew failed to check in on schedule—ten minutes after you'd entered your suite—I knew something was amiss. I knocked on your door, and when you didn't reply, I let myself into the suite. You weren't there, the mirror was open. . . . I knew immediately that there'd been a security breach."

"Damian roused the entire staff," Bill said. "He directed Mrs. Gammidge to the nursery to check on Andrew. He dispatched Kate to the village to fetch Dr. Tighe. He ordered Elliot to meet him at the side entrance, but Percy got there first because he hadn't gone to bed yet."

"Elliot showed up a few minutes later," said Damian. "I sent him around the headland while Sir Percy and I ran toward the overlook. We hadn't gone far when Will and Rob came tearing up, shouting for help. Sir Percy carried them back to the castle. I pulled out my gun and went after you." His gaze turned inward as the surreal scene unfolded before his mind's eye. "I was no more than ten yards from the overlook when Abaddon shot you. I saw you fall, saw him get to his feet and walk toward you. I took aim, my finger was on the trigger, but I never pulled it because at that moment"—he caught his breath and his eyes narrowed—"a single, blinding bolt of lightning dropped from the sky, as if it had

been hurled by an unseen hand. The overlook seemed to ex-
plode—there's a crater there now, where the cliff blew apart. The
concussion knocked me down, and when I looked again, Abaddon
was gone. I suspect that he fell into the sea, but it was as if he'd
simply vanished from the face of the earth." He shook his head,
bemused. "I don't know why you hired me, Bill. Lori already has
a bodyguard, and His aim is better than mine."

"Don't sell yourself short," said Bill. "My wife would have
bled to death if you hadn't reached her in time." He touched my
foot. "Damian improvised a compression bandage and carried you
back to the castle. He's quite the hero."

I shushed Bill frantically. "Don't use the H word around
Damian. He has a low opinion of heroes."

"Most true heroes do," Bill observed.

"If anyone's a hero," Damian said stolidly, "it's Dr. Tighe. He
saved you and Andrew, though the islanders helped as well. They
lined up to donate blood."

I peered up at the ceiling and said reflectively, "Normal
tourists bring shortbread home with them from Scotland. I'm
bringing fresh pints of B-positive blood."

"B-positive?" Damian's silvery eyes twinkled. "Is that your
blood type? Of course it is. *Be positive*—what else could possibly
flow through your veins?"

If Dr. Tighe had been listening at the door, he would have
thought the three of us were drunk. Our laughter was the laughter of release—it was too loud, and it went on much too long, but
every time we sobered up, we'd catch one another's eyes and start
again. We'd each endured a terrible ordeal, and though dark
memories would haunt our dreams, the waking world was ours
again, to do with as we liked. What better way to celebrate than
with laughter?

Epilogue

ndrew, Reginald, and I moved back to the castle the next day and stayed there for another two weeks, recuperating. Rob and Will played on the battlements with their father, Damian overhauled the castle's security system, and we invalids spent a lot of time lolling in the sunroom while Mrs. Gammidge waited on us hand and foot. Sir Percy spared us as much time as he could, but he was busy managing his island.

A flock of tabloid vultures roosted briefly at Dundrillin, but Sir Percy kept them so befuddled with effortless charm—and flowing whiskey—that Erinskil's curious prosperity went unnoticed.

Peter and Cassie contributed greatly to the press-distraction project by announcing their engagement. Since a wedding at Dundrillin would have drawn even more unwanted attention to the island, they regretfully rejected Will's sage advice and decided to be wed in the family chapel at Cassie's ancestral home in Kent.

Dr. Tighe declared Andrew and me medically unfit to comment on our experiences with Abaddon, and Bill referred all questions to Chief Superintendent Yarborough, whose answers were so blandly uninformative that the press had to resort to hounding Sir Rodney Spofford and laying siege to Brook House.

Jack Nunen's brutal concussion robbed him of all memories of his encounter with Abaddon, but it didn't stop him from writing an exclusive exposé about Sir Rodney's psychotic son. The story ran for two consecutive Sundays in the *Morning Mirror,* until yet another sex scandal took its place.

Chief Superintendent Yarborough wrapped up the investigation quietly and efficiently. No charges could be brought against the late Alfred Spofford, but Harold served time for supplying Alfred with a gun, and Sir Rodney was held to account for destroying the scrap of paper he'd found in the charred ruins of the summerhouse.

"Scotland Yard doesn't look kindly upon those who cover up cold-blooded murder," I commented to Aunt Dimity when I finally had a chance to speak with her.

I should think not. If Sir Rodney hadn't been so intent on protecting his family's reputation, much travail would have been avoided. And it was all for naught. The sad truth was revealed despite his ill-conceived efforts at concealment.

"I almost—*almost*—feel sorry for him," I said. "I don't know what I'd do if one of the twins went mad. Mental illness is a horrible thing."

You might call it mental illness. I call it evil. Alfred Spofford tortured animals and small children. He murdered his mother. He would have murdered your five-year-old sons if you hadn't stopped him, and he most certainly tried to murder you. After twenty years of the most intensive therapy, he crept back into the world craving blood, and he used sacred texts to justify his lust. When Damian ascribed Abaddon's death to the wrath of God, he was not being entirely facetious. I do not mourn the loss of Alfred Spofford. If ever anyone was evil, it was he.

I reflected that Alfred Spofford's timely demise had less to do with the wrath of God than with his unwise decision to stand in an exposed spot during a lightning storm while holding a hunk of metal at arm's length, but I had no doubt that he was evil. Something not quite human had peered back at me from the chilling emptiness of those coal-black eyes.

"Do you think he's . . . tainted the cottage?" I asked. "Bill wants to cut down the old hedge, Dimity. He says it'll always remind him of how close Abaddon came to killing us."

It's pointless to fight evil by destroying life.

"How *do* we fight it, then?" I demanded.

We kiss our children. We make sticky lemon cake for our husband. We cherish our friends. We leave the great hedge standing tall, to serve as a haven for birds and mice and spiders. We defeat evil every time we commit an act of kindness. When necessary, we hit it with a rock.

"I get it." I nodded slowly. "Fill each day with acts of grace, but keep a rock handy, just in case."

I couldn't have put it better myself. You must do it in needlepoint, my dear, as a reminder of a valuable lesson learned.

I'm still digesting the lessons I learned during my time on Erinskil, but the nightmares have grown fewer and I've almost lost my fear of thunderstorms. The twins, thankfully, have shown no ill effects from their ordeal. They expected me to rescue them from the bad man, and I did. End of story.

Much to their delight, I've taken a serious interest in cricket over the past few months. My batting still leaves much to be desired, but I can bowl a wicket clean nine times out of ten. I never miss a chance to strengthen my throwing arm.

Just in case.

Sir Percy's Favorite Sticky Lemon Cake

Lemon Syrup

½ cup sugar

¼ cup fresh lemon juice

Combine the sugar and lemon juice in a small bowl.
Whisk until the sugar dissolves.

Lemon Cake

¾ cup unsalted butter, at room temperature

1 cup sugar

1½ teaspoons grated lemon peel

2 large eggs

1¼ cups self-rising flour

optional toppings: whipped cream, clotted cream, lemon curd,
    or confectioner's sugar

Preheat the oven to 350 degrees Fahrenheit.
Butter an 8-inch-square metal baking pan.

Use an electric mixer to cream the butter in a large mixing
bowl until smooth. Add the sugar and lemon peel and beat until
fluffy. Beat in 1 egg, then half of the flour; repeat. Pour the batter
into the buttered baking pan. Bake about 25 minutes, or until a
toothpick inserted in the cake's center comes out clean. Place the
pan on a rack. Use a toothpick to poke holes all over the top of
the cake. Spoon the lemon syrup slowly over the cake, allowing
it to soak in. Cool the cake completely.

Sprinkle with confectioner's sugar or cut into squares and
serve with whipped cream, clotted cream, or lemon curd.